AGE OF ALIENS
SAFIRE & IGNEOUS

ARIA RANI SINDLEDECKER

Paperback ISBN-13: 978-1-7343800-8-8
eBook ISBN-13: 978-1-7343800-0-2

Special Acknowledgements:
Melody Reed
Sonja Solter
Naomi Kinsman

Cover art by Karen Chien
The text type was set in Palatino
Cover text font, Oh Now! by Syaf Rizal
Cover text font, Anita Semi-square by Gustavo Paz
https://creativecommons.org/licenses/by-sa/4.0/deed.en_US

For my Mom

Safire

CHAPTER 1

People that are normal *never* step in other's shoes. They really don't. They don't seem to have the least bit of empathy or sympathy.

I wish that every uncaring person that is normal would have a chance to be like me for once in their life.

You must be thinking, "Why did she say 'be like me'?" If YOU had any idea, you would see that I, Safire Waters, am not normal.

That's right. I'm *not* norm—

RING!!!

The sound of the class bell is always a daydream killer.

. . .

I was walking out of my last class of the day when I spotted her.

"Hey Marissa!"

We were in the school halls. I swung my backpack over my shoulder and skipped over to her.

"Did you finally finish your history homework, lazy pants?" she said. She turned around and smiled.

The way she smiled, the way her hazel eyes glittered and her black wavy hair bounced, made me happy. She always made me happy. If it were the saddest day of my life, the sight of her would cheer me up.

We were like sisters. We did most things together. I couldn't imagine my life without her.

"Yep, *finally*!" I smirked.

"I told you!" She gave me a playful punch.

I laughed and lightly punched her back.

"How did you do on your English test?" I asked.

"My dad is probably going to say, 'Marissa, you are very disappointing. You only got an A-minus? How horrible. Go to your room.'"

She talked with a funny accent that made me laugh so hard, my face turned red.

She grabbed my shoulder. "But as long as I have you…"

"Together we thrive!" we sang. The tune was from a commercial. It was the sort of thing we sang if we were happy.

And we were happy 99.99 percent of the time. There was just that 0.01 percent of the time that we weren't…and one of those super-rare moments was about to happen.

We started walking to the end of the hallway. I was really excited because my mom finally let me walk home with Marissa.

"Did you watch *Red Scar*?" Marissa asked.

"Oh yeah! I saw the first season," I said. "It was really good! It's like we are Bella and Ellie—"

"YOU WON'T BE WATCHING ANYTHING TODAY!" somebody said in a deep voice.

I turned around to see a man with a hoodie and jeans staring at us. He was looking straight at Marissa.

The tall man walked toward me and bumped me aside. He looked down at Marissa. He crossed his arms. "Hand over your paper!"

"D-Dad? W-what are you doing here?" Her face turned pale and her eyes widened and watered. She took a couple steps back.

I began to feel tired. My muscles began to protest. It felt like I had run a marathon. But at the same time, I wanted to jump on Marissa's dad and make him go away. *What should I do?*

My hands tightened into fists. My muscles stiffened. I knew from all the moments I've had with Marissa that she didn't deserve being yelled at. She didn't deserve to be broken-hearted. She especially didn't deserve this.

"HEY!" I shouted at her dad.

Marissa looked at me, horrified.

My veins felt like they were popping out of my head. "GO AWAY!" I yelled at him.

He didn't budge.

"GET AWAY FROM MY FRIEND!"

He looked confused. "Why are you telling me to get away from my own daughter?" he grumbled. "Plus, I'm older than you—you shouldn't be yelling at me like

3

that!"

I ignored him and I stomped. "I SAID, GET AWAY FROM MY FRIEND!!!"

I stared at him harshly, like he was my worst enemy. At the moment, he was. I felt like I had tunnel vision. I looked at his face to see any sign of weakness. The moment he cowered, I cracked my knuckles to threaten him silently. Nobody was going to mess with Marissa on my watch.

I looked around. Everyone was staring at me. Whispering.

Wow, I thought. *There is going to be a lot of gossip about this…but I don't care!*

I looked back at her dad again, starkly and straight into his eyes.

He actually looked horrified, as though I were a lioness and he were my prey. This time, he made a weird sound and ran away.

The people watching us walked away. Whispering even more. *WHAT IS THEIR PROBLEM?!*

I felt tired again. I felt so tired but satisfied. Then all of a sudden, I felt like an arrow went through my head. Pain crept all over my body. It was like lightning struck me.

I fell—but Marissa caught me.

. . .

The rest of the week was hazy and seemed to go by quickly. I really wanted to go to the doctor but my mom firmly said "NO" every time. I really wished she would give in.

"Safire! Safire! TURN DOWN YOUR MUSIC FOR ONCE IN YOUR LIFE!!!"

Yep, that's my mom. She'd been acting really weird lately. I didn't know what it was. Usually we were best friends and we hung out together. But she hadn't hung out with me as much and hadn't been super loving. She'd been really agitated, but I didn't think she was mad at *me* —

"DON'T GET ADDICTED TO YOUR MUSIC!!!" she yelled. "I'm about to take it away from you, if you don't come down in—"

ARRRG!!! I stopped my music and tossed my headphones into my backpack. I took my phone out of my pocket and laid it down on my bed.

I heard my mom walking up the stairs. But—

CREAK! The door slowly opened.

"Safire...what did I say?" she said.

I looked at her, annoyed.

She brushed her brown hair with green highlights from her face. Her hazel eyes bore into mine as she clutched the green pendant she always wore. After a moment of silence, she said, "Come on, Safire!"

This time, I walked downstairs.

"So, I decided..." my mom said, "that we will go to the neurologist, because you have been bugging me all week—"

"YES!!!" Yep, I was cheering and jumping around because I could go to the doctor. Weird, right? Most kids

5

would say, "NOOO, I DON'T WANT TO GO!"

Two seconds later I pulled my mom into the car.

Finally, I would get to the bottom of this strange pain.

. . .

"So, when did these headaches start?" asked the neurologist. He had a bright white lab coat and deep blue eyes. His freckles surrounded his soft smile and matched his super-spiky, strawberry blond hair. I guessed he actually had a good bedside manner.

"A couple days ago," my mom said.

"Do you…"

I stopped paying attention to the doctor. I didn't even know his name.

Blah, blah, blah…

I looked around the room. It was mostly just a white space with a couple of bookshelves and a mirror.

I looked at the mirror and caught my reflection. I saw my piercing, blue eyes and my pitch-black hair (with blue highlights) that covered both sides of my face. And then there was my forehead, with no acne and not a single line or crease.

That's right. I'd never ever had acne. Not even a single bump or sign of it. *My skin is as soft as a baby's butt.*

Out of nowhere, I saw something weird. My skin…was turning…

"YELLOOOOW!!!" I screamed. I jumped up and scratched my arms and legs.

6

"Yellow?" The neurologist looked up. "Are you feeling itchy? You look jaundiced…I've never seen it come on this quickly."

He looked at me with wide eyes, like I was a scientific wonder. "I think we need to run further tests."

When we returned to the car, I stared out the window, wondering about the whole yellow skin thing. It had gone away slowly over the course of an hour, thankfully, but I was still a little shaken by it.

First headaches, and now yellow skin?! What was going on with me?

I shook out my hands, trying to relax. When we got home, I went straight to my room to watch T.V.

I turned on the news and saw the headline:

ANOTHER SCHOOL SHOOTING

They showed pictures of kids screaming because they were so petrified and parents crying at the loss of their children. Every single picture showed sad and miserable people. All of them had suffered a loss. Their lives were a nightmare.

I couldn't look at it anymore. I couldn't help but bawl my eyes out. I couldn't stop.

Imagine you are in school and you hear shooting. You hear screaming. You run. You run and hide. But it seems like all is lost. Your best friends die. You never see them again. And your life is ruined forever. It is torn to pieces by a crazy person…

I couldn't stop feeling bad for them. Every time I

looked at one of their faces, I felt like I was experiencing what they were experiencing. I could actually feel their pain. I closed my eyes, trying to suppress the headache that suddenly seemed to consume my energy.

I turned off the T.V. and grabbed my head. Why was I feeling what they were feeling? Why had I never felt this before?

Nothing made sense anymore.

Igneous

CHAPTER 2

"Igneous…Igneous…Igneous!"

My eyes snapped open and bright artificial lights blinded me. My head was pounding like it never had before. "Nggg!" I whined. The world spun around me. My eyes slammed shut as I repeated my name and the planet I was on to stay awake.

My name is Igneous Stone and I live on Planet Magma. My name is Igneous Stone and I live on Planet Magma. My name is Igneous Stone and I live on Planet Magma—

"Igneous! Are you okay? A Lavaball just hit you!" A middle-aged person with a blue lacy shirt, dark freckles and deep ash eyes leaned over to help me up. Yep, that's my Lavaball coach. "Did you hear me? You got hit by a Lavaball…" she said.

I nodded my head slowly. Yep, we were training with dangerous Lavaballs. We never burn ourselves, and they weigh more than a Lavaboard. Thankfully all Magmians are adapted to lava so we can hold it; some can control it and we can also live in it! Lots of the things we used were made out of lava.

Well, my getting hit is another thing for the Jocks to laugh at me about. "HA HA HA HA HA HA!" I could hear the echoing of the other boys laughing at me.

I slowly got up while the world still spun around me.

After a few minutes, I got my bearings and didn't feel wobbly. We were in the middle of a huge meadow. The sun's warmth beat down on my back as I watched the Jocks in disgust. They were laughing, just as I had expected.

"Oh! Look who's mad now!" the Jocks sang. "HA HA HA! I guess Mr. Weakling is going to—"

"BE QUIET, MR. ENKI!" the training coach yelled at the Jocks. "Go to the office right now with your followers!"

Yep, that's my life. Every time anyone bullies me, I always get saved by one of the teachers, so the Jocks LOVED to pick on me even more. I can't even imagine what it's like to not have them on my back, bugging me.

"It's okay. The dean will deal with them," my coach told me.

The Jocks snorted and headed east, towards the school castle. That's right, our school is a boarding school and a castle. EVERYONE has to go to it. You start when you are eight and stay until you are seventeen. You only leave if you get a job earlier than expected.

Fortunately, I get good grades and the better the grade, the better the job. The only jobs you can get out of battle school are jobs appointed by Lord Obsidian Slag. (Lord Slag is our practically immortal ruler that has most of the power.)

My life is constantly being bullied, studying to ace every class and trying not to make a fool out of myself in extracurricular activities. I hoped I'd get out of this horrid life soon.

. . .

The next day I learned that I wasn't going to be invited to another Lavaball practice.

I was kinda relieved. My best friend, Xed, had been kicked off the team a while ago. He was excited I was kicked off, too. And then there were the Jocks. They were mad that I wasn't on the team anymore. I guess they liked having me as a punching bag.

Another good thing about being kicked off was having more time to study—and more time to be alone.

When I was a Little (that's what they call kids between four and seven years old), I used to be the most social person in the world! I had so many friends! But later I found out that lots of my friends were only my friends because I was smart. Most people weren't doing so well in school, so they wanted someone who could just tell them the answers.

That broke me down. Just one of the fifty friends I had was real.

The only friend I had that was friends with me because of my personality was Xed. (Xed was smart, too.)

Even though I knew I was closing myself off to others, I didn't change at all. I wouldn't change for anyone.

After I shut everyone out, Xed came up and sat down next to me. "Are you lonely?" (Yes, it was the cheesiest start to a friendship, but it was just so nice to have a real friend who actually cared about me and didn't take me for granted.)

Okay, back to the Jocks. I had a study hall for the first time in my life. It was weird, but nice. I didn't have the Jocks dumping my books in the water bucket in the corner of the hall. I knew I had to figure out how to get them to stop, but their bullying had become a normal part of my daily routine. So instead of using my time wisely, I imagined what would happen if the Jocks were there:

"Oh...are you studying?" The lead Jock, Scri, picks up my book. "I'm sorry. I didn't know you were reading more books!" He walks over to the water bucket. Before he can drop it, I grab the book and run away while the Jocks taunt me...

I quickly got out of my daydream and grabbed a history book to distract myself.

. . .

The rest of that day was sort of empty. Xed was sick and the Jocks were suspended. I was sort of on my own. The only exciting thing was the new Defense class I was taking.

"All right, class," the new teacher said. "Everyone is going to try every weapon we have here." He was wearing a suit with a purple bow tie and a black cape. His ash gray hair was pushed to one side and he smiled a lot.

"There are swords, axes, bows and arrows, daggers and many more. We need to figure out which weapon you connect with. Line up in four lines."

The room was empty except for the teacher's desk, a couple of long work tables and the weapons lined up on the wall.

I ended up in the dagger/pocket knife line. It took me a while to get to the front, but when I did, I had to throw a weapon at the target. My right hand was shaking, so I held it up with my left.

THRWAK! I was so close to the bullseye. My dagger was on the line between the red bullseye and the white ring outside of it. ARGH!

. . .

After class, I tried so many times to hit the bullseye. I had my heart set on getting ten in a row.

Hit!

    Miss.

    Miss.

Hit!

    Miss.

Hit!

    Miss.

    Miss.

    Miss.

Hit!

Hit!

Hit!

Hit!

Hit!

Hit!

Hit!

Hit!

Hit!

I aimed for my last shot so I could be done for the day...

HIT!

YES!

The rest of that day I was happy. I was alone, but starting to understand that being by myself was peaceful. You didn't have to worry someone was going to look at you weird or something.

. . .

That night I had a weird dream.

"Igneous, are you okay?" A girl with ice-blue eyes and pitch-black hair put her hand on my shoulder. "We have to go! He will catch us! Please! Igneous!"

The dream switched into a different one.

The same girl. We were in a red room with red walls and two red chairs. We were chained to the chairs, squirming to get free. "Did you hear him? We will be sentenced to death!" the girl's voice echoed.

The dream switched once again, making my head spin.

This time I felt an overwhelming sensation of loss. I was sitting in a chair and the girl was walking out of the front door. I got up and ran after her. "PLEASE!"

She turned around. "You said it yourself, this doesn't work. I'm sorry. With all our training…we weren't meant to be. I can't forgive you for those things…"

My eyes snapped open. I got up and realized I was in the boys' dormitory. I almost screamed but instead covered my mouth tightly with my hand. The sweat dripping from my forehead was blinding me.

"Whew," I whispered, as I uncovered my mouth.

The girl wasn't here and no more dreams, I thought to myself.

The girl wasn't here and no more dreams.

The girl wasn't here and no more dreams.

The girl wasn't here and no more dreams.

The image of the girl was swimming in my mind and I couldn't shake it away.

Who was she?

Why was she in my dreams?

Was I supposed to know who she was?

Does she know who I am?

Is she a real person?

Where does she live?

Were those dreams *the future*? They were so vivid.

Why her?

Why me?

I soon fell asleep again.

Safire

CHAPTER 3

"Please try harder next time." Ms. Pinelopi handed me my test: A-minus. Teachers always had high expectations.

I hung my head. At this point I was never gonna be at the top of my class. Well, maybe I might get to the top. Just need more studying. I love studying, but after a while it gets boring.

I walked out into the halls, passing kids. "Oh my god! Kevin just asked me to the dance next year!" said Susanna. She's a popular girl. Most Populars are mean, although she's sorta nice. Kevin is the leader in the Jocks group and likes Susanna since she's a cheerleader. I don't know how she likes him.

"Um…hey Susanna," I said as I passed her. "Good job cheerleading at the game last Friday."

"Um…thanks?" Then she stalked off. I tried my best to be friendly to people. It doesn't work.

People just don't care. But, sadly, I do.

I spotted Marissa in the distance. "Marissa! Wait up!"

She turned around and waved, but kept walking.

I quickly stumbled through the crowd. I put a hand on her shoulder and swung myself to her side.

"So! Your birthday is in a few weeks!" she clapped.

"Yeah, yeah. My mom is getting super emotional because I'm 'turning into a big girl now'."

Marissa snorted. "Well, we are throwing a party for you! So you need to dress your best! I can show you how to do your—" She glanced to her right and her face turned red. All of a sudden, she hung her head and walked away.

Lately all of my friends had been really weird. They just…walked away for some random reason.

. . .

I'm going to skip ahead a couple of days. It was May 3rd. 12:00 P.M. Lunchtime.

"Nobody heard about my weird illness, right?" I asked my friend Justin.

He turned around, and I could see my reflection in his glasses. "What?" Then he walked away.

It was like he was ignoring me. I closed my eyes, wanting to know so badly what was going on. Did I do something they didn't like? I was so fed up with all the secrecy.

So I texted my friends.

OceanBlue22

Hey guys. i just wanted to know why u

guys aren't texting
me. i feel like i did
something. Plz let me
know if i did
something.

Two minutes later:

JustInTime101
i don't know what u
are talking about. i
think everyone knows
someone has been
watching u lately.

                    OceanBlue22
                    Who? Why haven't u
                    guys told me? i'm
                    super creeped out
                    right now.

JustInTime101
IDK. But Marissa and
Ella might know. Maybe
ask them.

                    OceanBlue22
                    OK. i'll ask them.
                    SYL.

As I switched over to a different messaging chat, I
shuddered. I held back a scream, wishing I had a pillow

to punch. My hands began to get clammy as I texted Marissa and Ella. Why couldn't they just TELL me what was going on?!

I smashed my fingers into my phone and texted them.

OceanBlue22

Hey guys, J said that 1 of you should know who has been watching me. Do you know? Or is J just playing a trick...

Mars81

No. Justin is correct. But we got threatened that if we ever told u, he would do something horrible to us. Not a good deal. i probably talked to u too much, but honestly, i do not care. This guy doesn't seem like he is going to do anything. He hasn't done anything but threaten us a little.

Thinking about it, Marissa had been talking to me

a lot more than the others. But at the same time I was annoyed with her because she wasn't her usual self; she would just stop talking to me in the middle of conversations. I know if *I* had been in her place, I would have ignored the guy and still talked to her normally—and warned her.

NerdGirl30
Marissa is right, and LOL. :D But we can't tell u who.

> **OceanBlue22**
> Come on, he can't possibly be watching right now… Can he hack?

Mars81
IDK. I guess Ella can tell you. Ella can you please tell her. IDK the answer.

NerdGirl30
Fine. U know the guy in seat 30 in our Chemistry class.

> **OceanBlue22**
> Yeah. Steven.

NerdGirl30
Yeah, Steven. The guy
is his brother… Every1
has been saying he's
been acting weird
lately. It's almost
like he's possessed.
LOL

Mars81
STEVEN SPIELBERG!
LOLLOLLOLLOLLOL!

                   OceanBlue22
                   ???!!!

NerdGirl30
Anyways, his brother
goes to this school.
He does not speak and
only stares. IDK if
you know Safire. But
he stares at you all
the time.

                   OceanBlue22
                   That makes no sense
                   whatsoever.

NerdGirl30
I know. Listen. We
have to erase this in

21

case this guy sees it. Never talk about this again unless it's an emergency. Got it? I have drama club anyway with the stupid girl named Georgia. Bye.

OceanBlue22
Got it. Bye, see you tomorrow.

Mars81
Yeah, got it. SYL you guys.

We all deleted the conversation at the same time. My heart felt like it had been stabbed. The betrayal suddenly choked me. Why didn't she—

BZZZT! I looked in my messages app and found a couple of texts from Marissa.

Mars81
Hey, i'm really sorry i haven't been talking to you. I hope i can make it up to u. Just tell me if i can do anything 4 u. U know that i'm always there 4 u, even when u think i'm not, right? I know

u probably won't get
back to me… but at
least read this
message. I already
miss hanging out with
you.
P.S. the red scar
finale is on tonight!
Maybe we can talk
about it?

I stared at the message for a moment, thinking. But afterward, I sighed and put my phone away, feeling even worse.

I walked over to my locker. It's kind of decorated and has three pictures on the inside: A wave, a book and a peacock.

Other kids put up posters of singers, actors, famous people, photos of their crush, or mirrors to look at themselves.

Maybe I should tell you a little more about myself.

Me: Safire Waters.

Thirteen years old. In eighth grade.

Swimmer.

Favorite number is 83. Favorite animal is a peacock. Favorite color is black.

The peacock in my locker also happened to have a smell. It held a scent of the forest, so whenever I opened my locker, people caught a whiff of it.

I opened my locker, and a few people raised their heads and sniffed the air. Then everyone went back to their business. I pulled my books out and closed my locker. There were some high-pitched screams coming from the neighboring hall. At first I didn't really care, but then—

"RUNNNN!!! AHHHHHH!!!" A kid with a leather jacket, crazy leggings and a blue shirt ran through the halls, tracking blood with her shoes. My jaw dropped as everyone dumped their books and stepped forward to look at the blood.

Some chemistry nerds pushed their way through the crowd. "Get out of the way!" a kid with buckteeth shouted. They ended up getting stepped on as people got antsy.

"O.M.G! What is it?" a girl asked. "Is it lipstick?"

"Um…excuse me?" I gently pushed people out of the way. "May I get through?" I was getting tired of people doing stupid things and taking forever to figure out it was blood!

"Okay, people! This is blood. Not lipstick. Not water with food coloring. This is BLOOD." I looked closely at the spots of crimson liquid. I saw bits of silver. *Marissa…* Marissa had a problem when she was younger, and she had to inject lots of stuff into her blood. And it formed tiny, silver circles in her blood system…

My heart pumped as I started to panic. "Everybody RUN!" I blurted out.

All of a sudden my ears were pierced by the school fire alarm and girls screaming at the top of their lungs. The high-pitched sounds felt overwhelming. The seconds ticked by as floods of people ran down the halls, jumping over kids who had been pushed to the ground by other kids trying to get through. People were limping down the halls with blood trailing behind them.

Some kids were lying on the floor crying, bruised up, with kids trying to help them. A couple of fights broke out. Some kids tried to fit inside their lockers because they were too afraid to run, or something.

Meanwhile I just stood there with my back against a locker, staring at the other kids running down the school hallways in fear. This vicious sight froze me. I realized that life wasn't going to be so normal after this.

I felt like I was waiting for something. I was waiting for... My thoughts were too fuzzy and flew around in my mind.

I stood there for a few more minutes, feeling light-headed. My sight became blurry as I searched for something. No, *someone*. Then she came up right behind me.

I turned around to see Marissa in (what looked like) pain. Her hands trembled as blood dripped down the sides of her face.

"Safire...," she whispered. Her legs buckled and she collapsed. My arms flew out and caught her as she went limp. Her eyelids lowered slowly and her hair hung over my arm.

I don't know what happened after that. It was all a blur. I dragged Marissa through the halls, a line of blood dripped down onto the floor. My heart was so full of sadness that it seemed hard to breathe. All I remembered was getting outside.

Pain surged through my body. I collapsed from Marissa's weight and a bright light blinded me. My chest tightened as some men picked me up. I remember thrashing around in tears and shouting Marissa's name. My breathing became shallow as screams ripped across my ears.

My heartbeat was the background noise to a sudden terrible pain. It felt similar to the pain I felt when Marissa's dad yelled—but times ONE THOUSAND.

It felt like a movie.

Bright lights hit your eyes.

Screams and alarms from cars pierce your ears.

It almost feels like you are dying.

My heartbeat slowed to a weird sensation.

My body felt light, like I was flying.

My brain felt clear and my hands grew damp.

I let out an uncontrolled whimper. I heard some shuffling and felt something soft behind my back. I fell unconscious quickly.

. . .

I was sitting on a chair in a white room, thinking.

A boy barged into the room. "Safire!" He had pale skin and black and brown hair. "WE HAVE TO GO!"

The dream switched.

"I'm sorry, you've done things…," I said to the same guy. "Besides, we are needed to do different stuff. It's best if we split apart…"

The dream switched one last time.

"Did you hear, Safire? They are circling the planet," the same guy said to me. *"Our commanders are setting up escape ships for us. Maybe we should give ourselves to them?!"*

We rushed out the room.

. . .

I came back to reality after the set of short…dreams? I took my mind off of it and raced to figure out where I was.

Bright light smacked into my eyes, and my eyes felt really strained. My skin felt like it was being cracked to pieces. And it felt like a drummer was pounding on my head with drumsticks.

Tired…tired.

I looked around and saw a white room similar to a therapist's room. I was lying on a hospital bed next to two chairs and an end table. Wires and medications were hooked into my skin, and bandages were wrapped around my hands like white gloves.

My body heat rose and what felt like a warm blanket wrapped around me.

"Hello," said a voice. My head whipped around to locate the source. I didn't see anyone. "After four months in a coma, plus another month of being barely conscious while we tested you, I would say you are up to about 80 percent. But I think you are healthy enough to go back home—"

"Who are you?! Where is Marissa?!" I croaked. My heart raced and my hands quivered. *Four months? FOUR*

MONTHS!? How had I been knocked out for four months?

"I'm your doctor, Dr. Brown."

"Dr. Brown, where is my mother?"

"She's over there in the chair." My mother was sitting, staring out the window, trying to hold back tears. "But I would like to talk to you, directly."

A man with a white lab coat walked out from the shadows behind me and stepped in front of me, into the light. "We think you have brain damage. But we are only 10 percent sure." He kept talking. "We need to study our..."

I looked at my mom. She had a worried look plastered on her face. But she didn't seem worried about this medical condition; she seemed worried about something else. It was like she wasn't listening to him. It was weird.

Dr. Brown looked at me with his sharp, blue eyes. "We are trying our best to find out what it is, but this may take a while."

I raised my eyebrows, wanting to know more about this thing. But at the same time, I watched my mom, wondering why she seemed to be preoccupied. She glanced at me—

"Ahem! Ms. Waters, I'm talking to you!"

I nodded tightly as my face began to burn and turn red. "Oh yes...what's your name?" I asked with a sharp tone. This doctor was getting on my nerves. He had a higher-pitched voice than most guys, and he had no bedside manner at all.

"Dr. Brown." He calmed himself down. So did I, sort of.

"Whatever," I mumbled.

"As I was saying, can I please meet with you to run more tests?"

"Oh, I don't think that is necessary!" my mom butted in. She seemed stressed out.

"I just want to tell you if she does have brain damage," he said. "You can decide if you want to do further tests."

My mom seemed to like "no tests" better. "Fine."

When we walked to the car, I heard my mom mumbling. "They can't find out. They can't find out or they will take her away..." *Huh?* "HE will take her away..." *HE? Who will take me away?* "We will be destroyed..." *Who will be destroyed?*

I decided to keep these questions to myself and got into our car.

Igneous

CHAPTER 4

The day after I had the dream about the Girl, I told Xed about her.

He sucked in his cheeks. His round face turned into an oval while he thought about what I had said. "I think you are imagining your future girl," he said. His black eyes glimmered in the orange-lit room we stood in. "Why don't you just *not* think about her?" He shook out his shoulder-length hair, like he had a bug in it.

I slapped my head, trying to shake out of it. "You don't get it," I said. "If you imagined a girl saying all this stuff...," I slid a hand through my greasy hair. "Wouldn't you be thinking about her all the time?"

Xed shrugged and started to fidget. "I mean, is she cute?"

"Seriously, dude?" I laughed. "That's what you want to know?"

"I'm just asking!" he said, as he made a funny face.

"Well, sort of. I don't know..." I zoned out, staring at a random wall.

"Are you okay, dude?" Xed said.

"Oh, yeah, I'm fine!"

Xed started asking questions super quickly. "Are you sure? You were just staring off into space. Are you looking at something?"

"Can I go to the bathroom?" I said. Xed nodded and I ran out of Study Hall and into the nearest boys' bathroom. I dashed into a stall and slammed the door behind me. *Bang!*

I leaned on one of the walls of the stall. *What is going on with me? Am I hallucinating? Am I going crazy?* My hands covered my face as I slowly slid my back along the wall and crouched down.

I let out a quiet sob. Was I the only one this was happening to?

"Hello?" a voice said, right outside my stall.

I quickly flushed the toilet. I opened the door and saw no one. My chest tightened and my mind raced. *Whaaaat?* "Um...hello?" I stuttered. "Uh..." I frowned when there was no answer. I shuddered and opened my mouth to say something, but nothing came out.

I washed my hands and ran out the door. Nobody was in the halls. I looked at my watch: 1505M. How did I miss my last class by five minutes? It was 1490M when I went into the bathroom. How was I in there for fifteen minutes?!

. . .

That night I was reading a book in the empty library.

The librarian said I only had twenty minutes left.

31

She would be back soon to walk me out and lock up.

In the middle of reading my book, I heard the mysterious voice again. "Who are you?!"

I closed my eyes tightly. When I looked up, I saw the figure of the Girl.

"Why do you keep appearing in my dreams?!" she yelled. Her eyebrows curved down. I would have admired her if she hadn't looked like she were going to strangle me.

"What do you mean?" I yelled back. "You keep appearing in *my* dreams!"

"Sorry…" She cowered and put her hands up to her face. "I didn't know that." She scratched the back of her head. We stared at each other for a while, taking everything in. It felt really awkward.

"So…what did you see?" I said quietly.

"We separate, and then I—wait, why should I trust you? How do I know that you aren't behind all this?" She gestured to the room.

"Well, first of all, do you think I would have the power to do that?" I asked.

"I don't know," she stuttered. "Maybe you are some shapeshifter or a mad wizard." I started to laugh but saw that she had narrowed her eyes.

"Okay, listen," I said. "I know how it must feel to suddenly have someone talking to you through a Lavagraph."

"What's a Lavagraph?" she said.

What?! A Lavagraph is one of the most expensive technologies on my planet but also one of the most popular. How did she not know what a Lavagraph was? Even the Littles know what a Lavagraph is. A thought hit me: *Was she on another planet?*

"You don't know what a Lavagraph is?" I gulped.

"Am I supposed to—" She narrowed her eyes even more. "Wait. Is this seriously a scam?"

"What's a scam?" I responded. "Is it an acronym —"

"WHERE DO YOU LIVE!" she shouted.

"I live on Planet Magma," I said slowly.

"Wait, you're from another planet? There's life on other planets out there!" she said. "I mean, I always thought there would be. I just didn't know. I've gotta be dreaming." Her eyes were so wide that I could see the whites all the way around.

"Wait, where do you live?" I asked.

"On Earth," the girl whispered, confused.

Earth? EARTH? She didn't look like she was an Earthling. In Magmian school we learned about other planets. Earth was one of them. This girl was weird: she didn't have the normal skin color or hair color that Earthlings had.

"On Earth?" I asked.

"Yeah. On Earth."

"Oh," I said. I fought for the right words to say.

She narrowed her eyes. She opened her mouth to say something but nothing came out. As moments passed by without a single word shared between us, she began to fidget and squint. Every now and then she would shake her head. She seemed so confused. Maybe she was trying to figure things out. It was probably a lot for her. But I understood. I had felt that way many times.

"So you aren't a mad wizard?" she asked. She was probably trying to break the silence.

"NO!"

"Okay, okay…"

I was completely confused. My life was twisting around and around like a Lavacoaster. First, the Jocks weren't bugging me, then I started having dreams about a girl, and finally I met that girl and she happened to be on Earth.

"Why is everything called lava-*something* on your planet?" the girl asked.

"Lava is like our element on my planet," I explained. "The one who should be the leader is the only one with the lava powers. The problem is, our planet has been in total chaos because nobody has the power. Or maybe someone does have it but doesn't want to rule."

The girl nodded. She seemed to be interested in my planet. When we stopped talking, I finally began to admire her. The way she was so sure of herself, and the way she talked…it was so—*AM I SERIOUSLY CRUSHING ON SOMEONE I DON'T KNOW?!* I secretly yelled at myself. But she seemed so perfect. Unlike me. *Am I… jealous?*

"What are you staring at?" she said.

"Um, nothing!" I said apologetically. "Sorry…"

"Are you going to puke or something? Your face is completely pale, literally gray. It's been that way the whole time."

"Oh, well, since we are from different planets, we have different color skin tones," I said. She looked at me like I was crazy. "I should ask you the same. Why do you have *your* skin tone?" I snapped.

Her face softened a little. She looked down and sat on the floor. "I actually don't know…" She looked up and I started feeling really guilty for snapping at her. *WHAT IS IT WITH ME!* I yelled at myself again. *WHY DO I KEEP SAYING THE WRONG THING?!*

"What are your hobbies?" the girl spoke up.

"Knife throwing," I shrugged.

"Oh. I love reading and school."

I nodded slowly. "Nice."

"This is weird," the girl said, after a moment.

"Yeah."

"Sorry."

"It's okay."

"Yeah…" She trailed off.

"Can we just start with the basics?"

"Huh?"

"Like, our names, our favorite colors…"

"Sure?"

"You sound unsure…" I said.

"Just—what's your name?"

"Igneous."

"What's your favorite color?"

"I don't know."

"How do you not have a favorite color? Everyone has a favorite color!"

"I don't. Let's go on! What's *your* name?"

She closed her eyes. I figured she still didn't trust me. And then she said:

"Safire."

Safire

CHAPTER 5

Am I still dreaming?

I lay in my bed thinking about everything that happened in the last six months. The Incident at school, the dreams about that guy...

My mind wandered. Every thought led to another thought, like a tree. My thoughts were like the branches, splitting over and over again.

"Sweetie, start getting ready for the quick doctor's appointment!" my mom called from downstairs.

"OK!" I yelled back. Every day since The Incident had been so empty. I had no school to go to in the mornings, no homework I had to do. The days were mostly filled with lying around in my room, listening to music, watching seasons of shows like *Red Scar* and going downstairs to talk about random things with my brother or mom.

When I got up to go to the bathroom, I found myself stumbling into a strange room. It was too dark to see much. It was sort of like a library, but nothing like the ones I had ever seen.

At first I was confused and thought that I had fallen asleep. When I touched the shelves on the walls, I knew I wasn't dreaming—I could actually feel the shelves. It felt like I was on another planet, I don't know what it was. I wanted to scream so badly, but I kept quiet and walked around slowly.

Soon I got to the corner of the library and found a guy that looked like—no—*was* the guy in my dreams. "Who are you?!" I said. "Why do you keep appearing in my dreams?!"

"What do you mean?" he responded. "You keep appearing in MY dreams!"

Wait, what? "Sorry…I didn't know." I scratched the back of my head.

Before I knew it, we were asking each other about our dreams about each other. Over time, we talked about simple stuff like hobbies. I still didn't feel comfortable with this stranger but I dealt with it. I learned that the guy's name was Igneous.

"What's your name?" he asked.

I hesitated. "Safire."

I heard my mom yelling up to my room, "Safire, we need to get to that appointment!"

All of a sudden, Igneous and the library slowly faded from view, and I found myself back in my bed.

· · ·

"I'm afraid your daughter, *ahem*, has brain damage," Dr. Brown said.

It had been a week since I got out of the hospital; this was the follow-up visit Dr. Brown asked me to attend.

"What? Please—" my mom started.

"Brain damage?" I felt as if a knot were tied in my throat. "Is that why I have issues when I'm tired…" The world around me started spinning. I gripped onto the office desk as the ceiling lights blurred into one light.

"Yes. It is the reason. I want to send you a report that I typed up. Please look at it, and the link with it." Dr. Brown's face turned from a normal guy's everyday face to a glum and stressed-out face very quickly.

"Uhh…" I started. *Why did this feel so stressful?*

"What are you planning to do to help her, Dr. Brown?" my mom said quietly.

"I need you to come to the office so she can get an MRI," said Dr. Brown.

My mom looked at her hands and pinched her lips together so hard that I heard her squeal. "Should we go, Mom?" I asked politely.

"I'm sorry, Dr. Brown, but I don't trust your equipment…" She kept rattling off reasons why he shouldn't do any testing on me. When she stopped, I asked a question I wished I had asked a long time ago.

"Um…Brown? Dr. Brown?" My hands shook. I swallowed to ease the roughness in my throat. "How is my friend? Marissa Johnson?"

"She…she was in a lot of pain." His face turned even glummer as my mood sunk to the bottom.

"What do you mean by 'was'?" I asked.

"I mean that she was on life support when she got

to the hospital. She couldn't breath on her own. So her mother decided to not let her suffer any more..." He lowered his head.

"Y-you mean she's... *dead*?" I blinked over and over again to stop myself from crying. But my tears came down like a rainstorm.

I sobbed quietly and my mom hugged my head, even though I wet her shirt. I think she even started crying. I don't think she had realized Marissa was dead.

"If I—" Dr. Brown started.

"Thank you for your time," my mom interrupted. "We have to get home."

My mind blanked out as my mom dragged me out of the office, through the hospital, into the parking lot and into the car.

As soon as my butt touched the seat, the radio turned on. At first the internal crying in my mind drowned it out. It sounded like a series of mumbles, echoing in the background. But then I heard: "An incident occurred in San Francisco, California, four months ago."

My heart jumped out of my chest. Could it be? My mom pulled over next to a random apartment and turned up the volume. Biff, the reporter for GNN (Global News Network), usually annoyed me when I heard him on the radio. But this time, I leaned in close, my stomach bouncing around, to hear what he was about to say.

"*In John Adams Middle School, on a Friday, a fire alarm went off at 3:31 P.M. It was thought to be a school shooting. Firefighters rushed over to the school and found a thirteen-year-old girl, Safire Waters, stumbling out of the school carrying another thirteen-year-old-girl, Marissa Johnson, on her back…"*

My heartbeat skipped a beat. What did this mean?

"Firefighter Hankins will speak here tomorrow at 4:00 P.M. Pacific Time to provide further information. Now…"

For a moment I couldn't breathe. Tension was in the air. My mom and I just sat there, saying nothing. My eyes were wide with terror. My heartbeat grew louder and louder, and faster and faster, until I couldn't take it anymore.

"Mom? What happens now?" I whispered.

"I don't know, honey. I don't know…"

We sat in the car for a few more minutes. My mom finally turned off the radio. Complete silence washed over the car. All I could hear was the whirring of the engine as we sat in the parked car.

I felt as if a dodge ball hit me in the stomach real hard. Well, that pain *times ten.*

I thought about texting one of my friends. Maybe Ella, or Justin, or Marissa—

Sadness rushed through me. The thought of never seeing or talking to Marissa again made me feel nauseous. My head started to pound again. I knew I had to distract myself.

OceanBlue22
Hey. How are u guys… I

I couldn't type anymore. I didn't know what to say. I slowly tapped the "Delete Message" button and put my phone away.

"Mom, we're going to the lake RIGHT NOW!" I blurted out, for some random reason. My heart stopped. It *literally* stopped. I had never commanded my mom once in my life. "Sorry—"

"No, it's okay." She turned around to give me a kind and calming look. My thoughts froze. *WHAAAAAT?* Why was she being so nice? Was it because she was feeling sorry for me about Marissa? I turned away and looked out the window to gather my thoughts.

THUMP! A dent about the size of a basketball popped into the roof of the car.

My mom whipped her head around and swerved out of the parking spot and onto the street. She slowed down to the speed limit as if nothing had happened. Meanwhile, I was clutching onto my seatbelt and the coat hanger above the car window like an idiot. "It's okay," she said. "We are completely fine—"

THUMP!

"NOT SO FINE! THE BALL!!!" I screamed. What the heck was it?

"COME ON, *&%^ing car!!!" my mom cursed as she slammed her fist into the dashboard.

THUMP!

"MOM! GET OUT OF THE CAR!!!!" I shoved my door open the same time my mom did. We jumped out of the car as another ball came crashing down onto it. This time it went through the car. I started to panic. My legs and arms felt like lead. I was glued to the road. Cars stopped in every direction, their wheels screeching as they tried to turn around.

"MOM!!! WHERE ARE YOU?! MOM!!!" I screamed over the thumping of the balls. My vision became a tunnel. "MOM! MOM!" The thumping of the balls and the cars screeching faded to background noise. My heartbeat grew louder and louder until it was the only thing I could hear.

The car burst into flames.

I didn't know how I was still alive. I gathered enough energy to crawl through the flaming rubble. I made a chant to distract myself:

Right arm forward.
Left arm forward.
Right leg forward.
Left leg forward.
Right arm.
Left arm.
Right leg.
Left leg.
Right.
Left.
Right.
Left.
R.
L.
R.
L.
R
L

R
L

I repeated this chant over and over as I crawled around the pile of crud that used to be our car. I would have cried, but the flames dried my tears and dried out my eyes. I gasped for air as smoke filled my lungs. Flames scorched my clothes until they were brown and so delicate that, if I wiggled it, they might break.

"Mom…" I rasped. I couldn't talk.

I saw a head. Some hair. A nose. And lots of blood.

I realized it was my mom. I crawled over to her and put her head on my lap. The moment her head touched me, the blood in her hair soaked my lap and expanded like the universe.

My body began quaking as the world around me shook. I lay down next to her, knowing we would both be dead by the end of this.

"It's okay. We are together," I repeated. I closed my eyes as I shifted my head next to hers. My head felt heavy. It started throbbing again. *I'm going to die. We are going to die,* I thought calmly.

I saw something move. I got up to see a black car driven by a man with a face full of scars. His midnight black hair had streaks of silver—the same color as his scars. I spotted a camera peeking out the side window, taking pictures of my mom and me. Once the guy saw me watching him, the car sped away. I rushed to catch a glimpse of the license plate.

I found a shard of glass and put the tip in the

flames. Then I carved the license plate number into my left arm:

BB1437

I threw the knife into the flames as the characters on my arm filled with blood. I winced when my shaky right hand scraped it with a fingernail by mistake.

I crawled around in the ashes that were still sizzling. By now, I was used to the smoke. It's as if I was immune to it. *Weird. Why?*

I stumbled over to my mom. I put my head down on the concrete next to her. I felt barely alive. My chest slowly rose and fell.

Rise.

     Fall.

Rise.

     Fall.

Rise.

     Fall.

I tried to remember happy things to make myself go to sleep. To close my eyes for the last time.

If I had to die, this would be a good place: right next to my mother.

. . .

"Safire. Safire! SAFIRE!!!"

My eyes flew open. *What just happened?* Everything was blurry. Faces looked like strange circles with white lights on top of them.

Who is that odd and scary-looking man?

Lights looked like white, fuzzy spots in the air…

Am I dead?

Tools looked like silver lines…

Am I waking from a nightmare?

My mom looked like a ghost. Her pale, white face made me realize that this was all REAL. These strange occurrences were all part of my new normal.

The next moment, a sharp, metal device that felt like a tiger tooth was inserted into my tongue. I sank down into a bed. It was like I was in quicksand, slowly disappearing from the world. My eyes closed, and I fell into a deep, dreamless sleep.

. . .

I awoke, startled by the sound of voices.

"—have some X-rays of Safire's brain, Ms. Waters. We think she has a brain disease called…" I couldn't hear the name because the doctor spoke it too softly. "I think we shouldn't tell her about the disease or its possible effects," Dr. Brown said. "Please call it a brain tumor."

"Okay. Well…brain tumor it is," my mom said. She didn't seem that upset.

I stared at the blank ceiling. Questions ran through my mind. So many questions…

Where am I?

What do they mean? Why are they keeping secrets? Why don't they tell me everything?

What's happening to me?

What disease? Have I had it forever? Does it have to do with my dad?

Do I have cancer?

What should I do? What's going on? Why me?

Am I supposed to be different?

Why has my mom been acting weird? Why is she mumbling things about being destroyed? Why will I be taken away?

Who threw fireballs *on top of our car?*

Why can't I stop thinking?

I kept asking myself questions, losing track of how many there were. My mom leaned over me, but I couldn't hear what she was saying.

My thinking stopped. The questions stopped. A sleepiness washed over me. My eyes stayed closed as flashbacks suddenly wavered over me. They had a dreamlike feel, even though they were memories from my life.

I was with Marissa…

"Safire! I have to show you this paper!" Marissa said.

I was putting away my fourth period books in my locker and getting ready for lunch. "Let me guess," I said. "It's some chart…"

"Correct! Here it is."

It was a seating chart. The moment I saw that I got to sit with my best friends, I almost cried happy tears.

My friends had been with me my whole life. They always supported me…

The memory faded and another appeared.

I sat in a dining chair in our old house. I was seven years old. A man in a lab coat was asking me questions.

"Who is this Liginia?" he said. He smoothed down his fine hair.

"She is an alien of some kind," I growled. I felt that nobody believed me. "I don't know who exactly she is, but…"

Everything fell silent. I watched the man's lips move. What?!

All of a sudden, my body lurched forward, and I started punching the man. My mom cast a worried look and ran from the other side of the room to stop me.

The memory faded AGAIN. But I had just enough time to think: *Who was this Liginia person?* She was buried deep inside my brain.

That was the end of the random memories from the past. It was time to go back to the real world.

I realized I was in my house, and in my bed. I heard some shuffling. Then some huffing. And some puffing. And some stomping. And also some yelling.

"Safire!!! WAKE UP!!!" It was my brother, Aenon.

Oh, did I not tell you about him yet?

Pause.

Aenon Waters.

Fifteen going on sixteen years old. In tenth grade.

Lots of girls like him.

Football player. Quarterback. Jersey number nine.

Loves foxes. Loves orange.

REALLY ANNOYING!

Play.

"OKAY! I'M AWAKE!" I shouted back at him. I

opened my eyes to see Aenon's hazel eyes staring down at me. We may be two years apart, but we're pretty close. We fight a lot, but usually we end up sitting in my bedroom watching T.V. and hanging out.

"IT'S ALL BECAUSE OF YOU!" He stomped away.

My eyes narrowed. "What did I do?"

His footsteps stopped as if he were in thought. The footsteps started again and they got quieter as he walked down the stairs to the kitchen. "BECAUSE!" he yelled.

"Because *what*? Stop blaming me. And you don't need to yell. CALM DOWN!"

"Safire! Stop, for once in your life!" he shouted. "We need to talk!"

I grew quiet. "Why? What is it? What happened?" I fiddled with my hair as I waited for Aenon to say something.

"Um…well, you see, I haven't seen Mom or you for four months now." He scratched the back of his neck. "Mom hadn't visited the house for a while so I stayed at a friend's house a week after you left for the doctor's appointment and didn't come back." His eyes glistened like he was about to cry. "Um…and also, she only called me *once*, to let me know it might be a while before she came home…" Now tears came dripping down his face.

I sniffled. My throat dried up. My hands shook as I got up and hugged him tight.

"And…after a week, like I s-said…I went to my friends house for a week. But they didn't have enough food, and they said they would call Mom, so I ran away and came home. And I have had to survive every day…I had to use all of my allowance AND the money Mom gave me....plus, I had to go to the grocery store every day. AND I had to deal with football practice and school, on top of everything!" Aenon shook so much that my vision was getting blurry from the fast, tight movements.

"I-I never realized..." I wanted to ask him so many questions, but I didn't want to overwhelm him. So, just like I always did, I pushed the thousands of questions that swam around my head to the back of my brain.

I hugged him tighter as he cried and his tears soaked my shirt. I had never seen Aenon so sad. Usually he would just get back up again and wipe off his tears. I guess he had so much sorrow buried inside him, he was finally letting it all out.

"Aenon, Mom has been acting really weird. She said something about me being taken away if 'they' find out something about me. And then we will be destroyed. ...do you know what she means?" His jaw dropped. "I know," I said. "It's—"

The whites of his eyes turned bright red and he spoke in a commanding voice. "How do you know that?"

I flinched at the sight of his red eyes. "Wh—"

"Forget about it. Mom can never know you know."

"But tell me! What is going on?!"

"You can learn when you get older! For your sake, forget about it!" His eyes turned back to normal. I could tell he was fighting to look calm.

"What the heck? Why did your eyes turn red?" I asked. My hands shook.

"What are you talking about? The last thing I said

was what happened over the last four months."

For a moment, I felt like the whole world was against me. Why couldn't anyone tell me what was going on?! I didn't want to ask him more questions, afraid that he was going to turn into the red-eyed person again. I let go of him and ran to get him a blanket, trying to forget about the red eye thing. "Do you need anything?" I shivered.

"Water… soup…bread…sleep…"

"Okay…you rest here. I'll turn on my T.V. if you'd like…"

"Yeah. I'd like that." He gave me a pat on the shoulder.

I walked over to my T.V. and turned it on to a random movie called *The Gift of the Garden*. "And Safire?" Aenon croaked.

"Yeah?"

"Love you…"

"I love you, too, Aenon. Now get some rest. I'm sure you didn't get much sleep." I tried to push the freaky image of Aenon out of my mind. "I gotta deal with Mom…"

"Go get 'em!" he mumbled. And his eyes turned to the T.V.

My heartbeat quickened. I was ready to face my mom. But before I opened her bedroom door, the questions I wanted to ask Aenon popped up into my head and began to float around.

Why did Mom leave Aenon?
Why did Mom seem *dead when I found her after the car*

accident—but somehow turn out in better condition than me? Was she in the hospital, too?

Why did Mom have something to hide?

And, most importantly, did Aenon know about this thing that Mom seemed to be thinking about all the time?

Igneous

CHAPTER 6

I hadn't had any uncontrollable dreams about Safire since the day I met her. We hadn't met again because the Lavagraph wasn't working, or whatever connected us.

Every day, I wished that I would hear her voice. When I didn't, I thought that I must have gone crazy and imagined her. Every day, I dismissed the thought. The problem was, I couldn't get her out of my head. *HOW DO PEOPLE DEAL WITH THIS STUFF!?* I kept yelling at myself. I didn't understand why this was happening to me!

I stayed in my dorm all day and made the excuse that I was sick. When they checked me for a fever, I became so nervous that I got all sweaty, and they thought I actually *was* sick.

All day, and I mean *all day*, I watched L.S. (it means Lavascreening). I closed my eyes and listened.

"Today a thirty-year-old man with a long beard went to the Volcano and started cursing at The Guild, the top government officials. This man will be held in prison on serious charges.

"Now let's have a quick break. Jadgon, tell our watchers about our weather for this week."

Another announcer took over. "Yes, so, we have a high of one thousand mags this week, and it is going to be very cold. Our low is eight hundred ninety-nine mags and we will have many sear showers." (This is when we have lava fall from the sky and turn into sparks of fire.) "So, everyone get out your eelea jackets and get snuggled. This is going to be the coldest week ever!"

I switched the channel.

"This is episode ten of the Magic of Swedsing by Lob Poss. I hope you enjoy it."

Lob Poss came on. "So now you need to put some orange here to brighten the volcano and make it pop. Take this ash gray and lightly sweds the red sky. This shows the sky changing from the power of the volcano bursting."

I switched the channel.

"Are you in love with someone so much? Can you not control it?"

My heart started to pump fast. I opened my eyes to see a man talking on the screen.

"Then you should email me! I will give you the advice of a lifetime! Ask someone with the expert experience. It's just ten axer for one call!"

Really? I realized it was a scam. I closed my eyes again and switched the channel. After a while, I fell asleep. It was a dreamless sleep, thankfully, and soon my energy was almost fully restored.

· · ·

"Igneous!" I woke up and I saw Xed leaning over me, staring.

"It's time to get to our classes! You missed yesterday!" He helped me up. While I got ready, he filled me in on what I had missed (not much).

The day was mostly boring:

Schedule
850M to 950M: History
950M to 1050M: Math
1050M to 1150M: Planet Studies
1150M to 1250M: Science
1250M to 1300M: Lunch
1300M to 1400M: Language
1400M to 1500M: Study Hall
1500M to 1600M: Individual Practices

But when I went to study hall, nobody was there. I looked around. I looked at every single chair and table.

I felt a breath on my neck. I turned around—but nobody was there! It seemed like a horror movie: you stand in an empty room, with nobody else in there, and then something STRIKES!

"Hello?" a familiar voice said. "What is this place? Oh great, it's you again."

"Safire?" I asked.

"Yeah?"

"It seems like it's been forever—"

"Oh great, now I have to listen to your love

speech…" she said, sarcastically.

Color rose to my cheeks and I pursed my lips. "Sorry…where are you?" My voice weakened in embarrassment. "I don't see you."

"I'm right here!" All of a sudden, she appeared in a velvet seat on a table right in front of me. Safire stared hard at an open book in her hands. She flipped the pages but didn't seem to make out the words. "How do you read this?"

"Um…do you want me to teach you?" I asked.

Her face softened a little. "Uh…okay?"

I brought over a large Lavachalk board, which levitated above the floor. "The first word on the page? Look at it, and then write it here." I pointed at the board. Safire got up and wrote down the word:

勺 ♋ 勺

I wrote the meaning in English:

Did

Over an hour, I taught her all the letters of the Magmian alphabet:

A = ⅃	B = Ɓ	C = ɬ	D = 勺
E = Ƙ	F = Ᵽ	G = ʒ	H = H
I = ♋	J = ɟ	K = ᴐʒ	L =]
M = ⅄Ɪ	N = ⋃	O = θ	P = Ᵽ

Q = Q⁊	R = ಬುು	S = ş	T = Ť
U = ⱝ	V = ⸗	W = ꓧ	X = 㐅
Y = ⸰ö	Z = ꓑ

When the hour was almost over, she was able to read it!

"Good!" I said.

"Did…you…know…that…there…are 100 other… planets known that have…living things on them—

RRRRRIIIIIIINNNNNGGGG!!!

"What?" Safire looked up and freaked out. "Do they—do they know I'm here?" she asked.

"No! That's just a school bell!" I said.

"Oh…well, maybe I should go?"

I hesitated for a moment, but then I shrugged.

"Hey! Igneous! It's time for our next class!" I turned around and saw Xed running towards me.

I turned back around. "Safire—"

Safire had disappeared. It was like she had never even been there. I gathered my books and left.

. . .

During my last class of the day, I pondered and wondered so much about what was happening. I kept repeating the questions in my head: *Why her? Why me?* It was all I could think of. I didn't want to be dramatic, but if you were in the same place as me, wouldn't you think the same things?

That night, I stared at the ceiling of the boy's dormitory. I let my body sink into my bed in the corner of the room, away from all the doors. The other guys were joking around. Usually I did, too. At least, I did with them. But not that night.

"Hey! Ig!" one of the guys called out to me.

"Not right now!" I said.

"Okay! But...what's going on, dude? You've been really weird! I mean, you're always kinda weird, but not the weird you normally are."

"Um, I'm just tired from midterms," I said, half-lying and half-telling-the-truth. The guy gave me a look and walked away. I was surprised he was talking to me. Most of the time he just ignored me like everyone else, unless he wanted something from me.

I stared at the ceiling. My vision got blurry from looking at the same spot for too long. Dots of color danced across my vision.

I turned on my L.S. and listened to some sound channels. These channels were full of people making sounds to get you to fall asleep. The weird thing was, I had never used it before, because I thought it was dumb. Now I started to think it wasn't.

I soon fell asleep, like the people on the L.S. expected.

. . .

In my dreams, I was a child again.

I was in my cozy house with my older brothers who I

never really knew.

There was a knock on the door. One of my brothers got up to answer it. When he opened the door, he disappeared.

A younger version of Safire appeared at the door. She carried a heavy machine gun and started to shoot my other brother! I jumped in front of him, and she stopped. She then ran out the door. My brother lay dead at my feet.

I jolted awake with sweat pouring down my back. What was going on with me? Was Safire a killer in the real world? *NGGG!* Why did I believe my dreams? I stuffed my face into my pillow and cried. Luckily, everyone else was asleep by then. When I was done crying, I sat up and put a robe on. I quietly took a lava candle from my bedside table and walked out of the room.

I slowly walked down the hallway, passing doors to other dorm rooms. I was careful not to wake anyone. The lava candle glowed in the dark hall.

When I got to the end of the white-washed halls, I jumped over the railing that separated the hallway from the ground, seven feet below. My feet landed on the ground with a soft thud.

I looked around at the common room I had jumped into. The fireplace sat at the far side of the room. Red velvet chairs stood around a circular rug that sank under my feet. On the other side of the room, under a huge hallway, there were more velvet chairs and a long snack table. The walls were a dark red, and the carpet was like a cloud. I walked over to the snack table and sat down.

I picked up one of the snacks, labelled: "HOT AND

SPICY NACHOS!" When I put the first chip in my mouth, it exploded with flavor. I slowly savored it…

"Trooper! Are you IG-2283?"

I turned around and gulped. My squad leader stood behind me, with his dark eyes, dark hair and light skin. He tucked his uniform into his jeans.

There is one more thing I should tell you about. My boarding school was a military school. We all get troop numbers. We were trained to fight. We were only allowed to get six hours of sleep (except for when you were sick). Also, we had to have all A's, or you were moved to the Failer's School. Some people died at Failer's School. Many people try to run away, but the government always catches them, and that is that.

"Yes?" I stuttered. I hated my troop number. The man narrowed his eyes and watched my every move as he slowly walked back up the stairs. The squad leaders were always suspicious of some kids, but they had never been suspicious of me. This was the first time that they were. I trembled under his gaze. Fortunately, he didn't see.

When I was done with my snack, I walked to the door that went out into the large courtyard.

. . .

"ALL SOLDIERS, WAKE UP!" Yep, that's our fighters' 300M wake-up call.

I ran up the stairs and into my dorm, where others were getting up. I threw on my military outfit and grabbed my hat. *THUMP! THUMP! THUMP!* They jumped over the railing to get out of the room. *THUMP!* I joined them. We ran outside to the wide open grass field that we used as our training area.

"One hundred laps!" our commander said. Sheesh, this was easy. Usually we did two hundred laps! After a couple of minutes, we were on our last lap. The moment we finished, our commander shouted, "Fifty pushups! Then fifty burpees—"

BOOM!!! A gunshot sounded in the air.

Safire

CHAPTER 7

"Mom. We need to talk." I desperately needed to know why she left Aenon alone for so long. I shoved open her bedroom door to see her squinting over her laptop, her reading glasses on her bed. She looked up at me.

"No, I need to tell you something," she said. I tried to interrupt her, but she still kept talking. "That license plate number that you wrote down? It's useful. The police tracked 'em down. The guy who was in that car caused the fireballs. They don't know how he did this." She paused. I pursed my lips. "But they *do* know that he was…different. He had red eyes and scars all over his face. He also had weird hair. On his back, he had one tattoo that said, 'Safire,'" *Whaaat?* I scowled. "And another one in some type of language—they don't know what it means. But they did put him in jail." She seemed to be out of breath.

I forgot what I was about to say. So I just flopped to the floor. My mom was changing—or something was happening behind my back, and it was rocking my world like a cradle.

"Do they have a picture of him? Or do they have him?" I asked quietly.

She raised an eyebrow and stared at her mirror closet for a moment. "Well, before we get to that, I need to show you something." She moved the computer around so it was facing me. "Can you read this?" I looked at it.

The Unknown Objects from August 3rd
Recent studies show that the unknown objects that came down on August 3rd—the event that everyone remembers as the "catastrophe"—are aliens. The appearance of these aliens is classified. Their brains are called "yueoiuns." There have been some alien attacks on patients during certain medical procedures. "It's like a movie, but in real life and with real pain," Dr. Owen Brown said. "This is way more dangerous. This is real. If anything goes wrong, we might all die. I have a similar patient. My patient has yueoiuns in her brain. They twist around like worms—"

I stopped reading. *Wait... What?!* My mind couldn't seem to process the info.

I kept reading.

"...The worst part is that every test I run on her comes out as abnormal. I've never seen anything like it."

"Mom? Is the patient that he was talking about…
me?" I whispered.

"Yes, sweetie. I'm afraid it is true." She lowered
her head and got up onto her bed. She slouched over her
computer and sighed.

Tears filled my eyes. Why me? My headaches and
medical problems may have started recently, but I have
felt *different* all my life. For one thing, I never had a single
bite of ice cream, ever! (I haven't even had ANY sugar!)
Never ever in my life. When my mom and I went to
carnivals, I would see kids licking ice cream, and I would
cry and cry. After this happened three times, we never
went back. Though I never knew what it was that made
me different from everyone else.

I looked at my mom. She knew what I was
thinking. We always knew each other's thoughts, just like
the mom and daughter in *Billmore Girls*. But because my
mom was so understanding, she would take the blame for
all of this. It was nice, but none of this was her fault—or
was it? Was there something that she wasn't telling me?

I HATE MY LIFE, I thought to myself. *WHY DOES
MY LIFE HAVE TO BE SO HARD! Everyone else gets a
happy and normal life!*

"Mom?' I piped up. "Why me? Why did this have
to happen?"

"I don't know honey. I don't know." This would
have been more comforting if my mom hadn't looked like
she *knew* why. She glanced away, and looked back at me.
Did she know? I always felt like I could trust her before.
Now, I'm not so sure…

I decided to go back to my room to visit Aenon—but then I remembered why I came to my mom's room. "Mom. Why did you leave Aenon by himself here?! You didn't answer me earlier. You changed the subject. I want to know WHY," I said firmly, like nothing happened.

"Oh, sweetie. Did he tell you? I'm sorry. Now, shoo…"

My mother had never shooed me in my life; whether under pressure or not. It started to seem like she was somebody else. Like she was a creature in disguise. I kept telling myself she wasn't a different person, she's just confused. Confused, like I am.

"NO! Why was he left here all alone FOR FOUR MONTHS?" I shouted. "And was comforted with ONLY ONE CALL?"

"Safire, calm do—"

"NO! I HATE YOU! I wish I had never known you! I wish you were never in my life! YOU ARE THE WORST! MOTHER! EVER!"

With these hateful words, I turned and picked up a frame of my family and smashed it against the wall. The glass shattered to a million pieces, and the frame punched a hole in the wall. The leftovers fell to the ground. The picture was ripped up and could probably never be fixed. Not that I cared, in that moment. Ever since the headaches first started, my emotions were like a roller coaster. Was this puberty? I felt so angry at times, yet so sad at other times. Every emotion felt magnified times a million, lately.

I stomped out of the room like a madwoman. My steps echoed through the halls as I ran to my room. Aenon lay in my bed, clueless to what was going on. "What happened?" he slurred. "Why are you stomping around?"

"Mom doesn't care."

A knowing look passed his eyes. I cringed. It was just like the look my mom always made. I hated that look, because it meant secrets were being hidden from me.

"Food?" He looked at me with puppy dog eyes.

"Yeah, food," I said. "Let me go to the bathroom real quick." I walked out of the room and turned the corner, into the bathroom. I sat on top of the toilet cover, thinking random thoughts.

All of a sudden, a book appeared in my hands, and I was *teleported* to Igneous' world once again. This time I was in a big room with a loooooooong table and tons of chairs. I sat down and waited for Igneous.

Before I knew it, he rushed in. "I'm late, I'm—" He stopped at the end of the hall, confused. He stood there, sweating and combing his hair back with his hands, scanning every inch of the room with his eyes open wide. I figured that he probably expected there to be a lot more people in this hall. When he looked at me, I could almost see a hint of a smile on his lips.

"Oh great, it's you again." I said. "What is this place?"

"Safire?" A shiver ran up my spine. Why the heck did his saying my name make me feel good? I hoped I wasn't...never mind.

"Yeah?" I said.

"It seems like—"

"Oh great, I have to listen to your love speech

now?"

Like before, I grew more used to him. I began to… *like* him? He taught me how to read his language and cracked small jokes. I felt like we had known each other our whole lives…

RIIIN—dong! The sound the school bell in Igneous' world and the doorbell in my house on earth mixed together, scaring me. Everything immediately turned into the bathroom back at my home and I winced.

DING DONG! The doorbell kept going off.

Two seconds later, my mom rushed in the bathroom. My stomach jumped when she slammed open the door. *What the heck!* I thought. She looked disturbed when she found me just sitting on the toilet cover, not doing anything.

"Safire, you have to run away! Some crazy doctors that want to do more tests on you are *here*! Get the fire ladder! RUN! I WILL BE RIGHT BEHIND YOU!"

The moments that followed were scary. I moved like I was in a trance. I jumped over a pile of clothes and ran to my walk-in closet, where my escape ladder sat. My mother ran down the stairs, fiddling with her hair.

A loud piercing sound deafened me. I gasped. I felt a slight touch on my shoulder. I opened my eyes and found Aenon sitting on the edge of my bed next to me.

I pulled on Aenon's arm as hard as I could, to get him to come with me. But he didn't come. He just shook his head, silently saying "no." I cried for him to come with me. He was saying something I couldn't hear or understand.

He pushed me through my bedroom window. I flew out and landed on the ladder. I held on tightly and climbed down to the ground. Aenon threw me my backpack and a folder with some papers. I looked up to see my brother being taken away, dragged by his arms by the doctors with the blinding white coats.

I ran back towards the house shouting, "NO!" *Who were these bad doctors?* Why did they want me? Why did they want Aenon? How did my mom know they were different from Dr. Brown?

My hearing suddenly switched back on. I looked at the house, secretly saying goodbye. I had to leave. No matter how much pain it would cost me.

I had to leave.

Igneous

CHAPTER 8

"Attention!" a voice shouted. The air was filled with smoke…dust bombs. Everyone crouched down, coughing on the defense field. *Was this some joke?* All we were doing was warming up. "Commander Yeail, this is obviously a very weak squad!"

My mouth hung wide open, but nobody could see.

"W-well, this was unexpected!" For a second, I didn't know who this voice belonged to—but then I realized it was our commander, who never ever had a soft emotion. (She was always yelling.)

"Let's say I was an attacking squad. Of course they are going to attack unexpectedly!" the first voice said. *Who was that?* "It's a good thing I'm taking over this horrible thing!"

"Yes…" replied Commander Yeail. I couldn't hear the rest because I was drowned in the sound of coughing from the smoke of the dust bomb. My eyes strained to see any shape in front of me.

Once everyone recovered, we got in our "attention" positions. The dust cleared and we finally got to see our new commander.

A tall, muscular woman stood in front of us. She had piercing, navy eyes and gray hair. Her skin was a dark midnight blue. There weren't that many people on my planet that had blue skin. Most had pale skin that turned peach-ish brown sometimes. Her appearance almost freaked me out.

"Hello, everyone! I am your new commander. I am Commander Coal! Training is going to be much harder, but you will learn to work hard and get strong. Your new wake-up time is 100M! You will go to sleep no later than 1900M! If you want to be stronger, JOIN ME! Or you go to Failer's School!" she shouted. "I want you all to do one thousand laps! Then do two hundred pushups and five hundred burpees!"

I think everyone nearly fainted when they heard this. Because the day ends at 2000M, we will only have 200 minutes of sleep! Is Commander Coal crazy!?

After many hours of yelling, screaming, panting, pain and more, we were finally done. Everyone tried to stop themselves from crying. Our bodies ached so much that our arms and legs were red, and we all could barely walk. Thirty people had to sit out and were almost sentenced to Failer's School. Luckily I wasn't on the bench. There were still three hundred more people standing in my squad, and all of us were aching.

"Now! You are FINALLY done with the warm up," she said. Just the warm up? That was like, *twice* what we usually do in a whole day! We were never really tired at the end of morning practice. "We are going to follow a daily schedule. In the morning, practice will be about strength. And at night, practice will be about technique." Everyone sighed in happiness. "BUT! We are still going to do the same warm up!" Obviously she didn't want us to be happy.

After some arguing, she put ten more people on the bench (I wasn't one of them!). Then, we received a schedule:

Before Classes:
150 to 200—Warm up
200 to 400—Fist fighting
400 to 550—Fighting with weapons
550 to 700—Strength training
700 to 800—First aid/Cool down

After Classes:
Attacking
Defense
General Techniques (Weapons and fist fighting)

Fist fighting was EXHAUSTING. It was the worst thing. We didn't get any protection suits, because we needed to "muscle up." My fists turned white and dripped black blood. (Yeah, we have black blood instead of red, Earthly blood). My muscles began to feel overused, but I kept going.

Because the benches grew crowded, some people were sent to detention. Not just some: two hundred people! And only one hundred people were left.

After we finished our weapon fighting, Commander Coal called us to attention. "Now, there is no other squad here, correct?" We all nodded. "Well then! Everyone still here is backup until I choose the top fifty. They will be the best soldiers and the lead squad! I will choose again every two months!" My heart beat. I still had a chance to be in the top! "Attention!"

I puffed out my chest and let my eyes linger on the back of the soldier in front of me. The balls of my feet pressed into the hard soles of my shoes. My vision slowly got blurry. From the corner of my eye, I saw Commander Coal point at people and tell them to sit on the bench or on the grass—they would be backup.

After a while, she needed to eliminate two more people. I hoped with my heart that I wasn't one of them. (Also, Xed is a healer so he wasn't at this event) "ONE MORE PERSON! Be your best or you will be out!"

My heart beat when Commander Coal came near me. All of a sudden, her eyes snapped to me. I sucked in my breath. Her eyes lingered on me for a moment. Then she started to walk towards me. I realized that she held a knife in her hand. She began to scrape her fingernails on it. I glanced and saw that they were razor sharp. My eyes snapped forward. I heard her steps echo on the pavement. *CLICK, CLACK, CLICK, CLACK.* I felt the sudden urge to itch the back of my neck, but I locked my knees instead. One sudden move and I would be out.

When she was finally standing right next to me, it felt like my heartbeat stopped. Saliva filled my mouth. The world froze around me, except for the Commander.

She put her hand under my chin and stared at me. Her eyes bore into my eyes. The hair on my skin stood up. Up close, her muscular features were more obvious. Her creepy eyes had large red streaks across them, and she had one long brown strand of hair that weirdly twisted around her head. I tried not to cry; I kept my eyes open, drying my tears. An ultimate fear of failing shot through me—

"I trust that you can be good, right?" I nodded my head nervously. Abruptly, she took her hand off my chin and walked to a different student and sent him to the bench.

What was that about?

. . .

The next couple days, my run-in with Commander Coal was the new gossip. Before this, I didn't know that boys gossiped. Whenever I walked by, I would hear people whispering about me.

"Did you hear about what happened?"

"Yeah! That guy might be appointed by Lord Slag!"

"Eh, I don't know what will happen to him. He seems really weird."

After a few more days, it was like nothing had ever happened. Nobody thought about Commander Coal's behavior, except for me. It always lingered in my mind. When I was listening to lectures, when I was eating lunch and even when I was going to the bathroom! I couldn't forget about it. I started to get creeped out whenever Commander Coal got near me.

During lunch, an announcement took my mind off the event. "IG-2283 to the Office, IG-2283 to the Office please!" These words boomed through the loudspeaker.

When I got to the office, I was ushered in by a Lavagraph of the principal. I sat down on a seat in front of her Lavagraph. I cringed when she cleared her throat. "There are several people who have accused you of failing them," she said. "Is this true?"

Whaaaat? I was completely confused. Why would I fail people? "Huh? Who accused me?" I asked.

"Come on in!" the principal said. Behind me, the door opened and the Jocks stepped into the office. They sneered at me and even cursed at me.

"Mr. Enki! I can suspend you again, or send you to Failer's School if you don't shut your big fat mouth!" the principal screamed. "Now…explain why you think IG-2283 wronged you."

"Well, this big jerk has made fun of us our whole lives." There was a smirk in his voice. I opened my mouth in disbelief. "And we saw him talking to Commander Coal a couple of hours ago! He was talking about failing us!"

The principal looked back and forth between us in confusion. "Let me talk with you, separately…" She called the Jocks over, one by one, to meet with each of them in a separate room.

I sat there quietly, anxiously waiting for my turn. *How did I get into this mess?* First, the Jocks got suspended.

Then, I had dreams about a girl and met her. Then, we got a new commander (which never happens), and practices are a billion times harder. And *then*, I was getting accused of something I didn't do! *How many things could happen in a week?!*

My butt slowly sank into the velvet chair. I grew more drowsy from the hard workouts in the morning and evening. I just wished so much that my life would go back to normal, even if it meant the Jocks were going to bully me.

I could hear yelling in the room next door. It started to give me a headache. Did the Jocks really want to fight me about this? Couldn't we just move on with our lives? I just wished nothing had happened... I shifted around to try to find a comfortable spot. I closed my eyes and tried to sleep, but the sound of the Jocks yelling woke me up again and again.

"Why are you sitting in this weird room?" a familiar voice said. I turned around to see Safire walking towards me.

"I was accused of doing something I didn't..." I grumbled.

She walked over and sat in the Principal's seat. I wondered why I couldn't see the room that Safire was in. "Boring?" she asked.

"What do you mean?"

"Nevermind..." A moment passed. She was staring at a picture of Commander Coal and the Principal shaking hands. "Who is Commander Coal?" she asked.

"Our new training coach, who makes us do one

thousand laps, two hundred pushups and five hundred burpees!"

She looked at me like I was crazy and muttered, "I can barely do twenty pushups!"

We stared at each other for a while. Bored. I started to do it again. I focused on her pretty features. Her long eyelashes, her attentive eyes and—

"Why are you checking me out?"

I blinked quickly and stopped daydreaming. "I'm not!" I said. "Why would I?"

"I dunno." She looked down at her feet.

I fiddled with my fingers. "Um…and…" I trailed off, not knowing what to say.

She didn't look up. She started to fade away.

"Why are you fading?" I asked.

Her image went back to normal. "Probably because we haven't talked for a while?" she guessed.

"Do you want to play a game?" I asked. "I know one. You know…to get to know each other."

I was surprised when she nodded. "How do you play?"

"So, I will say something like, 'I have…pranked my mom five times.' If you have done that thing before, you clap your hands twice."

"Okay," she said. "I have never worn pink."

I clapped my hands. "I have been peed on by my pet!"

I smirked as Safire giggled and clapped twice. "A bunch of people started flirting with me out of nowhere."

I clapped twice. After a couple more rounds, I

suggested we get more personal, because we had only been saying funny things.

"Um…" Safire thought. "Lately, my life has been so weird. I mean, besides this meeting with you. And I don't just mean that a couple things happened at school…"

I clapped twice. There was an awkward silence. "Hey," I began. What—"

The door behind me slammed open, and Safire disappeared. *Why did she disappear?*

The principal rushed to her seat. "They were lying, thankfully." *Thankfully? Why thankfully?* "But I need to talk to you." Her voice got quiet. "Never tell anyone this, but I am…" Her figure turned into Commander Coal!

Shivers ran down my spine. My hands shook, but I tried to conceal it. "What? Why—"

"It's for your own good," she said. "If you tell someone, you will be sent to Failer's School. There, you will be treated as the worst and you will probably die in a month. So, DON'T tell anyone, or we will hunt them down and kill them."

"Why me?"

She laughed. "Right now is the only time to call Lord Slag…"

Safire

CHAPTER 9

I swung my backpack over my shoulder and looked at the open forest.

My path. This is my path.

I would give anything for everything to go back to normal.

My path. I will become my own person. I will fight through this.

I couldn't help but stare at the trees. For whatever reason, I felt connected to the quiet sounds of the forest. The songbirds humming. The snakes slithering. Woodpeckers, pecking in rhythm. The birds steadily flapping their wings. The grass waving in the air. It felt like a song. A peaceful song. The song of the woods. (Too bad other people had to ruin this by cutting down trees.)

This place reminded me of the Survival Games. I felt like Cat Deen standing in the arena, never knowing what will happen next.

People find it weird that, in books, I look for who (and what type of person) the main character is. Most people seem to read books just to find out what happens.

Not me. I feel connected to that main character. It's almost like I'm living out their feelings and emotions as I'm reading.

After a few minutes, I realized I needed to head on into the woods. I trembled and wished that I could hide or disappear. I struggled to breath normally. I felt so dizzy that if I didn't start walking, I would just topple over. So, without looking back at my house, I dragged myself into the forest.

As I walked, I kept pinching myself to test if this was actually real. But I knew it was. The ladder, the escape…the memories kept replaying in my head. The sorrow filled my chest so much that it choked me.

Don't be a baby. Don't be a baby. Don't be a baby, I said to myself.

I walked on through the forest for what felt like forever. The trees grew taller, redder and closer together, and started to make the forest much darker.

It was sort of creepy. I felt like somebody was breathing on my neck. But when I turned to check, there wasn't anyone there.

Don't let stuff get to you. Don't let stuff get to you, I thought to myself.

But I did. I did let stuff get to me. I pondered what was going on in the world. For the first time in my life, I thought, *what are other people doing?*

My thoughts were so random:

What is the President of the United States doing right now?

What is the world's richest man doing?

What's the person that loves music more than anyone in the world doing?

What are the kids who got the stuff I donated through charities doing?

And most importantly, *what is my family doing?*

I felt like my mom and brother were with me. I stopped and listened. I just heard the faint sound of leaves in the air.

I tried to busy myself. I flipped my backpack around and opened it. The contents of the bag were: a sleeping bag, a flashlight, the folder, one hundred dollars, an empty water thermos, a Swiss Army knife, a couple of bottles of water, my phone (which was useless because there wasn't any service) and hiking boots. At the bottom of the bag was a letter from Aenon. Gloomily, I pulled it out and opened it.

Dear Safire,

I don't have much time to write this letter. Listen, if you are reading this, you probably had to leave. And I'm sorry if I left you out in the woods. Believe me, Mom made me write this ever since the accident at your school two days ago. Hey—

Sorry, Mom is calling me. She said that she won't be home for a while, but I have to finish this letter today. And if everything goes back to normal, PLEASE don't tell anyone I know about this cheesy card...

Anyway, I wish you luck and I hope

everything we put in your bag will help you, BYE!
>w<

Love,
Aenon

The words surrounded me like a warm hug. I think I bawled my eyes out, because after that my vision was blurry for—I don't know how long. I later fell asleep in my sleeping bag.

I was standing in the park next to our house. My mom was laughing and pointing at something. I looked where she was pointing and saw a fire. I felt annoyed. It seemed like she was taunting me. I felt like yelling at her about leaving me behind. Anger bubbled up inside me. It felt like I ate too much and felt stuffed. But instead of food, I felt stuffed with anger and annoyance. I wasn't even sad.

Anger…
Stuffed…
Food…

I woke up, realizing I was hungry. I started panicking about not being able to find food. First of all, I didn't know how to tell the difference between poisonous and edible berries and nuts. Second of all, I would never be able to kill anything.

I pulled out the Swiss army knife from my bag and cut some bark off a tree. In books I had read, characters would eat bark because they had nothing else to eat. I hung the bark in front of my face with two fingers. *Don't think about it, just eat it!* I repeated in my head.

"ARRRGGG!!!" I shouted and shoved the bark in my mouth like a maniac. I sat there and munched on it like it was gum. It wasn't bad. It didn't taste like anything, but the texture was weird. I scraped some more bark off the tree. My stomach growled for more, so I ate more. Ten pieces more.

Big mistake. My stomach felt like I had eaten ten thousand eggs. AND I HATE EGGS!

I realized I had to start being realistic. I didn't want to, but I knew I had to. For some time, I sat on a tree stump and tried to figure out what to do next.

I pulled out a blank piece of paper from the folder and grabbed a pencil.

Things I probably need to do:

❏ Build shelter

❏ FIND MORE WATER!!! (besides the water that Aenon gave me)

❏ Make a fire

❏ Figure out some other way to eat

❏ Read the pages in my folder

❏ Make a bed to put my sleeping bag on (so I can be more comfortable)

❏ Figure out how to survive by myself for the rest of my life

❏ Make spear/weapon

My tongue and throat were starting to dry up. I realized I had gone a day and a half without water! I felt lightheaded and craved water. I finally connected with how poverty and homelessness would feel.

As I pulled myself together to search for water, I noticed my forearm. The license plate number was *gone*! My skin once again looked as new as a baby's bottom. How could it have possibly healed so quickly? It had only been a couple weeks since the car accident! I searched the rest of my skin for signs of cuts or scrapes. My skin was all clear. What was going on? Why was this all happening to me? Was this all connected? Were there things that my mother never told me?

I read this book called *Sword* when I was in fifth grade. It was about a boy named Ryan who had to survive in the wild. If only I had a magic sword thingy to make fires like he did...

The moon and sun switched places as Earth turned. And then, it was midnight. I looked up at the stars as I shivered in my sleeping bag. Everything felt peaceful for a moment. Me, looking up at the stars... by myself. I was truly alone, for what felt like the first time in my life. It was really lonely.

. . .

The next day I set out to hike for the day.

But first, as I promised myself, I made a spear. I put my things on the tree stump and walked over to a dead tree. I took out my Swiss Army knife and—suddenly I wanted a boomerang. The desire was uncontrollable. I didn't know *why* I wanted a boomerang, though. Maybe because it was a cool and unique weapon? Maybe because it seemed pretty easy to make? I took a couple of thick, semi-flat tree branches. Slowly, with care, I carved them into boomerangs.

SHHHHHICK! The wood made a loud noise each time I delicately struck my knife across it. *SHHHHHICK!* At last I had three boomerangs. Something about them didn't feel right. The feeling kept nagging me every time I tried to push it away.

When I first tried to throw a boomerang at a tree, it went up, then down and planted itself in the dirt. *THUMP!* I re-carved the boomerang and threw it like a frisbee. *THUMP!* It did the same exact thing. I pulled some grass out of the ground and threw it in frustration.

I started to wonder if the thing bugging me was the fact that I didn't know how to throw a boomerang. I breathed in deeply, so deeply that it made me cough. I blew out softly, carefully, so I wouldn't get lightheaded.

The next time I used a different boomerang. It did a little better: instead of going up, then down, it went past the tree. The rest of that day, I focused on trying to get the boomerang to hit the tree and come back to me. I even skipped two meals! I may have been in the zone, but I beat myself up every time I didn't succeed. My hands grew sweaty, making the boomerang slip out of my hands. I kicked the tree I was targeting, which hurt my feet. And I was so tired and thirsty from running to retrieve the boomerang each time I failed that I drank too much of my precious water.

I cringed as I remembered the doctor visit where I became exhausted. I began to feel a painful headache again. *Nggg...* I held my head and tried to think of other things.

Breathe in, breathe out.

Breathe in, breathe out...

It seemed to help. I made a mental note to do the same thing if I got the headaches again.

Breathe in, breathe out.

One step closer to surviving this horrid journey.

Breathe in, breathe out...

The smell of poop wafted into my nose. I pinched my nose and accidentally scraped my arm on the rough forest floor.

The sun began to set. I had been trying to master the boomerang for hours. I lay carelessly on the ground. One of the two water bottles Aenon gave me was now empty. *Ugh...* I resisted the urge to drink the last one.

Once again, the world around me turned into Igneous' world. There was no swirl of light—I just blinked and instantly was there. My eyes opened wide as I realized that except for my clothes, my things weren't with me. But I assumed that stuff didn't teleport with me.

This time I was in a room with two velvet chairs on either side of an official looking principal-like desk. Igneous sat with his head in his hands, closing his eyes.

"Why are you sitting in this weird room?" I asked.

Igneous turned around and stared at me. He

looked exhausted. "I was accused of something I didn't do…"

Igneous and I talked, but there was a lot of silence. When I started to fade away, we played a game to try to bring me back. Some of the things he said in the game were actually funny. He also seemed to be a good actor. But…what if all this was fake? Maybe he really was an actor…

All of a sudden, a door slammed open. I uncontrollably faded away and returned to the woods. I fell asleep almost immediately after. Traveling to a different world was tiring.

. . .

The next day, I tried my boomerang on another tree. I did a lot better because my hands weren't so sweaty, and I wasn't so tired like the day before.

"GRRRRR."

Say what now?

"GRRRR."

I pointed my boomerang in several different directions. "Who's there?"

"GRRRR."

"I feel stupid right now, so can you show yourself?"

"ROAR!" A big brown bear jumped out of the shadows. It towered over me. It had fierce eyes and a big nose. For a second, it didn't seem to notice me. Then it looked me straight in the eyes.

"Um…I'm just gonna go…" I said, as I turned and slowly tiptoed away. I hoped there wouldn't be loud footsteps following me. Or, worse yet, I hoped I wouldn't end up as an appetizer—

"Huh?" something said.

"Wait, what?" I raised an eyebrow. I shuddered and looked back at the bear.

"I said, huh?" the voice said again.

"W-who are you? Why are you stalking me?" I croaked. I tried to speak fast because I didn't trust my voice to give an "I'm powerful" impression.

"Why would I be stalking you? I'm just a bear." The bear tilted its head in what I thought was confusion. *"I'm just as confused as you are. I haven't been able to communicate with a human ever! It's weird, right?"*

"Yeah?" I frowned and massaged my palm.

I could suddenly see the softer side of a bear. Moments ago, he had been a beast. But now, his eyes weren't scary. They were kind, like Marissa's. I began to feel my stomach tumble around, and I started to sweat. My shoulders quaked as I tried to figure out what I was feeling…

Guilt. The guilt swam around in my stomach. But what was I guilty for? *That's right,* I thought to myself, *I could've saved Marissa.* There must have been something I could have done. Tears dripped down my cheeks. I closed my eyes and steadied my breathing.

. . .

The next day I went riding on the bear!

We had a really great time. We ran through the forest, the wind in our hair. I don't know if Bear was laughing, but I was. We traveled from where the trees were together, to where they were more apart. The sun rose and fell over the mountains.

Part of me hoped that I would see my house in the distance, the sun shining bright behind it. I would run all the way home with Bear. I would find my mom sitting on our couch, crying. (My brother would be panicking.) But I would come through the door, and everything would be alright. We would be a normal family from there on out.

Those are just dreams, right? *Hope is for suckers.* But don't listen to me. I've had a hard time in life, as you can see.

A quote from a book had been stuck in my mind this whole time in the forest: "You aren't identified by the battles you win or lose, but by the battles you dare to fight." I guess that kind of has to do with my life. Sort of.

I had a teacher named Ms. Yu for fourth grade. She went to a super good college (I forget which one), and she was SUUUUUUPER awesome. She was the best. She had this thing called "the quote of the day." Every day, in the morning, we would talk about a quote. The quote was always different. One time she let us make up quotes. My quote was, "Your life may be full of cupcakes and rainbows, but the people around you may not have as happy of a life. So appreciate your cupcakes and rainbows." I guess that applies to all of us…

Yeah, well, I could use some help now.

Help…
Mother…
Marissa.

I shuddered. My hands trembled. I was forced to control myself. My breath shook. I wished that Marissa was there with me. I wished…I wished so many things.

Marissa's eyes were so similar to Bear's. They both gave me the same warmth. When I communicated with Bear, it almost seemed like Marissa *was* Bear, watching over me. I felt bad about saying this, but it seemed like Bear was soothing my guilt.

The sun began to set. Bear and I watched the orange-blue sky turn to a midnight indigo. The sun cast a little yellow halo around itself and on the tops of the mountains in the distance. It almost seemed to say, "Goodbye, North America! See you tomorrow…"

I accidentally fell asleep on the bear sitting up. But for once, the nap was dreamless.

· · ·

Bear woke me up. *"I'm sorry, I have to go to my family, they will be worried…"* it said.

I smiled. "I have to go back to my family, too—" I stopped breathing. *Why did I say that?!* I asked myself. I gave the bear a weak smile, trying to hide all the tears that were unshed. Bear smiled back, and my tears dripped down my cheeks. But I didn't cry because I misspoke about my family, but because I would actually miss Bear. And Marissa, because Bear reminded me of her.

"Thank you," I whispered. There were many words of appreciation unspoken on my tongue. That's because, when Bear crawled away, I had the determination to keep going and keep living.

Igneous

CHAPTER 10

"Lord Slag?" I asked. *Why did we need to call Lord Obsidian Slag? (And why was Commander Coal pretending to be the principal?)*

"Yes, Lord Slag." Commander Coal paced around the office. "My mission was to take over the school so our Military wouldn't be so WEAK! But now, my mission is to recruit you as the newest spy! I used to be one, but now we need someone new. Someone able to sneak around, but also able to lead others!" She tapped her fingers on her knees.

This reminded me of how the guards always treated me. Sometimes it felt like they were acting whenever they treated me like the others. They were always mean to everyone. Maybe it was an act, because I was always a candidate to be the next spy?

"M-me?" I stuttered.

"Yes," she said. "Are you going to turn down this offer?!" I shook my head. "Good. There are other people who are trying to get this spot, too!"

"Um...why did the Jocks accuse me of—"

"It was just a way to talk to them. They are handy spies, by the way. And it was also a way to talk to you!"

She acted as if I was going to applaud her plan. I didn't really feel like it. "You were using them to spy on me?"

"I was just keeping an eye on you. It's fine."

"So all that bullying..."

"Yep, it was all an act. Now remember, meet me in the study hall tomorrow, 1800M sharp. Bye!" Her Lavagraph disappeared into thin air.

I sighed and walked to my next class, right as the bell rang. I felt weird. My stomach felt twisted around. I had no appetite. Also, I was having a huge brain fart: I couldn't seem to think or use my mind, whatsoever. I tried to deal with it throughout my classes, but I ended up skipping one period because I needed a break. Fortunately, the teacher of that class understood.

"Why did you need to go to the office?" Xed asked me at the end of the day. We were heading to the teaching part of the hospital wing, where healers taught fighters some first aid.

"The Jocks were just playing a stupid joke on me," I lied.

"Oh. Did you finish your lunch?" I nodded, and we entered the huge teaching hospital wing. We walked over to the closet where all the hospital coats are stored. We slipped ours on and strolled over to our station. "Hey, I feel like you aren't telling me something. What is on your mind?" Xed said, suspiciously.

"I'm just tired..." I had forgotten I had never told

Xed about meeting Safire, though. I had told him about the dreams. I slumped over the dummy that we practice healing on.

"Yeah, you are acting like you only slept two hours!" Xed said. I glared at him. "Oh, sorry, but you do."

I don't know why I ever chose to be a fighter. Healers don't have to wake up as early and their muscles don't ache. Xed said that his brain is fried everyday, though.

This is Xed's daily schedule:

- Wake up at 500M
- Go to doctor training
- Go to classes
- Study and do homework
- Doctor training
- Meet up with Igneous at the park to study and do homework together
- Teach Igneous doctor stuff
- Go to sleep at 1800M

Then there is *my* schedule:

- Wake up at 100M
- Go to fighter training
- Go to classes
- Study and do homework
- Go to fighter training
- Meet up with Xed at the park to study and do

homework
- Learn doctor stuff from Xed
- Go to Military Tactics class
- Go to sleep at 1900M. YAY!

See? Being a fighter is so much harder than being a doctor or healer. They don't have to wake up super early. I got so tired each day. Every day, I was extremely sore at the end. But ever since Commander Coal had come to the school, I was already sore before History class even started! It was a—

"DUDE!" Xed shouted at me. I must have been daydreaming.

"Sorry, sorry, sorry…" I trailed off.

"You look like you are about to get sick!" he said. My skin must have been growing peach, like a human from Earth. (For Magmians, when your skin "turns pale", it's actually turning peach or brown. It's the opposite of Earthlings.)

"I'm fine. I'm just so tired…" I said. It was true, I was tired. I was probably so tired that I could fall asleep standing up or on the flat, paved ground.

"I can tell. Why don't you skip practice—"

"NO!" I snapped. "I will be taken out of the best group!" I didn't mean to shout. It was a good thing most people had left.

"Oh…" Xed looked down. "Hey, I miss hanging out, I feel like you have been ignoring me lately. Because of…" He didn't need to say anymore; I knew what he was talking about. Commander Coal and my military training.

I felt that way, too.

"Yeah. We get no break. We constantly have pop quizzes that are, like, thirty questions long, about the different formations and tactics and stuff," I whispered. *NGGG!* My head and body ached. I really wanted to just sleep!

"Yeah. You are really lucky though. because so many people from squads lower than you are getting sent to Failer's School," Xed said slowly. "I think that Commander Coal is going to take over the healers, too…"

"Oh." I scratched my head. "But you are really good, I doubt that you will be sent to Failers School."

"I don't know…she seems really unpredictable." Xed looked really scared. I began to get worried about him.

"Dude, now *you* look pale," I said. A couple of people nearby looked at us. I glared, and they went back to work.

"Let's get out of here," Xed said. "Park?" I nodded my head and we headed out.

CLICK CLACK CLICK CLACK. That sound could only mean one thing.

"Mr. Igneous Stone!" a voice said.

I sighed and turned around. "Commander Coal!" I said. I puffed out my chest.

"I need to talk to you," she said, "but I see that you are talking to your…friend."

"Oh, no. I'm sure what you need him to do is WAY more important than me." Xed gave me a glare.

Wow. I looked at Xed with wide eyes. What the

heck? Why was he being such a jerk about it?! It was school after all, it wasn't some just extra stuff that wasn't important.

"Okay then! Igneous, come with me." With that she walked the other direction.

I nodded and left Xed. I could feel his eyes drilling into my back. I wished I could ignore the invite to Coal's office, but I would be kicked off the squad, and I wouldn't have a chance at being the newest spy. I glanced back and gave him an apologetic look. He didn't seem to accept it. Maybe, after all these years, he wasn't as nice as I thought he was.

I faced Coal and walked with the commander. When we got to the office, I felt guilt swish around like a liquid in my stomach. Why did I have to choose between a job and Xed? *WHY?!* I thought about the pros and cons of going with the job or staying with Xed. I felt torn. Honestly, Battle School wasn't that bad.

I stopped walking and focused on the room we were in. So this was her real office. "Master, this is him!" Commander Coal said.

A shadow appeared on the other side of her Lavawood desk. The Lavalamp on her desk clicked, and the room's walls were filled with pictures of me. I had heard about lava lamps before, but I had never seen one.

My attention shifted to the shadow. I could just make out a shape of a Magmian. "W-who are you?" I said.

"I am Lord Slag!"

Safire

CHAPTER 11

The day after Bear left me, I was lying on the ground in a tight ball when I heard something:

SHHHHHHHHHH...

What?

SHHHHHHHHH...

There it was again. I got up stiffly and squinted, still half asleep. I felt so weak from the little food I could get and the lack of water. "If there is anything out there... or anyone...please do not bother me!" My voice echoed through the trees. I shivered slightly.

The noise continued. At first, I thought it was a bird flying by. But there was nothing in the air—just a clear, blue sky. I walked around in circles in the clearing—nothing. I squinted and looked carefully at every inch of the place—nothing.

What am I doing wrong? I thought. *Why can't I figure it out—*

Suddenly, I could hear water. *WATERFALL!!!* WATERRRRRRRRRR... the sound made me so happy, but I was so delirious from the lack of sleep. Where was it coming from? I desperately needed water.

SHHHHHHHHHHHH…

"Where are you, waterfall?"

SHHHHHHHHHHHHHHHH…

"Stop doing that!"

SHHHHHHHHHHHHHHHHHHH…

"STOP, YOU STUPID WATERFALL!!!"

SHHHHHHHHHHHHHHHHHHHHHHH…

"STOP SHUSHING ME!!!!"

I decided to close my eyes and rely on the sound to guide me. I was on my last bottle of water; I needed water so bad. Just knowing there could be an endless stream of water, only feet away, made me even *more* thirsty.

When I got there, my mind filled with wonder. A turquoise pond shimmered in the sun. Cool water bounced off the wall of wet silver rock. The land encircling it closed in the shape of a "C."

The shimmering water reflected blue light onto the sand. The sand on the bank felt warm, like freshly-baked cookies. Around the water, there were tall fruit trees. The weather was perfect. The place felt like home.

I closed my eyes tightly and reopened them, trying to make sure it wasn't an illusion. I pinched myself. *Oww!* This was real, all right. I had found a place to call home, until I figured out the next step in my plan. I had to hide out for a while: I knew those crazy doctors could be looking for me.

I took my shoes off and sat down on the warm sand. I cooled off my feet until my toes began to get numb. I felt really tired. I had barely gotten much sleep the night before.

I slipped out my sleeping bag, settled down and looked at the stars.

Breathe in, breathe out…

One step closer to the end of this horrifying journey.

Breathe in, breathe out…

I felt peaceful for the first time in days. I drifted off.

. . .

I woke up. Of course, I didn't really want to…

I looked around, remembering that I really was alone in the woods. I cleared my throat and felt tears slowly drip down my cheeks. I kept thinking I was stupid to not go after my mom and brother. I tried to push the overwhelming thought to the back of my mind. I swallowed the lump in my throat as I got up.

I took the empty bottle and filled it up with water in the waterfall. I drank so much water, I began to feel bloated.

I walked around the little pond to find a place to put my stuff and build a shelter—a place with shade. I quickly planned on using the super steep hill to help support my house.

I threw my bag down and grabbed several logs that sat on the forest floor, like they were just waiting for me to use them. The logs felt heavy, but somehow I could run back and forth without my muscles getting too tired. I wasn't breathless. My legs felt no pain. It was…weird.

But I was too focused on creating the house. Every time something fell, I could easily tell what I did wrong and what I had to do to fix it. It was like I had magical speed in my legs, and my brain was working faster.

I placed the logs vertically on the ground. I buried them two feet into the sand for support. I kept doing this until I almost had a complete square, just leaving some space for a door that I thought about doing later.

After that, I rested for a little bit. I had a vision of everything in the area; it was like I was scanning everything and I was seeing the size of certain things and the weight of others. Soon, I was back up and working again. I created string from this weird, shaggy tree I found, and tied it around the logs so they would stand together. I created a tight roof by weaving leaves together, and I put in a small flippy door so I could crawl in. I created a bunch of baskets made out of leaves and string, for collecting rain.

When I was done, I lay in the new shelter and stared at the weaved ceiling. I hadn't realized how tired I was until then. I let myself sink into a deep sleep. I didn't even have to do the "breathe in, breathe out" routine.

. . .

Over the weeks, my site got better and better.

I planted seeds in the corner of my "campus" and got seedlings. I created a wooden fence made of logs and tree trunks around my camp and upgraded my boomerang, too. I also got better at killing blue booby birds. I mostly ate herbs: I just naturally figured out how to tell the difference between them.

Speaking of seeds, I *felt* like a seed. I felt like my family—other seeds—were far away, out of reach, and nobody was next to me. *How were they? What were they doing? Were they okay?* I tried to not think about my family. Dreams about them kept haunting me.

To make sure I didn't drink any dirty water, I bathed in the lake, and drank and watered my plants using rainwater. I didn't want to drink muddy water from the lake, but I did daily collect mud for securing my shelter. It was a good glue for gaps where the logs could fall down, and it made it impossible for small animals to get inside.

Overall, my camp was well maintained. I made a fishing pole even though there were not many fish. I created some shovels pierced with tiny holes for picking up mud and draining the water. I carved the tops of the logs into spikes. That way, if anything tried to climb up, it would not be able to get inside. No snakes and other predators came into my area.

I used string from the weird string tree to make a mesh covering for the plants. The mesh allowed the plants to get sunlight.

Ants were my biggest problem. They could get through the smallest holes in my fence and crawl along the walls of my shelter. They made little sounds: *tit tit tit.* It was hard to go to sleep. I felt like they were creeping and crawling all over me. It made me itchy.

After a week of critter problems, I decided I needed to do something. I took a spear and whacked it on the ground to scatter the ants. I took one of my plants that smelled like lemon juice and placed it in the middle of them. They ran off and eventually went away in that area.

That gave me an idea. I found several "lemon juice" plants, took their petals, put them into a bowl, smashed them up and poured water in. I poured this liquid all over my campus: the walls and floors of my main shelter, my main clearing, the fence and my garden —just not on the plants. It actually smelled really good.

After I had spread the mixture all around, the bugs crawled away, but I had no place to step that wouldn't make me slip. I slapped my head when I realized I should have left a path for myself. For the rest of the day, I had a knot in my stomach and I had no appetite.

The day after that, the ground was dry and I didn't slip anymore. Things seemed to settle down. I didn't know what was about to come, or the devastation I was about to face.

. . .

It was a bright, sunny day in the morning.

I was going to fetch my weekly meat. Birds hummed, and squirrels chattered. It was peaceful. I caught a mouse, a rabbit and a tiny bird.

When I returned to my campus, I locked the fence door behind me and set down my catch in a pile of new food. But something weird happened. The ground felt like it was shifting. In my shelter, my bed creaked and the water that was in woven baskets quivered.

BOOM! Thunder boomed from above. Clouds settled in the sky. A thin strip of lightning flashed. *BOOM!!!* The thunder got closer and rain started to fall.

BOOM!

SPLASH!

BOOM!!

SPLASH!

BOOM!!!

SPLASH!!!

BOOM!!!

SPLASH!!!

BOOM!!!

SPLASH!!!

BOOM!!!

SPLASH!!!

I put a woven tarp over the garden and pulled the fresh food inside of my shelter. I was not ready for this. I put another woven tarp over my shelter and stuffed everything on top of the bed. I took the sleeping bag out of my backpack and laid it on the floor. I took my boomerang collection and a dead bird inside a woven basket and stuffed them into my backpack. I filled up my water bottle with fresh water I had collected earlier that morning.

SWOOSH!!! It sounded like a hurricane.

SPLAT! Wait…

BLAM!

That wasn't the thunder. It was the door tumbling inward, because of—

"ACK!!!! AAAAH, FLOOOOOOOOOOODDDD!!!" I screamed uselessly.

CRASH! A wave flowed into my shelter with a *SHHHHHHHHH*. I sat at the farthest corner of my bed and watched in horror. *WHOOSH!!!* My bed slowly rose up two feet higher. Then three feet. Then four. It was like the ground was a pool.

I took the headboard and footboard off my bed. Then I quickly took my knife and carved some long sticks from my bed into paddles. I paddled to the front door and pushed a couple logs out of the way. The bed lurched forward into a horrible nightmare. Dead deer floated on the water's surface...a rabbit slowly drowning...a bird's nest with dead chicks clutching to it. It was a gross sight. (There was more, but I don't want to disturb you.)

I paddled to safely and laid down. I just stared at the stars. Hours later, I went to sleep.

· · ·

The next morning, I woke up, halfway in my bed and half in water.

"UGGGGGH!!!" I shouted when the sun blinded me. My head hit the pillow and the pillow EXPLODED! Leaves and string flew everywhere, like confetti at your birthday party. Just not at the right time.

"UGGGGGH!!!" I shouted again. I was cold, I had

cold water on half my body, and I had no pillow. This is when I really broke down.

Do not be a crybaby Safire, I told myself. *Do not be a crybaby, Safire.*

Life isn't fair. Why me?

I decided to clear my mind, so I went for a swim. I pulled off my clothes and bounced off my bed, into the water. The water was surprisingly not too gross or too deep. I stood on the flooded ground and relaxed. I let the sun warm my tired muscles and the cool water refresh me.

After my peaceful swim in the cool flood water, I made plans:

Updated Plans

If I find just flood water:

❏ Update bed to boat

❏ Make a paddle board for scavenging

❏ Make new weapons

If the flood stops:

❏ Make a new shelter, close to the lake and waterfall

❏ Make better walls that don't stop the water but protect me from it

❏ Make new weapons

❏ Make booby traps!

If I find a city:

❏ Go into the city

❏ Use money wisely

❏ GET AN APARTMENT SOMEHOW!!!

That was pretty much my plan. Not too big. I longed to find a city *so much.* I longed to see another human. Writing it down made it feel like it was more of a possibility.

. . .

At first, I had to use Plan A, because the flood was really bad.

I rowed around, extended my bed to a boat and made a paddleboard. I had made a platform on my bed for bonfires to keep warm, but there was no dry wood to start fires. I put a tarp over the platform, with some sticks to support it. But the wet wood that I collected and put under the tarp wouldn't dry. Luckily, every day the water got shallower and shallower, until it was finally gone!

Plan B: my favorite plan! BOOBY TRAPS! Over a week, I spent my time remaking a shelter.

Until one day, I thought I heard…human voices.

Igneous

CHAPTER 12

Lord Slag...Lord Slag? Lord Slag is, like, our all-time immortal ruler. Our supreme leader! *Why would he be visiting me?*

I looked around Commander Coal's office again, looking for answers. "Is this a scam?"

"What's a scam?" he said, in a low and crisp voice.

"Something that's not real, where people try to get money out of you..." I squinted, trying to see if he was—

"It's true," Commander Coal piped up. "He is Lord Slag."

I raised an eyebrow and nodded. I was almost convinced. I quickly swallowed a shout of glee. "Why do you need me?"

"I don't know if you know, Mr. Igneous Stone, but every Magmian gets a tracker when they turn one year old," the shadow explained to me.

If they could track me, did Coal and Lord Slag know about Safire? "What?"

"Yep, and every person has been 'spied on'. But when you turn twelve, your tracker destroys itself.

Sometimes, very rarely, we keep the tracker intact. We almost did for you." I let out a breath, knowing that Safire was still a secret. "Consider it an honor," Lord Slag said. "Now, I want to meet you in person in a few months, but first, train hard. I want you to come to this room every day for 100 minutes, at 0050M. Coal knows time tactics that pause time so that you still get your 200 minutes of sleep."

Whaaaaat? "OK…" I said. *Why more technique!?*

The shadow rose from his chair. When he stood up, he showed his full height, about nine feet tall! I shuddered, and he disappeared. *How rude,* I thought. *He can't even say 'goodbye' or 'see you in a few months'.*

"Well, I assume you want to get to your Military Tactics class, correct?" Commander Coal asked, coldly. I nodded my head. "That is good, I'm supposed to go there, too!"

I almost said, "That is *not* good." Instead, I said, "Um, I was planning on going to the bathroom first…" I really didn't want to go with her. Plus, my Lavaboard was in a nearby station.

"Okay. I will wait, Soldier." She was acting weird. She was still cold, but she was talking in less of a "commander" way.

I jogged over to the nearest bathroom and closed the door behind me. I was standing in a small room with a toilet and sink. Next to the door was a box. I opened the box and luckily found a board caller. It's a good thing people put them in bathrooms all the time because without a board caller, I would be doomed. I quickly said,

"Igneous Stone," into the top of it and pressed the button.

WHOOSH! My Lavaboard quickly sped into the room and I jumped on it. *WHOOSH!* I raced out the door, quickly balancing myself. I stayed low to the ground, hoping Commander Coal wouldn't see me.

I sneaked behind the classes, to the hospital wing. I found Xed walking out of the exit with his stuff in hand. "You need your Lavaboard?" I asked. I tossed him the caller, but he just ignored me. The caller crashed to the floor and split in half. I cringed but shifted my attention to Xed. "Hey, what—"

"You think you can just come to the rescue for everything, huh?" Xed said. "You think you are the best? You aren't a hero, Igneous. Leave me alone!" He looked at me with so much anger, but I saw something sad and deep in his eyes. A memory?

I lowered to the ground. "What? What are you talking about?"

"You know what I'm talking about. Ever since the 'top fifty soldiers' thing, you've been strutting around like you're the best. Just because Commander Coal is all interested in you…" Xed walked off.

I just stood there completely confused. *Life makes less and less sense every day—*

"Wow, I know what that feels like, when your best friend walks away from you because they are jealous."

I turned around. "Why are you spying on me, Safire?" I said.

"I just started looking," she said. "Listen, all you have to do is—"

"Why are you giving me advice?"

Her gaze softened. She looked down at her thumbs and twisted them.

"Is there something you aren't telling me?" I asked. When she looked up, I realized she was crying.

"My best friend, M-Marissa…she died. She died in my arms."

She explained what had happened. My eyes were wide open and my heart was pumping as I listened to her story. At first, I thought it was a fake, then I realized it was real. I couldn't imagine that happening to Xed. I almost cried.

"But I guess I have to live through it," she said.

There seemed to be something else she wasn't telling me.

. . .

The next morning, I told the teaching staff that I was sick.

Safire and I planned to spend some of the day practicing flying on Lavaboards. I said the day would cheer her up, but it was also nice to have a break from my classes and hard work. We were glad we knew how to schedule dates, and I had figured out how to control the Lavagraph for meetings because I needed a break from reality, and I could tell Safire did too. She had figured out that we needed to be away from people and loud noises. I kept asking where she was on Earth, but she never responded. I figured she wasn't at home. It worried me. I wanted to do something, but I couldn't.

"Here, take this suit. It'll protect you from the heat and keep your feet from burning." I handed her a special suit that I had brought with me.

"Okay, so step on your board and make sure that your footing is correct," I said. "If you don't have the correct footing, you will easily fall off."

We both were standing in the park outside of my school. It was one of the few places where no students patrolled the school. Safire carefully stepped on her board. *CICH!*

"It's okay," I said. "That means it is about to—"

"GAH!" Safire shouted as the board rose in midair.

"TRY TO STAY BALANCED!" I said.

THUMP! Safire fell onto her board and it tilted sideways.

She ended up falling ninety percent of the time. It was a good thing that we were covered by the trees, or else somebody would find out about all of this.

"Okay," I said. "Repeat these steps. Stand on the board with your foot in front of the other. Make sure your feet are on opposite halves of the board. Make sure you are balanced when you hear the *cich* sound. Grip the front edge of the board with your hands. Tilt your body from side to side to turn. Rock your board up or down to go up or down. And finally, think or say 'STOP' or 'FORWARD' to stop or go forward." My stomach flip-flopped as I thought about something bad happening to Safire.

"Um, okay?" She let out a breath. "Stand on the board…with one foot in front of the other." Safire walked onto the board cautiously. "Make sure I'm balanced when

I hear the *cich* sound." Safire wobbled for a moment, but quickly regained her balance. *CICH!* The board quickly shifted its gears and jumped up. "ACK! Um…uh…grip the front edge of the board with my hands…" Safire gripped the board so tight that her knuckles turned white. I quickly stepped on my board and rose to her level. She smiled. "Tilt your body from side to side to turn." She did a quick 360-degree turn. "Um…oh! Rock my board up or down to go up or down." Safire and her board went up, and back down to my level. She quickly turned away from me so she wouldn't crash into me during her next step. "And finally, think or say 'STOP' or 'FORWARD' to stop or go forward. FORWARD!" She sped away from me.

I quickly followed her. Air rushed past me as we sped through the forest. The world around me was a green blur with little bits of other colors in the mix. "Be careful, Safire!" I shouted to her. She didn't hear me so I went even faster. When I got to her side, I slowed to her speed and told her to stop.

"STOP!" she shouted. Nothing happened. "STOP!" She swerved up to miss hitting a tree and then swerved to the side. "SSSTOOOOOP!" she screamed at the top of her lungs. The board abruptly stopped, and Safire flew forward off her board.

I whistled her board to my side and told it to go to the ground. I sped to where Safire had fallen. I couldn't see her at first. "SAFIRE, ARE YOU OKAY?!" I shouted. *SHOOT! Why did I yell!? She's going to disappear now because I made a loud noise!* When I finally found her, she had almost disappeared, probably not knowing I was

112

there for her, then she was gone.

I stayed put for a while, feeling so lonely that it choked me. When I came to my senses, I rode my board back to my dorm. I lay on my bed, but I couldn't go to sleep. I kept feeling that it had been my fault that Safire fell and disappeared all alone.

. . .

After an hour of crying, screaming into my pillow and feeling horrible about myself, I got up and went to the common room. When I was about to jump over the railing, I heard a couple of teacher's voices. I stopped to listen.

"...Ms. Coal has been taking over the school, piece by piece. I mean, I don't know what to think of it. She keeps saying it's her duty. What does that even mean?" the first voice said in a quiet tone.

"She keeps coming to my class to 'check on how I'm teaching'," the second voice said. "I keep asking her to leave, but she keeps coming back!" Several other voices agreed and complained.

"I have arranged a meeting with Lord Slag," said a third voice. "He seems to be very busy since she joined us." She snorted.

"Do you think that he is a part of this plan?" said the first voice in the same quiet tone.

"He may or may not be," someone growled. "But I have been paying attention to Ms. Coal. She seems to be interested in IG-2283." I held my breath at the sound of my soldier name.

"Of all people, she is interested in Mr. Igneous Stone?" the second voice whined.

"Well, I understand. He is an A plus student, and he is good at sneaking around." I smiled. "But an important part of being a spy is strong hand-to-hand combat. He may be good with some weapons, but he can't fist fight." My smile faded. "What is it about him that she likes?"

"I don't know, but if it comes down to it, if we have to give Mr. Stone away to save our school, we will save our school in a heartbeat." My heart started to race.

"But if he is as good as she thinks he is, should we keep him in our army? We could still have Ms. Coal as Commander of the army. We could use her."

The conversation paused. I heard some quiet shuffling for a moment.

"Haven't you heard the things she makes them do? It is so hard on their bodies. There have been so many injuries from her practices." I nodded my head, agreeing with whoever said that.

"If they get used to the practices—"

"There is no getting used to those practices! Those practices have only made our soldiers weaker, not stronger! Their minds are so tired that they can't think!"

"Give it some time then!"

"I will not. Tomorrow I want to make a deal with her."

I raised an eyebrow. *Someone wants to challenge Commander Coal?*

"I really don't think we should! She should make the first move, so we have an idea how to get her out of this school."

"What if she just keeps taking over?"

"Well then, we will have to give her what she wants. Igneous Stone."

Safire

CHAPTER 13

I hated Igneous so much.

After I fell off a Lavaboard, did he come help me get up? No, he didn't! He just walked away. Every time I thought about it, I had to stuff it into the back of my mind. If I couldn't, I would go hunting for food to distract myself.

· · ·

I had always wondered if I would get to Plan C. And that is exactly what happened.

Let's back up. I was scavenging for some logs when I heard a whistle, then some quiet clapping. I probably wouldn't have heard it if my senses hadn't been sharpened in the forest. I smelled a wonderful meaty smell. *Barbecue.*

My mouth watered. I had not tasted that beautiful juicy meat in a long time. I could taste the sauce in the air. I grinned so wide that I had a small adrenaline rush.

Several skyscrapers shimmered in the sun. They all

stood behind a small strip of trees. I heard and saw people on top of the buildings; through the windows, I saw people inside, too. As the city sounds rushed into my ears, the honks and yelling made me smile.

My stomach growled, my brain shouted, and my heart raced.

I ran across a meadow, the only obstacle between me and the city. I heard the buzzing of a nearby bee's hive and the excitement of a bird cuckooing. My mind filled with positivity for me, myself and I.

I took my first steps into the city. I was surprised that there was no police officer stopping me. The city was amazing! The buildings shone in the sunlight. The pathways glittered, and the towers were all different colors. One building was blue, another was green, and another one was red! It was like the… *WAIT*… This was a weird city. What cities have different colored buildings?

I realized people were staring at me. *Oops.* I forgot I was covered in dirt. I stood there with my face completely red. "Um…hello-my-name-is-Safire-and-I-am-new-here-and-I-just-want-to-get-an-apartment-and-I-am-sorry-for-disturbing-you-I-came-from-a-camp-and-got-chased-by-wolves-and-I-ran-away-don't-mind-me. BYE!" I quickly ran to the nearest shop. I felt pretty good about my cover story.

BANG! I slid on the carpet and my butt and back hit the ground hard. The world spun around me as I tried to catch my bearings. I saw that I was in a small room with a glass counter that stretched from wall to wall. Small wooden figures were placed inside the glass cabinets. There was a small cash register and a bell on one side of the counter, and a brown and rusty door on the other. Around me were carpeted walls (*eww...*) with picture frames hanging with nothing in them.

The bell rang. I turned around and saw a plump lady with a buttoned-up pink dress. Her high heels hit the ground. *Click! Clack! Click! Clack!* She had her hair up in a bun. Her eyes wore a don't-waste-my-time look. Her makeup was so thick that it was a little creepy.

"Ahem!" She cleared her throat. *Wow, what an impatient lady!*

"Sorry, I was just trying to get...away...from the crowd?" I stuttered.

She looked at every inch of my body. "Take this," she blurted out. Her hand held a black pyramid with a circle carved on the bottom. "It will always tell the truth. All you have to do is ask a question, spin it like a top, and look at the bottom." I slowly walked to her and took the pyramid.

She pinched herself and opened the door behind her. "Bye." She slammed the door shut without any thought.

I stood in the room for a moment, holding the pyramid. It was sort of creepy being there all alone. I backed out of the room and ran out the door.

I ran past the shops with designer handbags and trendy clothes, the grocery stores with friendly people buying cheap fruit and canned food, and the little restaurants making delicious smells swim through the air.

I ran and ran until I came to a dead end. In front of

me was a beautiful beach with sand like powder. I took my shoes off and walked towards the water.

I held the magic pyramid tightly and closed my eyes. I spun it around and asked a question: "What would be the smartest thing to do right now?"

Get money and be smart.

"Um…okay? What—how should I get an apartment?"

Look at cheap things. Pawn shops. Think, what can you do with items like that?

I thought for a moment. I stared at the calming ocean that was rising up and crashing down onto the shore. Little kids played with their parents in the ocean. Parents… Family…

"Who is my father?" I asked quietly.

I'm not sure if I know what you mean. Ask me your question later.

"I said, who is my fa—" I stopped and sighed. "Never mind."

I stopped asking questions and crawled over to the ocean. I watched the water rise up and down. I imagined it was struggling. Struggling to get up on the beach. Coming up onto land, just to fall back down. Up and down. Up and down. I watched the waves, too. I imagined they were struggling, too. Struggling to reach the stars.

The more I thought about it, I was struggling, too. Struggling to fit in, struggling to live a normal life.

I put my magic pyramid in my backpack and took out the hundred dollars Aenon gave me. I rushed to the closest building that said "Clothing Store"—in giant, neon red block letters.

When I went inside, the smell of perfume filled my nose. The sad part was, the first t-shirt I saw in the teen section was $60. I looked at the buildings across the road. One said "PAWN SHOP." This gave me an idea...and I think it might have been the idea the pyramid had meant earlier.

I walked across the street to the little pawn shop. It had expensive-looking things—gold watches, diamond earrings, ruby frames—but things were cheap.

The guy at the counter wore a gray shirt with a pair of ripped jeans. He had a blob of matted hair, a tiny beard and brown, stone-like eyes that pierced into me. "WHAT DO YOU WANT?!" he boomed.

I stood my ground. "How much are those two gold watches?"

"Fifteen dollars!"

"Per watch?"

"YES!"

"Can I get them?"

"SURE! GIVE ME THIRTY DOLLARS!"

I fished into my pocket and got out thirty bucks. I held out the money. The man swiped it out of my hand and turned away. He counted the money over and over again and muttered that I could take the watches. I put the watches in a little bag and walked out of the store. I was surprised I made it out alive—in one piece.

I walked into the jeweler's store. At the front desk, I found a woman wearing a suit and a name tag that said

"RITA!"

"Hello! How can I help you?" she said.

"Can I sell you these watches for fifty dollars? So you can resell them?"

"Um…let me ask my manager."

After some talking and some waiting, the manager said yes. He would give me $50. I sort of expected to be carried away by the police!

I was up to $120. I got a pair of jeans and a pack of wipes. My shirt wasn't that dirty. I wiped and washed my face in the public bathroom until I looked clean in the mirror. I was down to $40. I sold a pair of earrings to the jewelers. I got back up to a hundred bucks since I paid $30 to the guy at the rundown pawn shop and earned $90 from the jewelry people. I bought a hair brush to not look like a homeless person. (Fortunately, I didn't.)

Also, I had been buying GOOD food. Well—just stuff to heat up, which wasn't really tiding me over. On day one, I ate fried rice with egg—a 'just add water' meal. Day two: bread—another 'just add water' meal.

Once, after I ate one of those lousy bread loaves, I barfed. Barfed on somebody walking ahead of me. "O.M.G!" The girl turned around. She was the same age as me and had on a pink, frilly beach dress. Her hair glittered gold and her soft blue eyes were just like the ocean behind her. Except…she wasn't so nice.

"OH! I'm so sorry!" I apologized. I buried my feet in the sand.

"You! You are in big trouble! MUM!" she shouted, in a heavy British accent.

"I can help clean—"

"Honey?" A woman that looked just like the sassy girl, but older, walked over to us. She looked at her daughter. Then at me. And back again. "Sweetie. Let's go, I'm sure it was a mistake."

"BUT IT WASN'T! Besides, even if it *was* a mistake, she is in *trouble!* NOBODY GETS TO *PUKE* ON ME!" The girl's mother apologized and pulled her away. A stream of insults tumbled out of the girl's mouth.

I just stared at her, bored. "Not sorry," I whispered.

I took out my magic pyramid. *It's been so long since I lived back in my house,* I thought to myself. *How much longer am I going to survive on my own?*

"Will I die soon?" I blurted out uncontrollably. I closed my eyes, wishing I hadn't asked that.

That's not the type of thing I'm made to tell. Ask me something else.

"Will I have a great ending, like most characters in books?"

I think so.

"Do you know how to have a conversation?"

Um…maybe? Let's try.

"Do you know how I got here?"

You were a girl with many problems back at home.

You had great friends. You protected them, until you couldn't save Marissa.

You were stuck in the hospital for four months.

You met a guy from a different planet and were uncontrollably transported to his planet.

You were in a car accident.

You were chased out of your own house by doctors, leaving your family behind. You were stuck in the woods and you had to survive there. You found an amazing waterfall, where you created your first house. Sadly, a flood came soon after that and you were forced again out of your home. You had to live on a boat.

The water cleared and you lived in an unfamiliar area.

You found this city. A bunch of people looked at you weird, so you made up a fake story about yourself.

Then you found me!

The end.

My jaw dropped. How did this magic pyramid know me so well? It was kind of scary.

Sorry, did I startle you?

I nodded.

Sorry.

"Well, I'm going to sleep." I stuffed the pyramid into my backpack before it could respond. I stared at the ocean in front of me. How did this pyramid know all about me? It almost seemed like someone was spying on me and programed the story of my life into the pyramid. My stomach twisted around when I thought about it.

Has it really been five months since Marissa died?

I needed sleep…

. . .

The next day was a short day. All I did was walk, eat, relax at the beach, nap, repeat. But by the end of the day, I had seen the whole city: buildings, dumpsters, houses, apartments, hotels, clothing stores, the mall, jewelry stores, bakeries, restaurants and the statues.

The day after that, my stomach began to growl, so I picked up some groceries. (Bananas, fruit snacks, crackers, hand sanitizer, lotion, fresh sandwiches, some chips, raisins and some fruit.) When I was heading back to the beach with my groceries, this little old woman was having trouble getting around, so I went up to her. She had tons of wrinkles and dark eyes that seemed to look straight through me. Her white hair was tied up in a tight bun, and she grasped onto a wooden stick that somehow supported her weight.

"Ma'am, do you need help?" I asked kindly.

"Y-yes, please. How come you are helping me? No one helps me..." she croaked. She handed me her groceries and told me to follow her.

We talked as we went. "So why doesn't anyone help you?" I asked.

"They all think a little old lady is helpless and stupid and useless. Imagine when they turn old. They better be laughing at themselves." The little old woman showed me her walking stick and swung it like a weapon at imaginary people.

"Oh, why do they say that? You aren't helpless— you are lonely because of those *brats!*" I grinned.

"Exactly." She smiled. "Why don't you come into my house? Let's have a cup of tea."

By then, we had gotten to what I thought was her house. It might have been just me, but her smile seemed really creepy. I had really wanted to go into her house, but now I knew I couldn't go inside. I didn't know what this lady was going to do to me.

"Oh, uhhh…I should probably go." I muttered. "And I don't drink tea." My gut twisted around with guilt. After so long, I really wanted to make a friend, but something just felt *off*.

"I see you don't live here." She had that faraway look, like she was planning something evil. *Evil!*

I shivered. I pretended to look at my watch. "Oh no! I have to go. My mom is going to pick me up at the beach! Sorry! I gotta go! Bye!" I sprinted out of there like I was being chased by a jaguar, my groceries in my arms.

"Okay. See you another time!" the little lady called after me. I could tell she was surprised because of the crack in her voice. I was definitely glad I didn't go into her house, but then again, it would have been nice to have a friend.

. . .

When I got back to the beach, I glugged a bunch of water and almost fell right to sleep as I hit the blanket. But something kept me from going to sleep.

Yep, I went to Igneous's world again, on purpose this time.

"I know what it feels like when your best friend walks away from you because they are jealous." I told him.

"Why are you spying on me, Safire?" he said.

"I just started looking. Listen, all you have to do

125

—"

"Why do you care?" Igneous said.

A lump formed in my throat. I closed my eyes and forced the tears to go away. *Marissa.* When I opened my eyes, I saw Igneous looking at me, concerned. I had to tell him. No matter how much it hurt me.

Then, for half a second, I saw Marissa standing next to Igneous. She gave me a thumbs up and walked straight into Igneous, standing where he stood. *What is she trying to show me?* I thought. I held my breath and realized that there were so many similarities between them. The kindness in their eyes were the same. They both cared about me and were always funny...

"M-my best friend died," I blurted out. "She died in my arms." The silence after that seemed to last forever.

Eventually I told him about it all. Even though there were some awkward pauses, I felt he really understood me.

"I thought *I* was your best friend!" he joked.

"Not funny!" I playfully punched him. The silence swept over us again.

"To cheer you up, I can teach you how to ride a Lavaboard tomorrow?"

I said yes.

. . .

The next day we hung out. It was nice to have a friend again. I felt that Igneous helped me open up to the world. Yes, he may just be a scam...which would suck, but he's helped me through my journey without knowing it.

That night after the Lavaboarding, I sat down on my beach chair and tried to calm my anger. While we were Lavaboarding, I had fallen off the board, but Igneous never came and found me. He left me laying on the ground by myself. I felt abandoned. I didn't want to be mad at him, but I couldn't help myself.

Once I calmed myself down a bit, I laid down and closed my eyes. The sounds of my surroundings at the beach disappeared and I fell into a dream state.

"Hello? Hello?" said a familiar voice. "Hello? My name is Liginia. Hello? We must go!"

"What—wait. What?!" I said, confused.

"Yes. You are on your—" Her words started cutting out for some reason.

There was a growl and a scream. Then there was a loud and gross noise. And more screams.

And my eyes opened.

Igneous

CHAPTER 14

The next day changed my life so much.

0100M
RIING! Yep, it's time to get up.

Everyone got up and quickly dressed while talking to their friends. The room was louder than usual. Everyone was shouting and trying to talk. All of a sudden, the loudspeaker turned on. I froze at the sound of the voice.

"HELLO, STUDENTS OF THIS BATTLE SCHOOL. AS YOU KNOW, MY NAME IS COMMANDER COAL. I AM THE COMMANDER OF YOUR MILITARY.

"MUCH GOSSIP HAS GONE AROUND ABOUT ME. PEOPLE HAVE BEEN WONDERING WHY I CAME TO THIS SCHOOL."

Everyone grew silent in my dorm.

"I HAVE SOME NEWS. RIGHT NOW, I WANT ALL OF THE TEACHERS AND STUDENTS—EVEN IF THEY ARE HEALERS—TO COME OUT TO THE MILITARY PRACTICE AREA. STAT!"

For a moment, everyone stood there, motionless. It turned back into chaos as everyone bounded into the halls, into the common room and out the door into the Military Area.

As we all marched to the area, I realized that so many people weren't there. How many people had gone to Failer's School? How many died?

Why did I not notice that before?

0175M

Commander Coal waited on the hard grass of the Defense Teaching Area. She stood straighter than ever, with her hands behind her back. She eyed every single person in the crowd.

"Thank you for joining me. I have some deals for the teachers. Many teachers say that all these decisions should be made in private, but I think differently," Commander Coal yelled to the crowd. "I think that students should have a say in things! You'll need to grow up and make decisions! So, either I get what I want, or I get the school!"

When she paused, one older kid raised his hand. "Why exactly do you get to do this, Commander?"

Commander Coal smiled and walked over to the kid. She looked at her nails; they were long, with blood-red nail polish. Then, she struck his face. Blood gushed out of the wound, and the crimson liquid poured down his face like tears, dripping onto the grass.

I winced and turned my attention back to Commander Coal. My heart beat fast. I hoped that, if I was going to be taken by her, I wouldn't do something horribly wrong—and have *that* happen to—

"Because I am powerful! And if anyone of you does something stupid, this will happen to you!" she pointed at the guy. Guilt twisted around in my stomach for no reason. "Sorry, pardon me. I tend to be a little vicious," she said coldly. Shivers went down my spine.

She began to look around. She was looking for someone…uh oh. Her eyes locked with mine, and she began to stagger over to me like a zombie. I swallowed hard while sweat rained down my back. My breathing became heavy. This started to feel like that one day in practice when Commander Coal became "interested" in me. The people around me shifted around, confused.

All of a sudden, my eyes rolled into the back of my head. I fell to the floor and dreamt of the past.

Bzz, bzz! The Lavaphone rang on the dining room table. I was six years old. I was sitting at the table with my family, quietly watching the Lavaphone. Two days before, I had applied for admission to school. This school had only a twenty percent acceptance rate.

"Hello?" I picked up the phone. "Who is this?"

"I'm the Principal of the Battle School," said the voice, through the phone. "Is your name Igneous Stone?"

"YES!" I said. A big smile lit up my face.

"Good. I have called to tell you that you got in."

She sounded so robotic, but I was so happy that I jumped up and down and said, "THANK YOU, THANK YOU, THANK YOU!"

The memory faded.

0300M

BEEP, BEEP! A machine sounded like an alarm clock.

I could hear a bunch of people frantically rushing around me. I struggled to stay conscious.

"He's awake, he's awake!" somebody said, happily. Sweat poured down my back. I tried to move and pain shot through me. I winced.

"Just try to relax..." The person talking to me was drowned out by the ringing in my ears. My vision was blurry. I tried to blink.

"Close your eyes..." someone calmly whispered in my ear. I tried to shift my head to look at them, but I couldn't move. I strained my muscle trying to move my arm.

"Nggg..." I let out a slight whimper.

"He can't move," a doctor shouted. "Give him the —"

His voice was drowned out by the ear-piercing ringing in my ears. I was so confused. *What is happening? Why am I here?* I repeated in my head.

Something was inserted into my arm, and I could no longer feel my arms and legs. I struggled to move as the feeling in my arms and legs came back again. I felt like I was strapped down to the bed, even though I wasn't. I started to panic as I realized from the sound of their voices that the doctors were stressed. That was never a good sign.

I tried blinking, and the water and crud in my eyes cleared up a little. At first, I could see shapes. Then, I could see bigger details, and soon I could see everything. All the doctors were running in and out of the room in a panic. One was hurriedly writing on a clipboard.

"HUTT! HUTT! HUTT!" one of the doctors yelled. All but one of the doctors rushed out of the room.

I still couldn't move. "Argg…" I whispered.

"Go to sleep!" said the remaining doctor.

Once again, something was inserted into my skin. "Go to…" My eyes closed and I fell asleep again.

0450M

I was still in the same room, but now it was dim. I opened my eyes a little to see two women talking beside my bed.

"…he can't miss the deal, Beranica!" said one woman. Her voice sounded familiar.

"I still don't understand why you care so much about him watching you make the 'deal,' Ms. Coal," Dr. Beranica said.

"I just want every student and teacher to witness it!" Commander Coal shouted.

"I don't care about this deal. This kid needs medical help—he just had a panic attack!" My jaw dropped. *A PANIC ATTACK?*

"Then we will wait. Can we do it tonight?" Coal said.

"Possibly. But are you his family?" the doctor asked.

Coal hesitated and shook her head.

The doctor looked at her clipboard, twisting her curled, dark gray hair around and around. "I don't know what to tell you then…" she said slowly.

Coal slapped herself on the forehead and muttered things under her breath. She looked at me. I closed my eyes. As I looked at the inside of my eyelids, I started to panic again. I calmed myself down and fell back to sleep.

0625M

"Hello, students!" said a voice over the loudspeaker. "We are sorry for the interruption this morning. We hope you will join us in the Defense Area for the delayed…um… deal? Commander Coal thinks that everyone should be there for the deal. So…that's it!"

The voice woke me up. The machine next to me said, "Awake, awake!"

A couple doctors rushed in. They began to shoot questions at me that I didn't have enough time to answer:

"Can you move?"

"Can you speak?"

"Are you okay?"

"Yes, I feel fine!" I finally said. Then they left me alone.

I moved my arms, legs and feet, feeling relieved and free. I had stretched enough that I could get up. When I first stepped onto the ground, I struggled to stay balanced. I kept falling and scratching up my knees and hands.

I focused back on trying to walk. It felt like I was learning how to ride a Lavaboard again. When I took my second step without falling, my foot twisted in pain, and I collapsed harshly to the floor. My foot felt paralyzed. I closed my eyes to ignore the pain.

Two doctors picked me up and put me into my bed.

0700M

When I woke up again, I waited for something to happen.

A doctor with a name tag that I couldn't read came into my room. She gave me crutches. As soon as I touched them, I was up and testing them out.

When I put the crutches right side up, the metal near the grip hit the ground hard. *CLANK!* I winced and pushed myself up. The rubber on the feet of the crutches hit the floor softly. *Thump.*

I realized that my foot was covered in a black bandage. The blackness seemed like a void. I wished I could fall inside it and sleep in it forever...

But I needed to learn how to walk again. I looked up and placed my feet on the floor. *Thump.* I breathed in slowly. At first, I could stand normally, but when I held up my paralyzed foot, my balance wavered. Unsteady, I clutched my crutches so hard my knuckles turned white.

Thump. I took a hop forward. Then another. And another. Every time I hopped forward, I had to take a huge breath to regain some confidence.

"Are you okay?" the kind woman asked. I squinted and finally read the name of her name tag: "Dr. Olsoion, Head Therapist."

"Yes, doctor," I answered.

1500M

"All students and teachers, now is the time for the announcement—er—deal! Everyone head to the Defense Area!"

1550M

I felt so tired standing there in my squad with my crutches. The sun beat down on me, and I wanted to sleep so badly.

Commander Coal proudly watched the crowd. She stood like before, but a little more annoyed. And then, the thing that I didn't want to happen, *happened.*

She started to look for me again. *Why did she have to say her whole "deal" in front of the entire school?* Couldn't she just say over the loudspeaker, "Can all the teachers and Igneous Stone come to the office!?" And then talk to us alone? Her eyes found mine and drilled into my face. I glanced away, trying to not look into her cold eyes.

"I have called all of you here," she said, "because I want to finish what I have started. I want to have a new generation in my team!" A bunch of people started to whisper. "ATTENTION!" she yelled. The whispering stopped immediately. The commander pointed at the guy who had gotten clawed 'til he was bloody.

"REMEMBER!" Everyone flinched. "Now," she continued, "remember how I changed this school into a better community. There are much better fighters and healers—"

All of a sudden, something bounced off her chest. Someone had *thrown* something at Commander Coal! She shot a fake smile at the crowd and picked up the item that was thrown at her. I closed my eyes and listened to the gasps of horror.

"WHO DID THAT?" she yelled. "WHAT IS YOUR NAME!" I opened my eyes to see her clutching the item.

A knife.

"Why should I tell you?"

The air was full of dust. I could see Commander Coal going crazy, throwing dust bombs all over the place to block people's vision. I closed my eyes. I could just imagine her creepy, bloodthirsty face.

I opened my eyes to see Commander Coal standing in front of me, wearing a wicked grin. She took my arm and dragged me to the front of the crowd. I tried to drag my crutches, but they got slippery from my sweat and fell out of my hands. I groaned as my paralyzed leg dragged on the ground. It didn't hurt, but the doctor said never to do anything crazy with my leg—and this was pretty crazy. Everyone was still coughing. A couple people looked at me, confused.

"IF YOU WANT NO MORE TROUBLE, GIVE ME IGNEOUS STONE!" she yelled to the crowd. The dust and smoke all disappeared, and a large Lavajet appeared in front of us. The navy blue jet was lined with clear pipes of Magmi Liquid. The jet's hatch opened. Something stood there on it, waiting.

"Thank you all, now good day and goodbye!" Commander Coal yelled. She twisted my arm and dragged me on my back toward the jet.

Someone behind me said, "You have done well, Commander Coal!"

She let me go and I got up. I brushed off the grass

on my butt and back. I turned around to see the shadow of Lord Slag. "Thank you, Coal."

"Didn't you want to wait a few months?" I asked, breathing heavily.

"No, we have some urgent problems," Lord Slag said. "Now, Coal, can you please wait here while I escort Igneous to his bedroom on the ship?"

"Yes, master."

"Now," he turned to me. "Ignore her. She has mental issues. Real ones."

"I do, too," I muttered under my breath. "It's true…"

"Yes, you do, and it is a lot for you. But from now on, think of me as your parent. You can tell me anything…and I am now in control of you."

I shuddered at that thought. "Okay? But—"

BOOM! A small explosion shook the ground. I looked back to see Commander Coal lying on the ground, dead. "Wha—"

Lord Slag turned my face away from the mess and kept making me go forward. "She has caused us many problems. Two years ago, she was our best fighter. Then, when she was battling someone, she got injured. She was no longer our best fighter. She went insane. Her mind was all over the place. It wasn't good. So, we sent her on this mission. We said that she could take over the school, but do us one favor: get *you*. And she agreed." He sighed. "She *had* been better lately."

If scratching and whipping kids was normal for Commander Coal, she must've been a killer before that fight two years ago. "I forgot to meet with her," I said.

"*She* forgot. And I'm sorry for the people she tortured in your school."

I got mad at him for saying that. He didn't even SEEM sorry. But I tried to keep my temper. He could kill me, after all. I tried to look him in the eye but couldn't make out his face. He was just a black 3D figure in the shape of a normal Magmian, only bulkier and fatter. "Is this your...real self?" I asked.

He nodded. I was bewildered. He was a shadow?

"So, are you ready to become the newest spy?"

Safire

CHAPTER 15

My heart raced. *Liginia? LIGINIA!?* What type of name was that? I have never ever met a Liginia in my life...but I *did* recognize it from my weird dreams about my childhood.

I kept replaying her 'message' in my head. There were growls...and screams...

It just seems weird. It's like she's a super spy! Who was she? The intensity was killing me.

. . .

It was 9:30 P.M. and the last rays of sunlight were disappearing, leaving the world and the ocean in almost complete darkness. The clouds floated away, revealing the bright moon in the middle of the ocean-like sky. The moon seemed to have a small halo around it. I thought back on my life.

I was about five years old. I was wrapped in a blanket, in my mother's arms, safe from the horrifying world. "I want to be an astronaut!!!" I said. I had big dreams back then.

"I'm sure you will be, sweetie. I'm sure you will…"

As young people, we all are shielded from the real world. The world isn't a safe place.

In fifth grade, we had a "poem" unit. At the end, we made poems on a theme based off of another poem. I really hated that part. It was like we were copying the writer.

I too, sing America,
The mask I hide behind,
Is all sweet and kind,
But they don't know me,
Because I need to change,
My thoughts are stuffed in my mind,
Never forgetting one thought,
But next time,
I won't be hidden behind a mask,
I will be my true self but better,
And others won't hate me,
They will understand,
I too deserve to be my true self,
I too sing America with everyone else…

I finally got out of my daydream—no, more like a nap. And one thought swam around in my mind: people here didn't look at me weird as much anymore. It was true, I didn't feel so different in the city. Maybe it was because people didn't realize I was different, or they didn't care. Or maybe they hadn't seen enough of me to confirm that I was weird and different—

"Oof!" I cried. I had forgotten I had to meet the

little old lady. Maybe this time I would learn something about her. I raced to the spot where the beach ended. Everything blurred around me. As I got to the more crowded areas, I could hear people's comments, "Look at her, she is so fast! She is like The Flash!" They were probably pointing. I grinned and ignored them and kept on going.

"There you are!" the little old lady said, when I got to the place where we had met the day before. She muttered something under her breath about not having a "complete first ability." She cleared her throat. "I think you should know who I really am. Let's go to my house for this."

I frowned. "Um…aren't you normal?"

"I will explain it all, once we get to my house," she said gruffly. "Please, you will realize what I've been doing once I explain it all to you." She walked off without a word, leading me to her house.

"Explain what?" I yelled. "Explain that you are a murderer trying to murder me or something?" *Was this woman trustworthy?*

"No! Please come with me!" The little old lady shrunk into a tiny version of herself, turned into a ball of light and rose up into the air. It twinkled in the sun. She turned back into the old lady, but no one else saw. "You see," she whispered, "we are both *aliens*…"

"LIGINIA?!" My jaw dropped, and my past memories of her flashed through my mind. "So, it's all true…and you didn't tell me. You didn't *tell* me I was an alien! You *lied* to me! For all this time!"

"You weren't ready," the little lady cackled. "You weren't mature enough. You hadn't even manifested an ability. You wouldn't believe us!"

"What do you mean?"

"There are many abilities. Every generation has one person per ability. The most powerful people have healing, or fire, or *multiple* abilities."

"What are the abilities?" I asked.

"Healing, Fire, Water, Control, Earth, Animals, Wind/Flying, Music, Shade, Strength, Electricity, Illusions, Ivy, Germ, Void, Dance, Genius, Love, Telekinetics, Dark, Light, Past, Present, Future. I can't tell you how many more there are. There are hundreds."

"Who were you in your generation?"

"I'm an illusionist!" Liginia scratched the back of her head.

"Waaaait...did you create this city?" I asked. She nodded. "So, you can make everyone else think one thing, when it really is...something else?"

She snapped her fingers and everything around us turned into the old forest. I heard screams from people nearby, who were confused as to why the whole city had just turned into a meadow. "This is what is really here," she explained. "But I can also make it into this." She snapped her fingers and suddenly we were in my house. I looked around, taking in memories and searching for my mom and Aenon. But they weren't there. Tears came to my eyes. Liginia snapped once again. The fake city slowly returned.

Honestly, I didn't care about the city being fake. I

could live in a fake city, for all I cared. But I was so mad about all the lies told to me for as long as I could remember. I felt like there was more that she wasn't telling me, but I didn't push it.

We slowly walked up the steps to her tiny cottage. "We need your help!" Liginia blurted out.

I stopped walking. "First, you lie to me, then you expect me to help you? Can't you help yourself, with your super cool powers?"

"I didn't say you had to help us. But you have two options—"

"You know what, crazy stranger? Get away from me!" I yelled. I didn't care if this woman was Liginia or not. I just wanted time to think.

"You have made a grave mistake," the little lady said. "You will regret it." I saw sadness in her face before she glittered away.

How could she just disappear *like that if she weren't the real Liginia?* I pinched myself, in case this was one of those dream illusions—but it wasn't. Honestly, I didn't care. I didn't want to be part of her schemes. I ran out of the cottage garden, in deep thought.

I heard the loudspeakers all around the city. "There is a free living space! Try to get it!" At first I was confused. *Living space…* And *free…* FREE LIVING SPACE!!! That was the thing I REALLY NEEDED!

Maybe, because this was a fake city, Liginia would give it to me. Because she wanted me to…er, live. But the magic pyramid had told me to get an apartment, so I assumed that I needed one. I bounced up and down a couple of times because I was so excited.

I bounce-ran to the living space office, the place to look at designs and stuff for your living space, and where you'd buy one. When I got there, I stood in front of a huge, sphere-shaped building. It was made of almost wall-to-wall windows. There were only narrow lines of brick in between the windows. The windows were tinted so you couldn't see into them. (Must have been one of those buildings where you can see out, but not in.) Anyways, the brick was stained white, and the roof was plastered with wallpaper that had "Living Spaces" in big block letters all over it.

I went inside, and the smell of fresh paint flew into my nose. One half of the room was filled with shelves of framed pictures, organized like bookshelves. The other half of the room had tables with samples of floors and tiles. On the very far end of the room, a man sat at a table. The sign behind him said, "Info."

Behind me, I heard other people come into the building. So I raced to the counter as quickly as I could. "Can I get this free living space?" I asked the guy at the counter.

"Wait." The man had soft, kind eyes and a red beard. He was wearing a Hawaiian shirt and some shorts. He spoke to the growing crowd. "Now please send one person from your family through this door so they may do the tests. Whoever wins the tests gets the living space. Further information will be given at the campsite. Ready? Follow me!"

The people chosen from each family rushed to the

door. But of course, I got there first. The Chosen and I scurried through an old tunnel, jumping at every sound, except for each other's footsteps. People pushed, fell and even punched as we went through. It reminded me of the halls back at school, when everyone was fighting to get out. My eyes became glossy but I fought off the tears.

We finally got out of the tunnel. I was still first, right behind the red-bearded man. We were outside, surrounded by greenery. There was a little campfire and even a classroom with desks. It looked like we were going to be camping while doing these tests.

"Ladies and gentlemen, welcome to the main campsite," the guy said. "Yes, we will be doing the tests and camping at the same time. Let's get to know one thing about each and every person in this campsite. Everyone, form a circle—and no pushing."

Everyone formed a circle. But no matter what the guy with the red, bushy beard said, everyone pushed to get into the circle faster.

"My name is Fred. Or, you can call me Counselor, since I will be leading you all during these ten days. I love adventures so much." His smile turned into a frown. He seemed pretty perky and happy. "Oh, by the way, according to the rules for this whole thing...if you are older than twenty-two, you must leave." A ton of people left, and I mean a *ton.* There were only half as many people. "And you must leave if you are under ten years old." Some kids left, and then there were only five of us.

"Let's introduce ourselves," Fred continued. "So, my name is Fred, and I love adventures!" He looked to the person on his right. "You go next."

A teenage girl in a crop top who looked about my age spoke up. "So, like, my name is Leslie, and I am, like, really famous on YouTube. So, like, yeah!" I had a feeling I wouldn't like this Leslie girl.

"Okay, nice. Next," Fred said.

A man with a tuxedo and a suitcase spoke in a strong and loud voice. "My name is Mr. Falone, and I am a professional businessman in the spy industry."

"Heh, heh, heh.," Fred laughed. "Hope you aren't spying on us. Next."

The next person was an athlete wearing sweatpants and a tank top. She had a low voice, but a kind one. "My name is Isabel, but you can call me Izzy. I have competed in the Olympics, where I earned a bronze medal in running." I don't know why, but she reminded me of my brother.

"Wow. Great job!" Fred cheered. "You are going to be a front *runner*. Get it? Next."

Then the fourth person spoke. Another man, but this one looked homeless. He had really long, gray hair on his chin and head, and super ripped-up, dirty clothes. You could barely see his face. "M-my n-name is Jon, and I am considering moving to the forest."

"Okay... Next."

Now it was my turn. "Um...my name is Safire... and, uh...I'm thirteen years old, soon to be fourteen..." I stammered. Not a good first impression. But I would only be with these people for a week. What harm could it do?

Leslie looked at me with a weird glare. *Huh?*

"Okay…I have seats right here for you. All of you have assigned seats, listed on the small blackboard on my desk."

This is what the blackboard said:

Front

Leslie	Safire	Izzy
Jon		Mr. Falone

"Okay. These will be your seats every time. No switching seats or anything. Okay, time for dinner!" Fred said. Once he said that, five servers came out from a building on a far hill and marched to the classroom. They placed plates full of juicy, awesome-smelling baby back ribs onto our wooden desks. *Yay! I love baby back ribs!*

"It's too messy…I need a fork and knife." Leslie moaned.

"You eat it with your hands. Not a fork and knife," I whispered back. "It's good to get messy." I devoured all the meat on the ribs and showed her my messy mouth.

"But my makeup! My makeup will get messed up! And my nails, too!"

"I'm sorry, but we don't have utensils here. You will eat it or starve," Fred grumbled.

"Then I will starve." Leslie whispered. She pushed her plate away from her. I gave Fred a look and pointed to her leftover food. Fred nodded, so I finished my plate and started eating Leslie's food.

Next to me, Izzy was asking for seconds and didn't

get any, so I shared Leslie's food with her. "You are a big eater," Izzy said to me, in between bites.

"Eh. My favorite food is pretty much ribs. So I never get stuffed eating them," I explained.

"Heh. Same," Izzy said. I smiled. I knew Izzy was pretty much going to be my only friend. I felt so happy that I could have a friend. But at the same time, I was nervous because she could end up being another alien.

Once everyone was done eating, Fred started talking. "Okay, friends! I hope you enjoyed that meal! Because it is time to get some rest for the ten days ahead of us!" He gestured to the campsite. "There are five tents, each a different color. You are all assigned one. There is a sleeping bag and some room to put away those backpacks of yours. I will wake you up in the morning at 5:00 A.M. I will give you all breakfast and explain the test of the day. You'll do it for seven hours or less." He smiled at us. "You will get break time and lunch while we count points for each and everyone of you. We will announce the points before we serve dinner. That will be the routine each day. So, find your tents and get lots of sleep."

ARRRRGGGG! I thought. I didn't realize this is what would happen, *just* to get a living space. Although, I had nothing better to do, so I didn't really care.

We got up from our desks and looked for our names on the tents. I got the teal tent. Leslie got the pink tent. Izzy got the blood red tent. Jon got the gray tent. And Mr. Falone got the black tent.

I said goodnight to Izzy and crawled into my tent. I set my backpack down and climbed into my magenta sleeping bag that was already laid out.

I took out my magic pyramid. I stared at it for a while. "How do you know everything about me?" I whispered. I spun the pyramid lightly.

The moment you touched me, I was informed of everything about you.

"By who?"

It happens every time someone touches me, but for some reason, all of your memories were less clear. It took a while to understand them.

"Is Liginia an alien?"

Yep.

"Am I an alien?"

I don't know…

Igneous

CHAPTER 16

"Good morning, Igneous!" said my alarm clock—

Hello, sorry. I didn't mean to confuse you. Let me back up a little...

The day before, I had gotten onto the ship and checked things out a little. There were two bedrooms, both had a dressing area, a bed, a robot station and a desk. Outside of the bedrooms, there was a storage and planning room, a robot pilot station (the robot in the driving system would drive anywhere you wanted), and two robot rooms (both had tons of shelves with robots, and an oiling and robot-fixing station).

"Come on, Igneous. I'm sure you are tired," Lord Slag had said. "Let me show you to your room."

When I got into the room, I ran to the bed straight away. But after a few minutes of not being able to sleep, I sat up. I shuddered when I looked at the room. It was bland, with white walls and hard brown floors. Overall, it was missing something.

"*Bleeeeep?*" I looked to my left and jumped back.

Next to me stood a small robot the size of three lavaballs on top of each other. It had three antennas and a black boxy head. It had one small circular red eye and a larger white eye. Throughout its whole body, it had all kinds of parts that probably did different things. And its lower half was a boxy shape that had six strong spider-like legs. I could hear the legs moving as it walked around my bed.

"Uh…" I said.

"Hello!" it said, in a light and bright tone. My shoulders relaxed a little. *"My name is Ezur!"*

"M-my name is Igneous," I stuttered. I didn't expect the robot to talk.

"Are you new here? Oh wait, I've heard about you before! You are the one who will get to own this ship if you get the newest spy job!" I frowned at the robot, trying to figure out why it was *so* energetic. I gave up trying to figure it out. I stuffed a pillow in my face and fell asleep.

Sorry, *now* let's go back to the present.

KNOCK KNOCK KNOCK! Somebody banged on the door. I jumped up, ignoring the look Ezur was giving me. "Okay, okay!" I yelled.

I opened the door, and the person who stood in front of me was *Lord Slag.* "Oh! I'm so sorry for keeping you waiting…" I pretended to look genuinely sorry. (But I wasn't.)

"Okay," he said, in a commanding tone.

"So, now what?" I asked.

"Now is the time you take a test!"

My jaw dropped. *A TEST?* "What—"

"You see, there are about ten others that are competing for the newest spy spot. But I understand that you are confused." I tried to interrupt, but he kept talking. "So, here, take this piece of paper. It lists the process to figure out which person is the best for the job." He handed me the paper quickly, urging me to read it.

- Test #1
  - Getting information from the target
- Short Interview
- Test #2 (if needed)
  - All about spying
- Acting Course (if needed)

My eyes were wide open. Dang...this might take a while.

"But I think you can do it" Lord Slag said, in a non-convincing tone. He must have said it to other people before. "Now, come with me to the planning area to take your test."

I slowly walked to the center of the ship with him. The moment I sat down at the table, the hairs on my arms rose. THE TEST WAS TEN PAGES LONG! *AHHHHHHHHHH!*

SPY TEST #1

1. If you are trying to listen to someone, but their back is to you, what should you do?
   A. Give up and go away.
   B. Walk over normally and say, "Whatcha

talking about?"

   C. Run to the person and shout, "I'm spying on you! Tell me what you are talking about!"

   D. Walk past the person normally, picking up parts of the conversation.

   E. Strain your ears to hear what they are saying.

2. You are talking to the person you are supposed to spy on. They are starting to tell you about themselves, like you want them to, but you don't have much time left before you need to report to your boss. What should you do?

   A. Ask questions that should lead the person into telling you what you want to know.

   B. Keep listening without saying a word.

   C. Give up and go away.

   D. Ask them directly what you want to know.

   E. Threaten them.

   F. Tell your boss to wait so you can become fake friends with the person, thinking that they will eventually tell you.

Most of the questions were like these. When I finished, Lord Slag became super happy. "That's good! Because we—"

THUMP! "We are docked, sir!" a robot said.

Lord Slag didn't finish his sentence. He just walked to the exit of the ship. When I didn't follow him, he looked at me and told me to follow him.

After we got outside and my eyes adjusted to the brightness, I saw a huge volcano with tons of lava leaking down the sides. The mountain was a dark ash brown that seemed like it was burning in the sun.

"Where are we going?" I asked.

"In that volcano." Lord Slag said this so casually, like it was normal to go inside a volcano. *WOW!* I started to jump up and down because I was so excited. Lord Slag just glared at me, and I stopped. "Now, we are about to meet The Guild. They are our government, so treat them with respect." I nodded, and we began to walk over to the volcano.

As we came nearer to the…um…volcano, I began to notice guards in semi-hidden spots. When we got to the entrance, there was a fancy person with a long dress robe with all types of sequins on it. His gray hair was clipped into a bob. I shivered when his soulless eyes looked into mine.

"We are here for the newest spy position," said Lord Slag. "This is Igneous Stone." Without a word, the man pushed part of the mountain behind him.

CREAK! I stepped inside, to be welcomed by the wonderful smell of lava-baked cookies. I looked around the big white room and cringed as the coldness wrapped around me. I tried to ignore the cold when I saw twelve bored-looking people sitting at a long, curved table in the middle of the room. The table curved around a small chair.

Tik, tik, tik. Somebody tapped a pen on their desk.

THUMP! I whipped my head around to see the doors behind me had closed. I tightened my fists and turned to face The Guild. I noticed that they all looked like Lord Slag. I quickly concluded that all powerful beings must look like that.

"AHEM!" somebody shouted from the corner. "THIS IS CANDIDATE NUMBER ELEVEN! PLEASE SIT DOWN, MR. IGNEOUS STONE!"

I slowly walked to the small chair and cautiously sat down.

"Please state your name, your date of birth and why you want to be the newest spy," one of The Guild members said.

"Um…I-Igneous. Igneous Stone. 23/145/345. I want to be the newest spy because…" Why did I want to be the newest spy? I didn't choose to be it; I was just brought into it. I hesitated. "B-because I'm good at spying on people. I love acting, and acting as a different person makes me forget reality, " I lied. *Well…the last part was sometimes true.*

"Okay, thank you. You may go." That's it? I slowly got up and walked out of the room. When I opened the door to leave, I heard a few murmurs about me.

"…he is pretty good, I think he might have the heart."

"Yes, but he was afraid and we don't need that…"

"He has potential…"

I closed the door, not wanting them to know I was listening. My heart started beating fast when the thought of getting the spot entered my mind.

Safire

CHAPTER 17

"Wake up everyone! It's the first day of testing!" Fred yelled in the morning.

I was already awake and quickly squirmed out of my sleeping bag and grabbed my backpack. I brushed my hair and headed out of the tent.

"Morning!" I said to everyone.

"Morning..." everyone (except for Fred) responded.

"Okay, everyone! Get to your assigned tables!" Fred said cheerfully. A big grin was pasted on his face. I almost said, "What could possibly be so good right now?"

Everyone dashed to their desks. The servers came with energy bars and sugar cubes. I didn't understand why we were having sugar cubes for breakfast.

"Finally something not messy! Like, yay!" Leslie exclaimed.

"Um...we only had one meal that was messy," I commented.

"Um, like, hello? I was talking to myself, you dork," Leslie said, looking grossed out. *How was I a dork?*

I ignored her and popped a sugar cube in my mouth. This reminded me that I had NEVER had sugar before. I tasted the magnificent flavor spread in my mouth. I closed my eyes and enjoyed it. But when I opened my eyes, my muscles tightened up. I couldn't move. My muscles strained against the pressure. The sugar made me feel so weird, it seemed like my weakness —my kryptonite.

"Hnnnggg…" A quiet whisper escaped my lips. Izzy turned around to face me.

"Are you okay?" she asked. I tried to get up to ask Fred for water, but I immediately fell to the ground. I was still conscious, so I rolled from my side to face upward. Everyone leaned over me.

"Safire, can you hear me?" Fred said.

"Hnnnggg," I whispered.

"Okay, well, there are doctors coming. But if you feel okay, we can tell them to go away."

"N-no…" I coughed. "I'm f-fine. C-call them off…" I said.

I soon felt much better. I just didn't eat anymore sugar. Izzy let me have half of her bar because she was able to eat her (and my) sugar cubes. Everyone finished breakfast.

"Okay! Eat up, because we have got to do our test," Fred started. "Today's test is…drumroll, please…"

Izzy and I drumrolled our fingers on our desks.

"We are doing running tests!" Fred said. "So I hope you all have good legs."

"Noooo! I hate running! It ruins my shoes," Leslie

whined. *GEEZ! I thought. When will that girl stop?*

"Well, you are in luck. You will all have new shoes for this. And you get to keep them. You will find the new shoes in your tents. They are all the right size, so don't worry about that," Fred said, as if he were the lead in a commercial. Very animated.

"Yes! New shoes. My shoes are wrecked," Jon cheered. Since he had been homeless, he probably never had new shoes in his whole life.

"Noooo! But I like my shoes! My shoes are sooo pretty," Leslie whined again. *What a big, fat baby,* I thought. I looked at her feet. She was wearing medium-sized semi-heels—not the *clippity clop* type—that were black with red swirls on them. I think they were leather. At least they had sneaker-shoe tread on the bottoms.

"Well, then you have to get your *nice* shoes dirty." Fred told Leslie. He turned to the rest of us. "If you didn't eat all your food, too bad. Because it is 6:00 A.M. and we need to start the test now. So go, run to your tents, grab your shoes and follow me!"

I speed-walked to the tents to save energy. To my right, Leslie was trying to decide if she was going to wear her nice shoes or the new shoes. She ended up wearing the new shoes.

"Follow me!" Fred cheered when everyone had gotten their shoes on. "Let's start by warming up! We are going to jog to the running track. Keep up!"

Maybe Izzy was a short-distance racer, because she was really fast at the beginning. Or maybe, it was just that all of those sugar cubes were kicking in.

She was a mile ahead of everyone, at first. Even when she weaved around the natural bushes and trees that were next to the path, she still beat us. But after five minutes, she started slowing down. At the ten-minute mark, she was behind everyone, except for Leslie.

Leslie was whining the minute we started running. "Can we rest? I have stuff in my shoes. I need to text my friends to let them know I am okay. This is so overrated and long. I don't deserve this. Excuse me? Are you even listening, Fred? Hello?! You guys are weirdos! Who needs to run when we have cars!" She sounded like she was plugging her nose when she was talking—that's how annoying it was.

I could see Fred's face was turning red. He stopped and turned around to look at Leslie. "Listen up, you! I don't care who you think you are! But you need to shape up! Or I will give you no chance of winning the living space! You hear me? Get it together!" Fred yelled.

I grinned and started running ahead of everyone. I ran fast. I ran so fast, that I felt adrenaline pump through my veins. I then slowed down for the others to catch up, so I wouldn't waste energy.

"Wow! That was crazy fast. You were like a blur," Fred said, five minutes after I had stopped running. "How do you run that fast?"

"Um…I guess, I just do?" I shrugged.

Izzy came up. "That seemed faster than Jastin Baitlen's fastest time. WOW!" she said.

"Um…who is Jastin Baitlen?" I asked, trying to change the subject.

"You don't know who he is? He is the fastest human on earth!" Izzy exclaimed.

"Isn't that Dsain Dolt?" I asked.

She looked at me like I was crazy. "Dsain Dolt has a time of 9.58 seconds. Jastin Baitlen beat him in the one hundred meter with a time of 9.45 seconds! So, Baitlen beats him by 0.13 seconds."

"Oh! Wow!" (Honestly, I really didn't care if I was super fast.)

"Okay, we're here," Fred said, trying to change the subject.

"WHAT IS THAT UGLY THING?" Leslie screamed.

I turned around. My eyes opened really wide. There was a clearing, with a long, smooth stick that marked the start and finish line. At its center was a statue about the size of my flooded shelter. It was a statue of a baby angel, standing on a large block of stone. The angel was crossing her arms and seemed to stare deep into my eyes. *What an unusual statue...* I shook my head. The rest of the clearing was sand, hard sand that surrounded the angel in a perfect circle. To the side was a small set of bleachers that would only fit nine to twelve people.

We stood near the finish line. "Welcome to where we will be running today!" Fred exclaimed. "I know this isn't much of a view, but who needs a view when you are running?"

"Um...of course I, like, need a view. A view like *me*," Leslie said. She tossed her hair and looked into her bag. She brought out a mirror. "Look at—AHHHHH!

Don't look at me! My hair is too frizzy! And my makeup…it's totally ruined! AHHHH!!! How could I not, like, *realize?!*" She took out wipes and wiped her face clean. Her face finally looked normal. "There, that's like a little better. Okay. Go on." I rolled my eyes when she started applying makeup again. She really caked it on.

"So…the first thing we will be doing is stretching," Fred said. "You must always stretch before you run fast. I want all of you to do *this*." We all copied him.

"Good job, everyone! Hold it a bit longer…" Fred praised.

"I can't do this! It's, like, too messy!" Leslie complained. She got up and sat on the benches nearby. She already had a bunch of sand in her hair. (Probably because she fell a million times.)

Fred rolled his eyes. "Good luck with that. Have a nice time trying to beat everybody," he said. "Okay. Get up, everyone. Now, do thirty jumping jacks."

While we exercised, he went and talked to Leslie. She smacked him. But after that, she flipped her hair and walked over to the other side of the benches. That's what dumb rich kids do—they do whatever they want, and they expect they will get their way in the end.

Fred looked like he wanted to punch her really bad.

Luckily we were almost done with our jumping jacks. "Twenty-five, twenty-six, twenty-seven, twenty-eight, twenty-nine, thirty!" we all huffed.

"Okay. Now, just shake it all out, then we are going to run." Fred said. We just shook our arms and legs out.

Then, Leslie came over to us.

"WHAT DO YOU WANT?!" Fred and I shouted.

"AHEM!" She started talking in a British accent. "You guys think I am so not strong and, like, so not smart. I'm going to prove I am *more* strong and smart than you guys. So...Bring. It. On."

I pulled out my magic pyramid. "Let's see what this says." I spoke to it. "Is Leslie going to actually outrun us all?"

Signs point to no.

"See?" I said. I showed everyone. *Good job, Safire,* I told myself. But then, I felt like a big bully.

"Now, everyone take a lap and get into your lanes," Fred instructed. "Choose whatever lane you want." He was really mad. Really, really mad. But he had been a little happier when Leslie's cheeks turned red after the magic pyramid's prediction. I returned the pyramid to my backpack and set it down by the bleachers.

We did a lap. At that point, I had no idea how Leslie was going to beat everyone. "Ugh... It's so gross and dusty here. I really wish I had my girls right now." she complained, *again.*

"Okay. We are going to get the short laps done first," Fred said.

"At least I will beat everyone in *that,*" Leslie said.

"Um...how are you going to do that, when you were so slow in the first run?" I asked. "And remember what the magic pyramid said?"

"I have my ways," she grinned. She looked like she was cooking up an evil plan. I don't think she remembered that we all knew she was creating a plan to win. After all, she told us a couple minutes before.

"Okay, I am going to say, 'Take your mark,' and you are going to get in the ready position," Fred said. "Then, I will blow the horn, and that will signal you to start. Any questions?" He was starting to sound impatient. The way he tapped his foot and fidgeted told me he was tired of coaching us.

I don't think Leslie cared though. "Um…excuse me? Aren't you going to, like, tell us, like, how to, like, get into the, like, ready position? *Hello?*" She went on, and on, and on, and on, *and on.* Fred glanced at his watch and raised his eyebrows.

"STOP!" Fred's face reddened, and he cracked his knuckles. "I can't tell you. Sorry."

"CAN WE START?!" I yelled.

Fred stepped back and nodded. "Take your mark."

I got in my position.

Then Fred blew into the horn.

All I heard was the sound of feet thudding on the ground. All I saw was a flash of color. Green, yellow, white, gray, yellow and green. All I felt was the pain in my muscles. And the pain in my heart was vanishing. Vanishing, like when Liginia left. Vanishing, like my happiness did when I had to escape from my house, and when Marissa died.

When I stopped at the finish line, the pain in my heart had gone, but my heart's happiness was still below zero. I felt dead. Dead in my mind, dead in my heart, and dead physically. I felt like someone was drowning me. I needed a fresh breath of air. But I felt that I wouldn't get that breath of air. I felt that it would never go away. I had no idea what was going to happen to me. I had no idea what I was in for. It was like when you watch a suspenseful movie where you have no idea what is going to happen. But you can skip the movie, if you want. You can't skip life. And that was never an option. Life is too precious.

I didn't even realize I was just standing on the finish line, staring at my feet. When I finally looked up, I found Izzy staring at me like I was crazy.

And I felt crazy.

At first, it looked like Izzy was just moving her lips. I realized she was talking.

"...Safire. Safire. Safire! SAFIRE! SAFIRE!!!" Izzy shouted at me.

"W-what?" I realized I was lying on the ground, and Izzy was looking down at me. "W-what's goin' on?" I mumbled. I was confused.

"You collapsed after you finished your race. Fred didn't even see it, because he went to the bathroom. You were standing there, just *standing there*, at the finish line." She pointed at it. "Then you just fell. I tried to wake you up. Your pulse is good. And you seem healthy. I guess you just might have been tired. So, yeah. You fell. And it was really odd. AND SO...I don't know what to say. If you are okay, then, do you want to still race, or—"

I cut her off. Izzy reminded me of Aenon again. Aenon would always say, "AND SO...I don't know what to say," whenever he had a loss for words. Tears tickled my eyes, waiting to slide down my face. "I'll do it," I said. I heaved myself up to a sitting position. Luckily, I didn't feel dizzy. So that was definitely good. Besides, I didn't want to lose the Living Space over falling down. I did the quick routine—*breathe in and breathe out*—and stood up.

Izzy started saying that I must be the child of the running gods.

"Um, who are the running gods?" I asked. The conversation was starting to get really awkward. For some weird reason, I just wanted to read a graphic novel in a little nook. I mean, we all have weird things that we want to do at weird times. Right? *Maybe* I wanted to escape into something I loved.

"YOU DON'T KNOW WHO THE RUNNING GODS ARE!?" Izzy said. But I think she understood that I didn't. She reminded me of Aenon again. She felt so passionate about running, like Aenon did with football. And they both seemed to think that anyone who didn't know much about their favorite sport was simply crazy.

"Yeah?" I got up and walked to the water fountain.

"Okay. You two need to take a break from talking about running stuff," Fred interrupted, as usual. "Fill your water bottles in the water fountain, and no, it isn't contaminated water. It's clean."

Everyone rushed to the fountain on the side of the track. As everyone was drinking tons of water, the dirt on Jon's face contaminated all the water. I think he was licking the water when dirt got washed off.

"Jon!" we all yelled.

"Sorry…" he said.

"What happened?" Fred asked, concerned.

"Jon contaminated the water," Mr. Falone said. I hadn't realized until now that Mr. Falone hadn't spoken yet. He had a low voice like a bass instrument.

"Why didn't you talk this whole time?" Leslie said to Mr. Falone. "Hello? What type of person does that?"

My anger rose up in my brain. I stopped thinking. Then I completely lost it. "What's your problem?!" I screamed at Leslie. "All you do is complain about what people are doing to you! Then you complain about your makeup and nail polish getting dirty! Who does that?" I was panting.

Leslie gave me an astonished look. "Who are you to talk about me like that?! Like, huh?"

"Who are *you* to complain about the stupidest things?! Huh?! Back at you!" I shouted.

"O.M.G! How could you say that! Ow…" She clutched her heart dramatically, as if she were in pain. It reminded me of melodramatic movies. I rolled my eyes. *Why couldn't she just go away and get out of my business?* I wished she would stop making me mad, so I wouldn't get busted.

"Split it up, you two!" Fred interrupted. "Get it together! We have to do these tests, so argue later." He pushed us apart. "Okay. Since we've had a little break, we shall now move on. Everyone, get in your original lanes."

Lane 1	Lane 2	Lane 3	Lane 4	Lane 5
Leslie	Safire	Izzy	Mr. Falone	Jon

"Take your mark," Fred said. "Get set. GO!"

We ran four more races, and the races got longer and longer:

Race 1 (one lap):
1st Place, Safire
2nd Place, Izzy
3rd Place, Jon

Race 2 (two laps):
1st Place, Safire
2nd Place, Izzy
3rd Place, Mr. Falone

Race 3 (four laps):
1st Place, Safire
2nd Place, Izzy
3rd Place, Leslie

Race 4 (eight laps):
1st Place, Safire
2nd Place, Mr. Falone

3rd Place, Leslie

Race 5 (ten laps):
1st Place, Safire
2nd Place, Mr. Falone
3rd Place, Jon

"Good job today, guys. You guys did excellent," Fred said, once we were done with all the races. "Now you can all rest. Take a nice walk back to the campsite. We are done for the day." Everyone walked back to the campsite.

"I'm going to lounge in my tent, Safire," Izzy said.

"Same," I said. Then everyone else went back into their tents.

When I got into my tent, I simply just laid there. Just thinking about things. I took my phone out. Izzy kept reminding me of Aenon, and I missed him. *I miss my old life. I miss my friends.* I switched my phone to offline mode immediately, just to be safe. Then I opened up my texts.

(Two months ago)

```
NerdGirl30
Hey guys, IDK if u
look at ur messages
anymore. But i wanna
tell u guys that i
miss u guys so much.
And safire, is marissa
dead? Um... If u guys
```

can respond, that
would b so nice.
Thank u…):

(Two months ago)

JustInTime
Hey peeps, i am
moving. I just wanna
say i wasn't at school
when the thing
happened. Something
happened at my house.
My cat died. I am so
sorry. Marissa
wouldn't have been
dead if i had been
there.
So yeah. Bye…

I had been trying to forget about everything I had
to leave behind. I decided to write back, knowing I
couldn't hit the "Send" button, in case someone tracked
me.

OceanBlue22
Hi guys…
I'm sure you guys
probably forgot about
me… But our lives have
fallen apart. One of
us has died, Mar Mar,

169

and something happened at our school. So yeah, I don't think we will ever see each other again...

I immediately regretted even thinking about using my phone because the doctors that attacked my house could have tracked down where I was. I was glad I hadn't used it before. I put my phone away, having fresh memories of that day. The day it all fell apart. The day when I saw Marissa bloody. The day she died. Before that, my life was as normal as it would ever be. I missed my therapist bugging me. I missed knowing what Marissa was going to say, every time. And the doctor appointments...who knew I was gonna miss those? I blinked back my tears and crawled out of my tent.

Everyone was outside eating snacks. *FOOD!* I looked at the sky, trying to tell what time of day it was, but I just confused myself, because the sun was starting to set, and the sky turned from a normal sky blue to a lazy orange. My stomach growled. I wished I hadn't missed my snack.

"Everyone! Quiet down." Fred said. "Okay so in fifth place, Leslie Watts." Everyone cheered. "In fourth place, Jon Washington and Mr. Falone in third." Everyone cheered. "And in first place is...Safire Waters!" Everyone cheered. "Oh! And Isabel Porgeta is second." No one cheered. Why did Fred forget about Izzy and jump to my place?

"Ugh…a homeless guy beat *me,* the YouTube queen? Ugh…" Leslie moaned.

"Izzy almost didn't get her place announced," I said. "Quit whining."

"Easy for you to say," Leslie said. She ignored the part about Izzy.

"What's Leslie doing now?" Izzy said. We watched as Leslie kept shouting at me. All I did was wave and turn towards Izzy.

"She's overreacting." I said.

"Got it. Nice!" Izzy said.

I felt like I was a bully, again.

"Time for dinner, guys!" Fred called out.

Everyone rushed to their tables and was ready, straight away.

The servers came with plates of steak and potatoes. *Yum!*

"Good night!" I said to Izzy, when we were all heading to the tents. "And I forgot to say to you, sorry that—"

"Good night!" Izzy said, before I had the chance to say that it was strange that they forgot about her.

Igneous

CHAPTER 18

I had been waiting all day to know the results.

I had been sitting in my bed on the ship, talking to Ezur. I never thought I would. Apparently he was a new robot, and he was made to be a personal assistant. *"IGNEOUS,"* Ezur said, all of a sudden. *"I got an alert from Lord Slag that it's time for you to go to the Volcano!"* I stared at him with my mouth and eyes wide open, and ran out the door, out of the jet, across the flat field and to the volcano.

"IT'S ME!" I panted to the doorman. He quickly pushed the door open and I ran into the room. I really didn't want to give up the only job that would get me out of Battle School. Besides, I wanted to help my people. Whenever I did anything that helped them, I felt good. I hoped I could change the world.

"SORRY, I'M LATE!" I said to The Guild. After a moment of silence that felt like an hour, I asked, "Actually, *am* I late?" One of The Guild members nodded. "Did everyone already hear who the spy is?" He shook his head. "Who is it?" I demanded.

He glared at me. "We don't know, and it won't be you…" *I knew it,* I thought to myself. "BUT! It's not official. A ceremony will be held in town at the National Announcement Center later tonight." My eyes opened wide. *WHAT?* Why did I have to wait?! My life seemed like I was always waiting.

I walked out of the room, a little annoyed.

. . .

"LADIES AND GENTLEMEN, WELCOME TO THE NATIONAL ANNOUNCEMENT CENTER!"

The crowd roared. I cringed as the sound crashed through the auditorium. Even the huge auditorium with velvet seats and huge theater boxes couldn't handle the sound. The floor even vibrated.

"As you know, the big thing of the day is the choosing of the newest spy! So let's get right to that! IF I CALL YOUR NAME, PLEASE STAND UP!

"MADU GESIOUN!

"WEB NESINE!

"VEIK REMOLIAN!

"QUESAINOE SLELD!"

Six more names were called up, and then—

"AND IGNEOUS STONE!"

I stood up slowly. My heart beat so fast, it felt like the time when I had a panic attack. Bad memories. I tried to get the whole…dying thing…out of my head.

"NOW, ALL OF YOU, COME UP HERE!"

We all walked nervously to the stage. When we

finally lined up across the stage, behind the shouting announcer, he took out an envelope.

"THE NEWEST SPY IS...IGNEOUS STONE!"

I stood there for a second, the thoughts in my mind racing. I thought I wasn't going to get it at all! Even The Guild said it! I looked up at The Guild's theater box, trying to meet eyes with one of them. Well... I couldn't see their eyes though because they were shadows...

"COME OVER HERE!"

I snapped out of the daze and walked to the announcer. I bowed as he did some rituals that crowned me "the newest spy." I still didn't believe it was real though.

After the show, Lord Slag greeted me. He didn't sound proud of me when he greeted me. "I have a task for you! But first, I need you to take some lessons." *Arg...* No congratulations or pat on the back? "We just need to walk a little to get there," he said.

We arrived at a gray building, with no windows that I could see. We stepped inside to a small room with a lady at a desk that said "Front Desk."

"OH! Lord Slag!" she whispered. She snapped her fingers. To the side of the desk was a door that I hadn't noticed before. It opened quickly and we stepped through.

"WOW!" I said. I looked around at the huge room. Many people were—

"This room has many Lavagraphs," Lord Slag said. All of a sudden, he clapped, and every single person disappeared, except for one. This man was obviously a

Supreme, because he was a shadow, too. "Igneous, this is the Supreme Teacher."

The Supreme Teacher was the best teacher in the world. Usually only 0.0001 percent of the people who ask to train with him are accepted.

"WHAT?!" I said.

"Nice to meet you, Mr. Igneous Stone." The man suddenly appeared at my side. The figure towered over me and I winced. "Huh. You are showing signs of weakness already," he said strictly. I frowned. *Did I seriously have to be like a soldier again?*

"Well, I will leave you to it," Lord Slag said and disappeared. What was the deal with everyone teleporting around?

"Now," said the Supreme Teacher, "since you are under my instruction, we are going to start tomorrow."

. . .

The next day, at 0600M, I was standing in the teaching area, right in front of the guy (I had no idea what to call him).

"First thing's first. Defense and fighting. What would you say you are better at, weapons or fist fighting?" he asked.

"Weapons."

"Okay. But you need to be good at both."

I let out a breath that I didn't know I was holding in. "But I'm skinny and weak." It was true—my body was way less strong than my mind.

"You can be flexible and be a good fighter. Are you flexible?" he told me.

"A little."

"We can focus on fist-fighting later, during Fit Studies."

I frowned. "What exactly is Fit Studies?" I asked slowly.

"We work on things you need extra help with." He stepped to his left and revealed a table with many different weapons. "Choose a weapon."

I picked up a couple of daggers.

"I don't think you should use those," he said in a commanding voice.

I still picked up a knife. I slowly played around with the knife. "What do you usually use?" I asked.

He seemed a little annoyed that I was prying into this business. I could hear a quiet growl come out of his mouth. "Axes, usually..." he hesitated. "Now, try that dummy." He pointed at a small dummy that had circles on its chest, stomach and forehead. He probably wanted me to fail to prove a point.

I threw a knife effortlessly at the chest. *Clank!* It hit the dummy right in the chest.

"Close your eyes, spin around for ten seconds fast, and then hit it in the chest."

I closed my eyes and began to spin. One-two-three-four-five-six-seven-eight-nine-ten. I opened my eyes and quickly hit the dummy square in the chest again. (Good thing I practiced back in my old school.)

"Close your eyes and throw it." I closed my eyes

and threw it exactly the way I did before. "Hmph…you are decent."

I opened my eyes to see the knife perfectly in the center of the dummy's chest.

"Most students I teach throw the dagger at their leg by mistake," he said. He didn't seem that impressed with me, though. "I think you are a natural. Let's try 'Lights Out.' You have to listen for the dummy—a sound will turn on inside it. It is your job to hit it in the chest. You can only use one knife, so you only get one shot. Got it?"

I nodded and the lights turned off.

Eeeepp. Eepp! The sound began to echo through the room. I shook my head and listened closely. I took a step forward and heard the sound getting louder, but at the same time my heart beat so fast, I could feel the blood pumping through my veins. *Eeeepp. Eepp!* The sound reminded me of something, but I shook it out of my head and aimed.

THUMP! The lights turned on, and I saw that I hit the dummy right in the chest again. *Wow!*

"That was okay," the Supreme Teacher said. "Let's keep going. My big goal today is to see how far you go. Let's try a Lavagram task. Come with me into this room." He pointed at a transparent door.

We walked in and I stared in wonder at the room. On the ceiling, on every wall and even on the ground were small electronic orange circles. "What—"

"This room is a simulator. It creates figures that try to kill you. It's like a game. You will have one life. If you get hit by one figure, you die. Meanwhile, you will try to kill all of the Lavagrams. Instead of actually throwing knives, just pretend. The simulator will make Lavagrams of knives appear in your hands. And don't worry—for now, you have an unlimited amount of knives," he explained.

"Should I start now?" I asked. He nodded and left me in the room.

The lights dimmed and the first figure appeared.

Clang! Thump! I hit two targets that were next to me, at the same time, without looking.

I watched the next two figures appear. *Clang! Thump!* I spun around, throwing a knife through my legs; it went through both figures. My other hand threw two knives up at a jumping target. *Clang! Thump!*

I did a quick cartwheel and used my hands to throw myself up in the air. While I was airborne, I hit five targets. I landed and hit the ground hard. I got hit by an arrow. "Ow…" I said. I clasped my shoulder.

The game said, "You lose!"

The Supreme Teacher opened the door. "Igneous, you have to use the pain."

"Huh?" I said.

"You are going to get hurt many times, but a true hero gets up every time, no matter how many times they are hit to the ground. Get up." I frowned, but slowly got up. The Supreme Teacher spoke again. "Try again."

So I did.

I stood in the room once more. My Lavagram knife was ready.

Clang! Thump! I hit a couple of targets that I heard behind me. I dodged an arrow that whizzed past my face, shot from a figure in front of me.

Clang! Thump! I threw five knives in all different directions. Each of them hit one figure.

Clang! Thump! I laid myself flat against the floor as a huge bomb soared over the place I had stood half a second before. I winced as it crashed into the opposite wall.

Clang! Thump! I threw knives as I jumped up.

Clang! Thump! I took a deep breath as I hit a bunch of targets. Like before, I cartwheeled, using my hands to push off the ground as hard as possible.

Clang! Thump! Everything turned into slow motion as I flipped in the air, shooting knife after knife.

Clang! Thump! I hit the ground with my feet, staggering a little. Again, I threw knives between my legs, behind my back, up and down, and while I was airborne.

And then the simulator stopped. "You won!"

My eyes were wide open. I was super proud of myself. I didn't know I could do that! I didn't know if this was a new power I had, or if all my training from back at school kicked in at once.

"Wow…I haven't had a single person I know do that," the Supreme Teacher said. "But it was only decent. You can still go much faster—and also, you don't need to use that many knives. In real battle, you will have a limited number. In the game you have an infinite amount —"

But he was cut off by a voice. "Hello? Hello?" It

was Lord Slag. The Supreme Teacher ran out to Lord Slag, who was standing next to the food court area. I tried to listen to their conversation.

"…is he ready?" Lord Slag asked.

"I think he is. I have looked through his records. I can tell that he is a good actor. He's amazing with knives," the Supreme Teacher said.

"Should we tell him?"

"Yes…"

"IGNEOUS!"

I ran to them, throwing open the door. I walked politely, pretending I hadn't heard anything.

"We have a mission for you," the Supreme Teacher said. "You see, you are the same age as the person we are trying to capture, and we think you could do it."

"What?" I said, confused.

"You see, we are fighting a quiet war right now. In order to win the war, we need a girl. Her name is Safire."

Safire? The Safire I "connected" with through a Lavagraph?

"Why do we need her in particular?" I asked, curious.

"Because she is very powerful. If we can contain her powers, we would definitely win the war. Besides, we could use her in the long run."

As I heard more about this plan, I felt like it was an evil plan, not a virtuous one. "Huh…" I said.

"We need you to go to Earth," Lord Slag said. "If anyone asks you about your skin, say you were born that way. Do you understand?"

"Yes. I am going *now?*"

Lord Slag nodded.

Safire

CHAPTER 19

"Wake up! Wake up everyone! We have a surprise today!" Fred said.

"Morning," I said, when I got out of my tent. "So what's the surprise?"

"I will tell the surprise once. Not twice," Fred said. Everyone popped their heads out of their tents. We ran to our desks and stared at Fred. "Okay. So, um…Leslie, don't give me that look," Fred pointed out.

Izzy and I shared an annoyed glance. "Um… Fred?" I asked.

"Sorry, back to what I was saying," Fred said. "Let's get breakfast first." This time everyone shared an annoyed glance. But we went on with our day. "Today's breakfast is bananas," Fred announced. "Eat up." Everyone rushed eating their bananas. Even Leslie rushed.

"Okay, I'm done!" we all shouted in unison, when we finished our bananas.

"So, what's the surprise?" I asked.

"Um…" Fred said.

"Come on, Fred," Izzy said. "We have been waiting forever for *whatever* it is!"

"Okay, okay. Igneous, come out," Fred said.

"Igneous? What type of name is Igneous?" Leslie asked.

This Igneous guy came out of the bushes on the left side of the camp. He had on a denim jacket, a blue shirt and ripped, dark blue jeans. The light gray of his skin matched the light gray streaks in his dark brown hair. His eyes were stone gray. If he looked at you, it felt like his eyes bore through your soul.

"Uh…hi?" Igneous said, as his eyes darted to me. He looked at me like he had seen me before. He squinted at me, as if he needed glasses.

Wait, could this be the same Igneous I've been hanging out with? Why is he on Earth? I thought he was on another planet. Could he have been deceiving me this whole time?

"So, what is the test today, Fred?" I said, trying to change the subject.

"First, Igneous needs to take a seat. Please take the seat behind Safire," Fred demanded.

Igneous grinned, but only for a second. Our eyes met, and his eyes were filled with so much sorrow. I looked away quickly. My mind swirled with thoughts and confusion. I really didn't know if this guy was the same Igneous. He talked the same way, and he looked the same…*but Igneous is on his own planet.* This couldn't be him. Why would he be on Earth? I remembered falling off a Lavaboard—that was when he left me. He didn't help me get up or anything…

"Okay, the test today is…healing!" Fred announced. For a second, we were all dumbfounded. *Healing,* I thought? *I can't heal a thing!*

"Yes, yes, I know that none of you are doctors, but this test is all about problem solving! So let's get to work." Everyone got a first aid kit, a dying bird and a worktable. "YOUR TIME STARTS…NOW!"

I opened the first aid kit. My thoughts raced when I saw all the bottles of medicine, bandages and medical scissors. "WHAT?" I whispered. I looked around and saw other people freaking out. Their eyes were wide open in horror. It was like we had opened up bags and saw our worst nightmares in them. A slight breeze chilled my bones and helped me deal with the sun beaming down on my back.

"*Squaaa…help…*" I looked at the squawking bird. Why was it talking? Was I losing my mind? All of a sudden, its pain gave me an adrenaline rush. I felt the way it felt. I felt like I *was* that bird. Just like the school attacks on the news and the fight with Marissa's dad, my head felt like a knife was stabbing through it. I closed my eyes, trying to conceal the pain. Every time I looked at the bird again, it seemed like another knife stabbed through my head.

Finally, I couldn't take it anymore. I grabbed a random thing from the bag and glanced at the label. It said:

Numbing—only use for stitching and surgery

I looked at the bird and saw that its leg was bleeding. I felt overwhelmed. I closed my eyes and breathed in a couple times, ignoring the frustrated yelling around me. In the blank space behind my eyelids, X-rays and pictures of the bird's leg flashed, with labels everywhere explaining what was what and what I needed to do. I may not have seen everything, but when I opened my eyes, I was in the mode, and I knew EXACTLY what to do.

I pulled out a medical towel and dried the bird's blood with it. When I finished lightly patting its leg, I found a bad wound. It wouldn't stop bleeding, so I dabbed the blood away and quickly got out the medical stapler. My hands shook as I lowered it down. I got the bird ready, trying to be careful not to hurt its bones and muscles.

CHA CHING! I pressed the two sides of the stapler together. The bird was fine. Well, it wasn't bleeding anymore. I inspected my work slowly, making sure that I didn't staple the wrong place. "FRED!" I called.

He ran to my bird and nodded. "Good job! I'm really—surprised! Usually nobody finishes…"

"Does every single person get a bird with a broken leg?" I asked.

Fred nodded. "Okay, everyone, get back to your desks." Everyone sighed and frowned at Fred. "I didn't expect everyone to finish. Some vets will come over and help the birds. But good job today." Everyone went back to their desks, disappointed. "Since the tests have been so

185

much work, you all get a really long break. It stretches from now to the time I announce who is winning the contest so far. Have fun, relax and recharge."

Several others and I returned to our tents. The only one who stayed outside was Mr. Falone. He was just sitting there, whistling. This seemed weird and almost made me think that he was spying on us—or that he was really Liginia with her "illusion" powers.

While I was in my tent (for about forty-five minutes), I thought about everything, from Liginia to Igneous to everything I left behind. I spent a good deal of time crying about Marissa. But I was quick to wipe away my tears when Fred announced that he was going to tell us who was winning. Metaphorically, I put on my mask that hid my emotions from the others.

"I'm guessing you all already have an idea of who is winning and losing," Fred said. Everyone nodded. "In last place, Jon." Jon started whining. "Tied for third place are Izzy, Leslie and Mr. Falone." They all cringed. "And in second place is…Igneous!" I glanced at Igneous, trying to figure out if I just didn't want to accept the truth that it was really him. "So, Safire, you are winning!"

Everyone cheered except Leslie. "Ugh," she said.

How was Igneous in second place? He just showed up!?
"Fred?" I asked. "How is Igneous in second place if he just got here?" I asked.

He looked startled. "Oh! Oh yeah…he did the tests right before I introduced you guys to him," Fred said hesitantly.

"Okay, everyone! Round up and get to your

tables." Fred said. "Today's dinner is fish 'n chips!"

"Bleh. That's finger food. Do we ever *not* get finger foods?" Leslie moaned. Then she went off in her own world, probably thinking of makeup and popularity.

The servers came out from the hills, on the far right side of the camp. They gently set the plates on our desks. When everyone had finished eating, Fred called out, "Okay, good night, everybody. Time to sleep."

"Okay," everyone responded.

I headed to my tent and waited. Once everyone went into their own tents, and Fred had gone into the hills, I went back to my desk in the classroom. I rested my legs and feet on the desk and tilted my chair back to look at the sky.

There was a full moon, and it lit up the sky. It reminded me of when my brother, my mom and I would look up at the stars.

Once, when my brother wasn't there, I asked my mom about a forbidden topic in our house. "Mommy? What happened to Daddy?" I asked.

My mom glared at me. "Don't you dare talk about that!" my mom yelled.

I sank into my seat. "But—"

"We will never talk about this subject again! You hear me, Safire?" my mom said. She buried her face into her hands and wept.

I was only seven then. That day, I had presented a family tree to my class. Everyone except for me had a dad. I didn't even know what a "Dad" was.

I'd spent five years wondering what had happened

to my dad, or if I had a dad at all. A shooting star raced across the sky. I quietly wished to find out if I had a dad and what had happened to him. I sighed and got up.

"Hey."

I looked over my shoulder to see Igneous walking towards me. "Oh, hey." I really didn't want to talk to him. I also didn't want to keep wondering whether he was the same Igneous I've been meeting.

"I wanted to ask you—do I know you?" he asked.

My muscles tightened. Maybe this Igneous *was* the guy…but I didn't trust him after the Lavaboard incident. I shook my head, and I ran into my tent.

I didn't go to sleep automatically. I actually tried to stay awake. I retrieved my backpack and dug out my folder. I looked at the papers and found one with small handwriting which looked like my mom's.

Look at the sky,

The stars are the key.

Follow the North to the west.

The first star that way,

Will point down,

To home,

But your homes,

Are like two lines next to each other,

Worlds.

What was my mom trying to tell me, and why did

she have to write a riddle? I immediately assumed that it was important, because the poem didn't just say what she was trying to tell me. I began to decode the riddle, still confused as to why this seemed like a big secret.

> Look at the sky,
> The stars are the key...

The poem has to do with the stars.

> Follow the North to the west,
> The first star that way...

Look at the North Star, then draw a line that leads to the west, and find the star that is first on that line.

> Will point down,
> To home...

Look at the star that is right below the west star.

> But your homes,
> Are like two lines next to each other,
> Worlds.

My homes are parallel...worlds?
I never thought that parallel worlds could be a

thing. I felt so confused. I put the paper away and tried to forget about it, thinking I was just dreaming.

I fell asleep.

Igneous

CHAPTER 20

"And so…that was my first day," I said to the Lavagraph of Lord Slag.

"Well done, Igneous," Lord Slag said. "You did a pretty good job. But you must stay up."

"Um…I sorta got to get some sleep, I am really tired and—"

"Ahem. Who are you talking to?" Lord Slag asked.

"Sorry, my Lord," I said, as I laid down at the Lavagraph's feet. The tent had no cloth or anything to separate me from the ground, so I ended up getting a bunch of grass stains on my clothes.

"Exactly. Just because you have a higher position, doesn't mean you are higher than me," Lord Slag reminded me. "And always remember who you are talking to. You hear me?"

"Yes, I understand, my Lord." I swallowed hard. *I deserve some respect*, I thought.

"Okay, come close. Let me tell you your mission," Lord Slag said. "Your small mission is to see what goes on at that camp in those hills."

. . .

"Yes...finally! I—that...was...hard," I said, in between each breath. (I was running to the hills after I had finished my meeting with Lord Slag.)

I am not the toughest person ever. If you think I am some big, buff guy, well, you are completely wrong. Well, not completely—I am strong enough, but I don't have these big, bulky muscles. I'm fit, but skinny. I am *cut.*

I was running into the hills. Actually, I was running *alongside* the hills. But still, it's pretty much the same thing. The hills had lots of overgrown grass that went up to my knees. There were very few bushes and no trees. The hills were super round on top, and it was hard to find a spot where you could sneak up on the camp without using the entrance.

As I went around the hills, the sides of the mountain had more and more soil. It went on like that until it seemed as if the hills were made out of soil. I fell from the excitement and bit my lip. It started bleeding.

After what seemed like a decade, I found a big cave in the hills. I studied it, made my decision, and went in. Dark stone lined the walls and darkness swallowed me. The ceilings of this dark hole had pointed fangs that faced down to the ground.

Gulp. "Um...hello? Ouch!" A sharp piece of stone had pierced my shoe. When I finally got the stone out of my shoe, I kicked it away. More blood.

"HELLO, LITTLE BOY!" a booming voice said.

I slipped in fright. "Um…h-hello? I-I'm not a little boy," I stuttered.

"COMPARED TO ME? THE BIG, BAD—" the voice echoed down the dark and creepy cave. I couldn't see a single thing now that I had turned away from the entrance of the cave.

"Excuse me? The big, bad *what?*" I teased. Lord Slag would never want me to be scared, and I wanted to please Lord Slag, so I just joked around to distract myself. I stood firmly and clutched the knife that hid in my boot.

"I WAS SAYING, LITTLE BOY," the voice grumbled, "THAT I AM THE BIG, BAD, AMAZING, SCARY—"

"Wait, sorry, I was tying my shoes. The big, bad, amazing, scary *what?*" I joked.

"GRR!" the voice warned.

"Okay. Let me get this straight," I said. "So you are the big, bad, amazing, scary *growl?* Wh—AHHHHHHHH!!!!" I screamed and curled my lip.

The Big Bad Growl had jumped out from behind one of the cave walls. It had poop-brown eyes, a weird mohawk on his head and wrinkles like an old granny. He also had dust-gray skin that looked like it was going to fall off, so I was going to see his GUTS! "Who is scared now?" the monster thing said.

But then—he shrank. Then, he *changed.* He was a man with crazy white hair, wearing a Hawaiian shirt and gray shorts. To top it all off, he had on cheap sunglasses. "Surprised?" said the now not-a-monster thing.

"Who are you?" I asked.

"My name is Livinius," the man said in a low, crispy voice. "What is yours?"

"Igneous," I stuttered. *Could I trust this guy?* I thought.

"Ah. I see. You are on that guy Slag's side. The dark shadow?" the man asked. He seemed a little trustworthy.

"Yes, I am. I just started working for him," I explained.

"Very well then, I am at your service," Livinius said.

"Um...what?"

"You see, I am a shape shifter," Livinius explained. "I had this sister named Liginia. She and her minions kicked me off our planet. So I came here and hid for a long time. For 12,894,387 years and eleven months, to be exact. Oh wait—and two days."

My jaw dropped. "So, let me get this straight: you have been in this cave for 12,894,387 years, eleven months and *two days!?*" He simply nodded, as if it were nothing. I slowly rubbed my hand on the popcorn ceiling. "Soooo... how do you live here?"

"Potions," Livinius answered. He said to follow him. *Was this really real?* "Okay. Right down this narrow hall, and to the left, and down that narrow hall, and through the last door to the right," Livinius instructed. I did that and came to another hallway. "Down the hallway, take a right and go down the next hallway." The directions swam around in my head, but I did what he said, and I came to another hallway. The odd part was, there were white wooden doors along the way, and the farther we went, the less cavelike it was.

"Why can't we use the doors?" I asked.

"Traps," he muttered. My heart stopped. I really hoped we didn't end up going through the wrong door, or we could die. After five minutes of walking, we came to the door that led to his lab.

It was a huge room that had shelves covering all the walls. They were filled with bottles of potions and antidotes. In the middle of the room, there was a table with empty bottles, bottles of herbs and other ingredients, and some tubes and vials. The herbs gave the room a clean smell. "WOW!" I gasped.

"This is my lab. Let me show you around. So, here are the strength potions, the healing…" *Blah blah blah…* Livinius went on and on. "And this—follow me."

I followed Livinius to a small closet in the back. When he opened it, it was full of bottles of some pink liquid, plus a huge canister of the same stuff. "This is the strongest potion in the universe. The antilectory potion. You know what that is?" Livinius asked. I shook my head. "It is a…I will tell you later. Wait, no—you should guess it."

"What?" I asked. Why wouldn't he tell me?

"I am sure you will figure it out. I will not tell you anything more until you guess what it is. So out, out, out. Come back when you have the answer." Then Livinius pushed me all the way out of the cave. It was hard to keep track of which way we were going because he was pushing me so fast. I think he was using the same route he had me take to get to the potions room. Then, he vanished.

"What?" I yelled after him. I tried run back into the cave, but some invisible force was blocking me. After a few tries, I quit and decided to head back to camp.

When I got back to camp, I started heading to my tent. I looked at Safire's tent and remembered my main mission.

Then it hit me. I knew what the potion was!

Safire

CHAPTER 21

"Okay, everyone get up!" Fred announced.

It was the third morning we had spent in that campsite. I was feeling really good because I was winning and nothing really bad had happened so far. I jumped up, stretched and crawled out of my tent.

"So, Fred, what are we doing today?" I asked gleefully, my head up high.

"Something you might like. Everyone, gather up. Get a quick protein bar and gather up!" Fred shouted. He shot everybody an impatient look. "Today we are going to go swimming. Not me, but you guys." He pointed at us. "We need to hike to the river where we are going to swim. You guys get a couple minutes to finish your snacks and gather everything you need to bring. Got it?"

We all nodded and went to our tents to retrieve our bags. Before I knew it, we were already hiking down the trail, and our surroundings got less and less familiar.

During a break, Leslie pulled me to the side of the trail and behind a thin tree. "Hey, like…good job back there." She rubbed the back of her neck.

197

"Thanks. Uh…you too," I muttered. This was awkward. "You seem different."

"Oh. Yeah. Can I tell you something? You just seem…nice. Nobody listens to me," she stuttered.

A feeling of sadness pushed me to ask her to tell me. I knew it would make her feel a lot better. "You can tell me, " I responded, as kindness overwhelmed me. I began to feel like I *was* Leslie.

"Thanks," she said. "So, I have really rich parents that live a state away because of work, but they didn't let me move with them. They don't even visit me! I have to be by myself, every day. Well, I had my parent's house all to myself, and since they don't approve of me, I started my own World Wide Video channel. I got more and more subscribers every day. But sometimes, comments from random people broke me down. I had absolutely nobody to really talk to." She sighed. "Some odd men started flirting with me because I'm blond and naturally pretty." She was saying true things. Her skin *was* perfect. Not a wrinkle or a scar anywhere.

She kept talking, with very few breaths in between. "Then one time, when I was twelve—I'm fifteen now—I was stupid and took a video with my house in the background. Two days later, somebody knocked on my door and called my name. He was almost taunting me. I looked out my bedroom window. I didn't see anybody there. I went down the grand stairs to the front door and opened it. There was nobody there, either. But when I closed the door, I heard the beeping of a smoke alarm. I ran up to my room and saw that it was on fire. My bed, my bathroom, most of my things were burning. I would have died if the water sprinklers hadn't turned on. The firefighters came and took care of the rest. I was sent to the police station. I cried and cried. I called my parents multiple times, but they hung up, saying, 'I'm busy.'"

I looked at her confused. "How could your parents not listen to your pleas?"

"I don't know. Anyways, after that, I did more and more videos of myself. I probably did about ten videos a day."

"What?!"

"Yep! And you know what's worse? A year later I found out that my parents had divorced two years earlier! We hadn't had a single conversation since the day they left me, when I was ten years old." Leslie's eyes started watering. I patted her on the back.

"I begged for one of them to come live with me. But they said no. I haven't talked to my parents for two years. I haven't even spoken a word to them. I do go to school though, but nobody treats me the same as others. I'm known as 'the video girl with no friends.' All the videos I made damaged me, one by one. The comments got darker. Before, they were like, 'Oh! This is amazing!' But then, it got to them saying, 'Just stop wasting your time, rich girl.' I was soon old news. I created a different account and dressed up as a brunette. But people figured out the trick. One day, someone hacked into my account. They made me look like a *murderer*. People started visiting my house and pounded on my door. So I escaped. And I came to the city. It's weird...there isn't any name for it. It started off as meadow, and after I blinked, there was just this large city before my eyes. So, I have lived there for a month. And yeah, that's my—WAAAAAAA!" All of a sudden she broke down crying.

I rubbed her back and softly whispered, "It's okay, Leslie. It's okay…"

"Everyone! This was our last stop! We are almost there!" said Fred. I turned around to see everyone lining up to keep hiking.

"Leslie, we have to go," I whispered in her ear. She looked up and wiped her tears away and nodded. We walked over to the line. I felt overwhelming sadness and loneliness. It was as if I was sucking the emotions out of her and putting them into myself.

. . .

We reached the river Fred had been talking about. The river was semi-deep, from the looks of it, and it was dark and blue. There was a hill on the other side of the river, and the trees danced in the wind. The pebbles poked at the soles of my shoes as we walked.

I put my finger in the river and coldness crept up my finger, down my arm and into my body. I caught Igneous staring at me. I glared at him and he stepped back. *He wasn't trustworthy.* When I needed him, he wasn't there. When I fell off the Lavaboard, he just ran away. I really needed someone who I could trust because so many people have disappeared from my life. Not to mention, my dad couldn't even stick around long enough for me to meet him.

"Okay, we have swimsuits for you guys. We just need to know your size," Fred said joyfully. I think he was glad he didn't have to swim—the water was cold.

It took a while for us to get our swimsuits and put them on. Everyone got a black suit. And Leslie didn't whine. I was glad she was changing her personality. But at the same time, if she hadn't changed, I would be fine with it. Her experiences shaped her. She was unsure of herself and wanted to be like any other kid. She just wanted a caring family. She just wanted to be normal, and I knew that feeling all too well.

"OKAY!" Fred shouted. "Everyone is going to dive in at the sound of my voice—but first, I'm going to whistle to tell you to get in your places!"

TWEEEET!

This was going to be easy. I don't know if I mentioned it before, but I used to be a swimmer in middle school. (AND I was at the top of my age group!) I acted like this was a normal swim meet. I took my place at the edge of the river. I didn't look to the side. I didn't see the competitive swimmer glares, but I could feel there were a lot of them.

"GO!" Fred yelled. I dove in. The others were already so far behind me. When I reached the surface, I heard a distant *splash* and a yelp.

"He—"

Somebody was drowning! I turned around and saw Leslie struggling for air. "What the heck, people! Leslie is drowning!" I shouted at the others. They had picked their heads up for a second but still continued swimming.

I swam in the opposite direction. "Leslie! Leslie!" Her head disappeared under water. I got to the spot where she had been and I did a relay start that launched me into the water.

Leslie's body was slowly sinking. "LESLIE!" I shouted under water. I kicked and slowly went downward. Her body settled on the bottom of the lake. She was unconscious. I stretched forward, trying to grab her. "LESLIE!" I shouted again, as I swiped and grabbed her arm. I was running out of air—I had never gone this long without air. "NGGG!" I adjusted my grip on her and kicked as hard as I could. My heart felt like it stopped beating. I kicked and kicked, until I couldn't kick anymore. I was so stiff, I couldn't move. My eyes closed. I let go of Leslie.

All of a sudden, something tugged my hand. I opened my eyes and saw a figure trying to pull Leslie and me up. *Izzy?*

My lungs gave out and I fell unconscious.

. . .

When I woke up, I was lying next to Leslie (who I think was unconscious). We were on the pebbly ground, and the river water was tickling my feet.

"L-leslie?" I croaked. I got up. Everyone—Izzy, Fred, Igneous, Jon and Mr. Falone—was staring at me. "W-what happened?" I stuttered.

Fred spoke up. "You were underwater for two whole minutes. I told everyone to stop racing, and that someone had to help you guys. So, Igneous dove down and saved you!"

I glanced at Igneous. Now I had to give my thanks to this guy?! Well…I hated to admit it, but I was a little grateful. *He really saved our butts out there…* "What about Leslie?" I asked. I realized there was a blanket wrapped around me. Leslie didn't have one, so I wrapped mine around her.

"Leslie woke up when we got her out of the water. She seemed fine. She just wanted to say thanks for trying to save her," Fred said.

"Oh." I looked at Leslie with love, like I always did with Marissa…*NO! Leslie could never replace Marissa!* I thought, as my breath became shallow.

"We are postponing the race till tomorrow," Fred said. He walked away, and Izzy, Jon and Mr. Falone followed his lead. But Igneous didn't.

"What are you doing here?" I said.

"I volunteered to take you guys back to camp when you guys are ready." He turned his attention to a nearby leaf.

"You just take every chance to be near me, don't you?" I said.

"Yes. I want to know the truth," he said simply.

"About?"

He froze and didn't respond. He seemed angry, scared and sad, like somebody was threatening him or something. But he was still so eager and curious, he tried to break the awkwardness. "About the whole communication thing...I know you are the person on the other side of the 'call' thing..."

"Yeah," I finally admitted.

"Why are you so mad at me?" he asked suddenly.

I narrowed my eyes, trying to keep the boiling blood from erupting out my ears.

"You *left* me..." I growled quietly.

"I—what?" he asked.

I shook my head. I didn't want to get into this. As far as I knew, we were never going to be friends. I could never trust him again...ever. "Should I just wake Leslie up, so we can go?" I said.

He nodded and soon we were strolling down the path with Leslie. Nobody spoke. After a long and silent hike with no breaks, we got back to the camp. It was starting to get dark. Everyone was sitting quietly at their desks. Fred looked at us in silence.

"You guys took a while..." Izzy said.

. . .

The next day we got our swimsuits on and ran quickly to the river.

"GO!" Fred shouted. We dove into the water and swam. Once again, in the middle of the race, I stopped and made sure Leslie was okay. She was doing better. I swam some more, then I stopped. I remembered her story. *She needs to have something that boosts her confidence,* I thought to myself.

So I waited. I waited until the others were within a few yards from me. I stared them down. Just like I did with Marissa's dad. Fred looked at me from the trees. He stood a good distance away from the water for some odd reason. I shook my head and glared at him. Izzy looked at me. I shook my head and glared at her. I knew my anger and empathy would keep them from winning. Leslie needed this.

I pretended I was tired, while using all my hope and *sending* it to Leslie. She started picking up the pace. Soon enough, she was swimming just as fast as me.

Is there someone in my generation that has this Empath ability? Maybe this is one of the abilities, that Liginia was talking about!

When Leslie zoomed by, I stopped casting my glare on the others. Izzy looked up at me confused. I smiled. I did it! I really did it! I used my powers to help Leslie! Maybe I really can help people.

As I got out of the river, I realized that I did have powers. I wasn't confused anymore. Back in the city, Liginia had said, *'You haven't even manifested an ability yet!'* I guess I've proven her wrong again.

The happiness swallowed me. I had forgotten all my worries. I had even forgotten about Igneous.

Igneous

CHAPTER 22

"So, do you have the answer?" Livinius asked.

I was standing at the front of the cave talking to him, my muscles aching from saving Safire and Leslie earlier. The night before, I had figured out what the potion was. "Yes. It is a…l-love potion," I answered proudly, but nervously.

"CORRECT!!! Good job, *boy!*" Livinius ruffled my hair in praise.

"What? Did I—"

"You-must-promise-me-you-will-never-use-it-or-tell-a-soul-about-it." Livinius spoke without breathing.

"Wait, what? Say that again, slower," I asked politely.

"I said, Y-O-U, as in *you*, M-U-S-T, as in—"

"YOU KNOW WHAT I MEAN!" I yelled.

"You must promise me you will never use the potion or tell a soul about it," he said simply.

"Okay," I said. "I promise."

"Good. Now get out." He pushed me out again, like the day before.

"See you later?" I said, as he walked back into the cave and disappeared.

· · ·

I was walking back to the camp.

If only I could use the potion...but on who? I said to myself. *I don't* have *to use it...wait. I have to get her on Lord Slag's side. Hmm...I can use the love potion to make her do anything for...* me. My first good plan. I knew I would be going against Livinius' rule, but I also knew I had to follow Lord Slag.

With my plan in mind, I raced back to the cave to get the potion. But then I remembered I couldn't get through. This pause made me think about just going back to the camp and forgetting about it. I didn't want to do this to Safire. I closed my eyes tightly. But, then again, Safire already doesn't trust me, so I guess I *should* do it?

I thought it over. I could help one person, or millions of people. I wanted to cry from the weight of the decision on my shoulders. It felt like something as heavy as a Lavabus was sitting on my shoulders. But I knew what I had to do in order to help my planet. I needed to follow my people.

Soon, I was trying to get into the cave entrance again. It took me a while to figure out how I would do it, but once I got going, nothing could stop me. I found out that, on the left side of the cave entrance, there was a hole in the magic wall, so I squeezed through it.

Once I got through the hole, I went through the

shadows and down the hallways to the lab. I got to the door and peeked through it to see if the coast was clear. It was.

I slowly opened the door and closed it behind me. I tiptoed over to the closet with the potions. A sweet, comfortable feeling came over me as I pulled out the love potion. I almost let the potion take control of me, but I snapped myself to consciousness. *Wow, this stuff is strong,* I thought. I looked around for some instructions, or a little booklet on how to use the potion, and surprisingly, I found one:

Instructions: Antilectory Potion

Dispensing it on Another
Keep in mind that while trying to dispense this powerful potion on another, you may accidentally dispense it on yourself. When dispensing this, you must take the mini shooter and load it with the little balls of antilectory. Don't touch it too long or its effects will start going into you. A glove is recommended. When using the mini shooter, hit the button above the trigger to melt the antilectory balls into a liquid. Then pull the trigger.
For extra safety, read the bottom. Be safe.

Shivers went up my spine as I read this. This potion could be a life or death thing. Especially since I could get caught by Livinius. I took a deep breath, quickly loaded the mini shooter and set out like a soldier of war.

I planned to complete the mission that night while Safire slept. Once I got to the campsite, I quietly unzipped her tent. I hesitated, aimed the mini shooter at her and—

CRASH!

"OW!!!" I yelled. "L-love...I love ME!!! I am so awesome—AHH!!! I love me! AHH!!! I am so awesome—AHH!!!" My words were stuck in a loop. When I triggered the mini shooter, the potion somehow bounced off Safire and onto me, so *I* was taking in the effects of the potion. I tried fighting it off, but it wasn't working.

I stumbled out of the tent, out of the campsite and out into the woods. I heard a human voice. "Hello? Hello? Who's there?" It was a girl. I couldn't seem to place her voice, but for a second, it led me back to my childhood.

I blacked out.

.   .   .

"Get up!" a voice yelled. "Who are you and what do you want? This campsite is not a place where you try and kill people. Unless you want to go to jail!"

Then someone shook me and brought me back to consciousness.

"I wasn't trying to k-kill you..." I said, dreamily. I realized that all of the test participants were there, standing around me, with furious faces. All except for Leslie. She had a hurt look on her face, as if her boyfriend had broken up with her.

"Heh…" I laughed, deliriously, even in sadness. And I think Safire noticed that. She smacked me really hard in my face and made me bleed. The potion finally stopped working. I wasn't so delirious anymore, but the sadness was still there. I wasn't myself, but I knew what I had done was wrong.

"I would say we should report this to Fred," Izzy said.

"Yeah, but I would like to finish the first part of his punishment," Safire argued. Then she slapped my wound hard. All I could do was sit there. I agreed with her: I shouldn't have tried the potion on her. I would take the punishment I deserved.

Lord Slag would be greatly disappointed in me.

Safire kept hitting me in fury and became almost uncontrollable. The others tried to drag her away, but she escaped their hands. She threw everyone out of her way, and they were knocked unconscious. Safire charged at me, but as soon as she got five feet away from me, she fell down unconscious. *Whaaaat? What the—*

"Don't you dare come closer to my girl." A silhouette of an old woman appeared.

"I—"

"Don't you come close, don't you come close, don't you come close…" she echoed and then turned into a ball of light and glittered away.

"What?" I said. No answer.

I was too tired and beat up to go on. I laid my head back down and fell into a deep sleep.

. . .

"Welcome to jail, newcomers," a voice said.

My eyes fluttered open.

"Yeah," another voice said.

I sat up and looked around. I was in a stone room with a stone table in the middle and stone couches lining the walls. I was lying on one of the couches. There was an iron bar door on one wall that had a tiny handle. I jumped off the hard couch and tried to open the door, but it didn't work, it was locked. That's when I noticed that I had gray, dusty clothes on—and that a person was watching me.

It was Safire. She was in the same clothes, too. "Thanks a lot. You just got us in jail," she said.

"Where?" I asked.

"*Jail.* You know that I came here because of you, because I attacked you. So…" She gave me a hateful look, then laid down and looked at the stone ceiling. "You know we are going to have to deal with each other for a long time," she went on. "And we both hate each other, right?"

"I don't hate you—" I started. But then she was right next to me at light speed, ready to punch me. "Um…"

"Get out!" she said.

"I can't…" I said. *I mean, how can I?*

"Use your mind. Go to your own corner. I preferred it when you were asleep," she growled.

"Okay," I said, as I went back to my corner and she went to hers. What was this place and why was I here?

Safire said that this place was a jail…

Safire

CHAPTER 23

"Lunch is served, *cons!*" the lunch lady said. She slid two plates under the stone door.

I got up from my cold bed to get the food. As I munched down on the food, Igneous got up. "Rise and shine Igneous the Stupid," I called.

"Lunch served?" he asked, ignoring the name I called him.

"Yeah. Stupid ham sandwiches," I answered. I didn't care what I said. We were in prison. "Oh, and by the way, *jerk*, we are now convicts. Thanks to you."

"I was just asking to see if you…whatever."

"Whatever is right," I muttered.

Igneous got up in a position to face me. "This is boring."

"Don't even start."

"What?" he asked.

I frowned at him. "Don't. Even. Start."

"Humf."

"Arg…"

We started to make sounds, just to distract

ourselves.

CLANK!

THUD!

Rumble.

Whistle…

"This is not working," Igneous mumbled.

"For me it is! So shut it," I ordered. Probably too harshly.

"Okay, little princess. Whatever you say," he said slyly. Yesterday his tone was nice, but I could tell he was getting angry.

Well, I was, too. I ignored him and tried to climb the walls to find things I could use to escape. But of course, all I found was more stone. I dropped down to the ground and lay on my stone bed. *Sigh.*

"Where is the food?" Igneous asked.

"I ate it all," I answered. "You should wake up on time, next time." My eyes turned to slits from anger. I sat down in a little ball and closed my eyes.

Memories from camp raced through my head:

"I love me — AHH…"

"I need to finish his punishment…"

"I wasn't trying to kill you…"

"Look at the north star…"

"How is Igneous in second place if…"

"To where you find HOME…"

I looked up. I started sweating at the sight of the jail bars. My breathing quickened. My eyesight became blurry.

And I lost it. My world went black.

. . .

"Safire? Safire!? Safire?!!"

I swiftly jumped to my feet in confusion. It was nighttime. Igneous was asleep. Who was talking to me? I felt I was going crazy. I slowly sat down on my bed.

The moonlight crept into the room through the barred window. It cast a creepy glow on the ground. My shadow was stretched across the floor. The room was silent. The only sound was my steady breathing.

I used the cracks in the walls to climb up.

. . .

After what seemed like forever, we finally got to take a break from our stone cage and roam around the prison.

In the hours we spent outside, I mostly ran away from Igneous and explored places people never went, like the unused rooms at the back of the jail. But, there was one place, a place where no one wanted to go, that we luckily didn't go to.

"Yeah. The bro died. But he wasn't one of us battle bros," a con said one day, as Igneous and I passed his table in the cafeteria.

"…he was trying to get out. And that's the only way us cons can get out…" another said.

"…I would try it, but it's way too dangerous. We need to trick the pigs" the third one said.

"What are pigs?" Igneous whispered, as we

listened at the table next to theirs.

"Shh…" I said.

"Convicts from section 13579, please return to your rooms. I repeat, convicts from section 13579, please return to your rooms," the announcer said. *"Convicts from 1357911 and 1357912, please come to the main office."* Two cons got up from their tables and walked over to a door on the west side of the stone cafeteria. Everyone else went through the main entrance of the café to their cells.

It was weird, because just then, I thought I saw someone familiar working in the cafeteria booths. "Um… meet me by our jail cells. I'll be back," I said to Igneous. He nodded and walked to our cells. But I could feel his eyes linger on me as I walked to the cafeteria booth.

I made sure that I was in the crowd, a safe distance away from the familiar stranger. I scanned the room, seeing several guards lurking around. I tightened up my shoulders and walked by the booth, alongside several others in my section. I carefully peeked at the man just as we passed him. His face was full of scars and he had black hair with silver streaks in it…and the color of his scars matched the color of the streaks in his hair…

I searched my memories for anyone who looked similar. It took me a while, but then I remembered the car accident with my mom and me and the fiery balls.

Memories flashed through my head:

"MOM! We are going to the lake right now!" I yelled. *"Sorry…"*

"No, it's okay."

THUMP! *SWERVE!*

216

"It's okay, we are completely — " my mom said calmly.
THUMP!
"NOT SO FINE! THE BALL!" I screamed.
"COME ON #@*&ING CAR!" my mom cursed.
THUMP!
"MOM! GET OUT OF THE CAR!"
THUMP!
"MOM! WHERE ARE YOU! MOM!"
THUMP!
"Mom…" I rasped. *I choked.*

That memory was clear as day. Why was *he* here? The anger escalated in me. I stopped walking with the people in my section. I stared at the guy. He still hadn't seen *my stare*. The stare that I knew would make him feel scared. I felt the same anger I did toward Marissa's dad. Pain shot through my head as I began to step towards—

"No, Safire, don't get noticed!" Somebody grabbed my hand. I turned around and found Igneous pulling me towards our cell. "What was that?" he asked quietly.

"Nothing."

· · ·

Igneous and I were sitting on the benches in our cell.

"I wonder what happens when you get through the doors…and what awaits you on the other side…" I thought out loud.

"Yeah," Igneous agreed. I was starting to feel more comfortable with Igneous because I was pretty much stuck with him.

"When are we going to get out of this prison…" I trailed off.

"I don't know."

"I wish—wait! What if we figure out how we can get through that place? The place that we can get out of jail?!" I said. "Nah, that's jailbreak. Great…"

"Hey, do you hear that yelling sound?" Igneous said, out of the blue.

"No. Wait! Yeah, I hear it. What—"

"…I have kids and a wife! I can't just give that up! What do you think?! I had to do that for them!" It was the voice of an innocent citizen, not a con. "And that isn't even close to breaking the law! Have you all of a sudden changed a law?! Because if you did, I didn't see it…come on…FOR MY FAMILY!!!" the voice yelled.

Soon enough, the yelling man was thrown into the empty cell facing us. Igneous and I raced to the bars, looking out at the man. He wore the same dusty clothes as us and had an unshaven beard, a long, curled mustache and a bald head. He had kind, brown eyes with tears falling from them. "Please! Please! For my f-family!" he yelled after the guards. When they disappeared from sight, he dropped to the ground crying and mumbling.

Igneous and I glanced at each other, thinking the exact same thing.

"Um…excuse me?" I said in a kind voice.

"G-get away—children? What are you k-kids doing here?" the man said.

"That's a story for another time," Igneous said. "We didn't really break the law. The question is, how did *you* get here?"

"W-well, first, my name is Joe. What are your names?" he asked.

"I am Safire and this is Igneous," I said. "So...now what?"

"Well, I do not know," Joe said. "I just like to have company—"

"SHHH!!! Lunch lady coming," Igneous interrupted.

Joe, Igneous and I ran back to our stone beds. I was sort of confused, because we had just eaten in the cafeteria. The lunch lady wouldn't need to come because we already had food. But she just walked on past.

. . .

Over the weeks, we became weaker and thinner and more hungry. We talked, we stretched, we ate, and we drank. We did everything to keep ourselves from getting bored. We did everything to keep ourselves in shape.

We decided we had to do something about it. And the opportunity came to us.

It was our free hour to roam around. Joe, Igneous and I were talking about random stuff at a cafeteria table.

"I'm so tired of this!" I exaggerated.

Joe and Igneous silently agreed. "I haven't heard how long we are supposed to be here..." Igneous said.

"I'm starting to feel a little crazy..." Joe trailed off.

"Cons 13579345, 13579346 and 13579347, please come to the main office!" someone said over the loudspeaker. We

all squinted at our uniform numbers.

"Um, guys? I think they are calling us!" I whisper-shouted. Igneous and Joe raised an eyebrow and looked at their uniform numbers. They glanced at each other with wide eyes when they realized I was right.

"I really hope we are going to get out of here," Joe said with a shaky voice.

"Yeah," Igneous agreed.

We silently walked to the main office. A woman with black hair tied up in a tight bun greeted us. "We have your clothes—you can change into them quickly, then you can get out of here. Some police will meet you and give you some of your other belongings. Good luck on your journey home." She gave us a tight smile and led us into small changing rooms. All three of us changed quickly, not uttering a word to each other. We were all so bewildered.

A random police officer gave Joe his things. "Here is your wallet. It's is all that I am supposed to give you." He then pointed at the door that led outside.

"Thanks?" Joe started, but Igneous and I were already pulling him to the door. I wondered why they didn't give me my magic pyramid back. Or my phone. They didn't give me *anything* back! This was madness!

But I couldn't say anything because they had already pushed us out of the building. We were outside! We were free! But why?

And why so suddenly?

Igneous

CHAPTER 24

It had been two days since we were freed.

We luckily got a suite using Joe's money, so Safire didn't have to change in front of us… (Bleh! I never said that!) That day, Safire sat at the desk in the room pondering. Meanwhile, I was organizing everything because Joe kept throwing his stuff around.

"What's going on?" I asked Safire.

She sighed. "Haven't you thought about Joe?" She had bags under her eyes.

Why was she so tired? "Yeah, I've been thinking about his unorganized mess in the other room!" I pointed out. I crossed my arms, wondering what made Safire bring this up.

"No, no, no…I mean, like his *family.* The sadness might finally be getting to him. That might be why he's been so…weird lately. Back in jail he had stuff to do. But now, when we sit in this room *bored,* he might be thinking about them and all the things he misses about them." She sighed as she stared at a blank notepad in front of her.

"Um, are you kidding me? In jail we had nothing

to do! We just sat in our cells all day," I said.

"But there were more things to worry about back then. We didn't know if we were even going to get out of there alive!"

I shook my head. "Even now we have things to worry about!"

"I never said that there isn't anything to worry about—just his mind has decided NOW is the time to think about it!" she snapped.

"Fine, fine," I held my hands up like I was surrendering. "By the way, where is he now?"

"Getting groceries."

"Um…" I thought about what to say.

"We have only so much money, Igneous," she blurted out.

"Huh? Oh yeah…"

"We need to figure out a different way to survive."

"Okay." I yawned.

"Igneous! Are you listening to me?"

"Sorry…I think I need some sleep…" I blinked hard. But truthfully, I was just so sick of everything, I wanted a mental break. I kept one eye open as I lay in my bed.

Safire hummed, thinking about something or writing something down. I let the sound of her voice pull me into a daze. It relaxed me.

BANG! The door smashed open. Joe stood in the doorway, holding a paper bag with canned foods and vegetables.

"JOE! WHAT HAPPENED?!" Safire yelled.

I jumped up and stared at him. He looked normal. Why was Safire so upset?

"I'm fine," Joe said. "Here are the groceries."

"Well, Joe, I was thinking about…getting you back to your family." When she said "family," she looked like she had been punched in the gut.

"W-what? You guys…need help. You need me," Joe mumbled.

Safire rushed to his side. "No, Joe! We can take care of ourselves! We are thirteen years old. We aren't babies."

He dropped the groceries. I kneeled down and quickly caught them. "You really would help me get back to my family?" he asked, as he grabbed the groceries from me.

"Yep!"

Before I knew it, they were out the door, leaving me with the room to clean.

After that, all I did was stare at the ceiling, trying to organize the annoying thoughts I had pushed to the back of my mind. I racked my brain, thinking of things to do.

I made a mental list:

Problem: Obsidian Slag
Solutions:
    a. Abandon him
    b. Wait for him to talk to me, then decide what to do
    c. When he gets mad at me for not completing the mission, say it was all a mistake—he

must have not gotten the correct information

d. Do nothing

Problem: Safire not knowing about mission or where I came from
Solutions:

a. Talk to her about it, even though she is going to freak
b. Do nothing

I kept going through these thoughts until I got to the last one.

Problem: My crush on Safire
Solutions: None

Usually I can find solutions for things, but not this one. I pushed the thought away once more and waited for her to get back.

VVV PPP! All of a sudden, a shadow appeared in front of me.

"Lord Slag," I said.

"Hello. I see that you are doing some...*not correct* things!" It was so obvious he was mad.

"If you have been watching me, well—I just don't know what to do."

"It's young love," he said. "But it must stop. You are better than her. She is trash. Don't even think about her."

"Yes, sir. Sorry, I must end the call—we are having dinner soon. I know what to do." The Lavagraph disappeared. I felt so glad that I got away from him quickly. I rolled my eyes, annoyed with him. I turned around and—

Horror struck me so hard, I almost fell over. There stood Safire, dumbfounded and betrayed. *This was the last thing I wanted to happen.* I shook as she turned away from me and ran. Automatically, I ran after her.

Pain shot through my heart. She would never trust me again.

Safire

CHAPTER 25

When I got back from helping Joe, I remembered we had left Igneous.

I ran up to our joint suite, my feet making soft thumps. I opened the door that led to my room, with my pull-out sofa bed and the only desk. I heard a voice that was talking to Igneous in his room. I quietly tiptoed to the suite door that led to his room.

"I just don't know what to do," Igneous said.

"It's young love. But it must stop. You are better than her. She is trash. Don't even think about her."

I moved around to figure out who was talking—but then I could see two things:

1. Igneous sitting on his bed
2. A shadow that stood in front of him (I think the shadow was *talking* to him)

"Yes, sir. Sorry, I must end the call—we're having dinner soon. I know what to do." With that, he ended the call, got up and turned around.

When he saw me, there was horror on his face. It was all I saw before I ran out of the suite and down the hall to the stairs. And, of course, he ran after me. Anger infiltrated me. I could feel my blood boiling. I KNEW I couldn't trust him.

"Please! You don't understand! I'm not with him!" he yelled.

"Yeah, right!" I shouted back at him. "Of course you are with whoever that was!"

"I can't do anything else but *pretend* to trust him or I will die! You would do the same thing!"

"But I would tell you about it! I would sit down with you, and talk about it, and answer every single question you had!"

Without waiting for him to say another word, I ran as fast as my tired legs could carry me. I pretty much *blasted off...* but I couldn't see where I was going. All I could see were colors—gray, red, black, yellow, green... *Green?*

I stopped running at the edge of a random street to catch my breath. Gray two story homes surrounded me. I walked down the quiet, peaceful street.

In the distance, I can see a brown and gray three story house. Ivy crawls up the sides of the house and tall grass sways in the wind in the front yard. There was something familiar about the large windows and the colors of the house.

I began to quicken my walk. Was it really... My old house? Where I lived with my Mom... my brother... and had a kind of normal life? The place where I grew up, but was also hidden from my true identity?

Thump... Thump... Thump... My feet hit the floor

quietly as I walked across the wooden porch of my old house. Without thinking, my hand reached for the door knob. The copper knob was cold and seemed like it hadn't been used for a long time.

My hand turned the knob slowly and pushed the door open. I put my hand in my pocket as I stared into my old dark house.

I could see the shapes of the steep carpeted stairs, the dining room table on the far end of the house and the kitchen island on my right.

I tried to flip the lights on, but the house stayed dark and cold. And so I started my walk around the house, memories slowly becoming as clear as glass.

I wanted to cry. I wanted to cry and cry and cry until I couldn't cry anymore. I wanted to not be brave and strong. I wanted to be weak. But the weakness didn't come. My eyes were too dry. I felt like a monster within me was clawing my heart, making it turn into stone.

THUMP! A large noise coming from the floor above shook the weak and thin ceiling. Dust fell from the ceiling making me want to cough even more.

THUMP! When the noise came again, I ran up the stairs on my toes with a stick of wood that had fallen from the ceiling. Who would possibly want to be in this old house that hasn't been lived in for months? When I reach the top of the stairs, I find my old bedroom door wide open. Human shoe foot prints lead me into the room.

I look up to see a faint shadow sitting on the edge of my bed with a flashlight at their feet. The flashlight dimly lit up the room, illuminating the person on my bed a little. I took a step into the room and I clasped my hand over my mouth in disbelief.

"M-mom?" I stuttered. My stomach flip flopped as the figure turned around.

There she sat with her beautiful straight brown hair and large purple eyes with golden flecks. I had never been so torn about feeling something.

Should I have been happy to see her? Mad maybe? Sappy? Happy should have been the answer, but she never looked for me. For a year she never looked for me... I wanted to believe that something had gone wrong and she couldn't find me. But my guts told me that she had everything she needed to find me.

"Where have you been all this time?" I asked her softly. She turned back away from me.

"There are some things you need to be protected from," she replied.

"You didn't answer my question," I said, starting to raise my voice.

"You were safe out there. I thought I could protect you, but the truth is... You are fine by yourself. But you need to stop making reckless decisions," she said softly.

"What... do you mean?"

"Sigh... Safire," she turned to me. "You need to be protected. How? I don't know. But—"

"Who are you Mom? What are you really? Are you really my Mom? STOP KEEPING SECRETS FROM ME!" I began to get louder and louder until I was screaming at the top of my lungs. When I was done yelling, I tried to catch my breath while my mom stared at her hands with deep regret in her eyes.

"Safire... I know I haven't been the best person ever... And that I've kept too many secrets from you, which you still didn't need to know. And one of those secrets is..." she paused and I looked up from my feet. She stared into my eyes. "I am... Liginia." I could barely hear the last word.

"Wait, what?!"

"I am... Liginia and—" She stopped talking and looked so guilty.

"A-and I am your mother."

The world spun around me. Finally everything was clear, but at the same time, it was all as clear as mud.

"Safire," my mom said in distress.

"LEAVE ME ALONE!" I screamed at her. She jerked back and I ran out of the house once again, this time, it was my choice to leave.

Here I was, running from my life again. Running from everything I know. This time I ran with my eyes closed, wishing that I could just disappear from the world.

CLANG! And just like that, I knocked my head into something and fell unconscious. I started dreaming...

I was in a completely white room. Nothing was there except for me.

"Tell me what you want to search for!" said a voice.

"Igneous Stone," I said, without hesitation.

The room vanished, and a bunch of screens and pictures of Igneous appeared. Color surrounded me, and all the pictures of Igneous stared down at me. One of the pictures showed

Igneous being named "the newest spy." Another showed him training in a sweaty t-shirt, which made me blush. I clenched my fists, annoyed with myself.

"Pick which article you want to view."

I spun around and the images slowly turned into weblinks that popped up in blue writing. "I want to view the 'All About Me' website."

"Okay." All the images vanished and were replaced by words.

Full name: Igneous Meta Stone
Birth Date: Unknown
Age: 13
Parents: Unknown
Average Grade: A+
School: National Magmian Battle School
Home Location: NVBS (National Magmian Battle School)
Birth Place: National Magmian Hospital

I skipped a few lines, and then…

Love Interest: None

"This is the end of the page, do you want to refresh it?"
"Sure?"
BZZZZT. *"New information confirmed."*
I quickly scrolled back down the page using my fingers.

Love Interest: Safire Waters

I nearly fainted…

"AHH!!!" I shrieked. I woke up in reality. The moment I opened my eyes, I could smell the fresh, sweet scent of flowers.

The dream bothered me. *How could it be a dream, when there was information I didn't know?* What I dreamed would never happen—at least I thought so?

I realized I was in a huge grassland meadow that stretched pretty far. At the end of it, there were tons of trees obscuring what laid beyond.

There was a metal pole next to me. As soon as I tried to get up, tons of blood rushed up to my head and I fell back down.

"Ugh. RAHHH!!!" I screamed. I just lay there, looking at the blue sky, the floating clouds, everything. But I couldn't stay there. Soon, I was all better. I slowly got up to standing—it seemed like it took hours—and stayed put.

"Hello? Is anyone there?" I asked. No response. "Hello? Is anyone there?" I repeated. No response. "If anyone is there, I'm going now." I turned a random direction and strolled through the meadows. My hand started quivering.

At first, I didn't hear the sound coming from behind a tree.

And then—"Hi, little girl!"

"Ai-yee? AIIIIIIYEEEEEE!!!" I screamed. I turned around. My thoughts swam around. I could barely think.

I saw a sight that nearly made me pee my pants.

Igneous

CHAPTER 26

"You have FAILED!!!" Lord Slag shouted at me.

His voice echoed through the stone throne room he had transported me to. It sent a shiver down my spine. "You have completely FAILED!!!" he shrieked. He towered over me, and I could only imagine what his face would look like, if he had one. "You know how bad you are?! YOU HAVE FAILED YOUR FIRST MISSION!!!" he screamed. "Do you know how hard it is to gain my trust? DO YOU KNOW HOW HARD IT IS TO GAIN MY TRUST, BOY?!?!"

"Yes sir. V-very hard. The hardest thing to do..." I mumbled in fright. *Was I gonna die?*

"YOU, BOY, YOU HAVE MESSED UP YOUR HARD WORK! YOU ARE A FAILURE! YOU ALWAYS HAVE BEEN!" he boomed. This time the windows shattered from their stone frames, leaving holes in the walls. Now my heart was beating so loudly, I was sure that Lord Slag could hear it. "You now shall feel the wrath of the Colossi!!!" He snapped his fingers, and his guards brought him a stick with golden designs on it. It had a glowing blue ball at the top. Lord Slag took the Staff of the Colossi and put it inches from my face. My legs trembled, barely holding my weight.

"Please...I could explain!" I begged. I thought I was going to die because of my stupid crush on Safire!

But he ignored me. "Let the wrath of the Colossi unravel you!!!"

Then a super bright, bluish light blasted into my face.

At first, I was in some sort of dimension with no shapes, no matter, no sound, no space, not a single thing...except for oxygen.

To test it out, I walked forward for a long time. But I didn't hit a wall or anything. It didn't seem like I was *really* walking—I was sort of making walking movements in midair. I tried moving my hands around, to see if anything was there. (I knew there was nothing. But I was testing, just in case.) To my horror, just like I had suspected, not a single thing was there. There was no matter. It was just a dark world that was just like space.

My heart started pumping. I started thinking I was dead. I thought that this place was the afterworld and that I had to live in it.

But then, the dimension changed into something else. The void disappeared and turned into an Earthly library. The library had fifty-foot walls. And, of course, there were bookshelves covering all but one foot of wallspace. There was a hardwood floor with a blue carpet in the middle.

I quickly looked around for any sign of life,

anything that could be watching me. I went over to the wall with the large fancy window. Next to the window was a patch of wall measuring four feet square. Since I thought that there probably would be trap doors that would lead somewhere, I pushed it. Nothing happened. I pushed it again.

This time, something did happen. All of a sudden, an image of a girl (who was *not* Safire) flashed through my head. I couldn't tell who she was, but I had a feeling this girl wasn't a good person. A message flashed on the wall:

WELCOME

"Um...welcome to what?" I asked out loud.

Welcome to the Tunnels. The
Tunnels hold our Ancestors, The
Colossi.
Please put your hand on this pad
to enter the tunnel.

"Um...okay?" So I slowly lowered my hand onto the cold, glassy surface.

Thank you. Hello, IGNEOUS. We
have great things in store for
you.

```
You must be thankful that this
is not a prison.
Please sit on this chair so we
may check you for weapons.
```

"W-why do you need to check me for weapons?" I said to the screen.

```
Because you are going to see our
ancestors.
Again, please sit on this chair
so we may check you for weapons.
```

"Got it." I cautiously sat down in the chair that had just appeared. I had no idea if this screen was trustworthy or not. Then the red scanner above the chair set to work, checking me. After what seemed like forever, the chair turned away from the library until it was facing the wall. The screen disappeared and reappeared on my lap. I clutched onto it, closing my eyes.

The chair lunged forward into the darkness of the Tunnel. Pressure beat down on my chest, making it hard to breathe. I coughed. I wheezed, "What is— happening…"

```
Please relax. The Colossi will
see you soon.
```

"I-I can't r-relax!" I croaked, coughing some more.

Please relax.

All of a sudden, the chair stopped. The screen turned off.

The world was pitch black.

Safire

CHAPTER 27

A tall man stood over me in the meadow and smirked.

"AH—*MFFF!!*" Before I knew it, he had put tape over my mouth and a bag over my head. I struggled to get out of his grasp as he pulled and dragged me across the ground. I pinched myself, trying to make sure that this wasn't real life—but it was.

I managed to peek through a couple holes in the brown bag. We came to a truck loaded with a ton of crates and other things. There were animals in there. I shivered and cried silently as he put me into a cage. All of a sudden, something hit the back of my head super hard.

. . .

When I woke up, the truck creaked to a stop. I heard a couple of whines from the animals around me. I couldn't see anything because the area was pitch black and blocked off by the doors.

THUMP! I'd just been thrown into a room. A blinding light beamed inside my cage. I looked over at the door and saw a man with ragged, factory worker clothes on. "HNNNGGG!" I whined. He began to lift crates of animals and haul them onto a rolling cart. My breathing became heavy as I looked for an escape. I was too late—before I knew it, my cage was being pulled into the cart.

THUMP! The guy slammed the cart doors shut. I didn't want to say a thing, because he would realize that I could be a threat. I needed a way to get myself and the animals out.

After the doors to the truck were locked, the man rolled the cart out into a garage filled with tons of trucks that looked like the one I was just in. *CREAK!* He opened a door and pushed the cart through. We rode into a huge room with animals in crates and cages. *Was I destined to stay there forever?* It gave me shivers thinking about all of this.

THUMP! The man pushed all the crates off the cart and walked out of the room. I sat there helpless, feeling so bored and useless.

. . .

I was guessing that days had passed.

I tried to sleep but I couldn't, so I looked around, inspecting every inch of the place. I wanted food and water so badly, but I didn't get any. I wanted to escape. The problem was, every once in a while, there would be another group of cages brought in. How was I supposed to get out, when a guy could just come in when I was trying to execute my plan?

. . .

One day, I was done with being starved.

Every minute, my tongue would swell up even more. I waited till the next person came and went.

CREAK! The same guy who had dropped me off came into the room.

THUMP! He pushed off the cages and grabbed the rolling cart. He did a quick check of the room and slowly walked out.

THUMP! The door closed. I waited a second to make sure he wasn't going to open the door and check the room again.

One, one thousand.

Two, one thousand.

Three, one thousand.

Four, one thousand.

Five, one thousand.

I began to put my plan into action. First I looked around for any security cameras. Unfortunately, there were about four of them. I didn't know how I didn't see them before. All of them were at the top corners of the room, wedged in between the ceiling and the wall. *VSSSSPP!* I could hear them moving around, inspecting every single inch of the room.

I knew that they wouldn't understand me if I talked to the animals. "Hey! *PSST...*" I said to a couple of baby cheetahs next to me. They looked at me like I was crazy. "I know it's crazy that I can talk to you, but I can help you get out of here! I can help everyone else too! You just have to listen to me," I whispered.

"How do we know you aren't one of them?" one of the cheetahs said. I'm pretty sure he was the older one—he had a gray tuft of hair.

"Because those guys would be the last people on Earth that would possibly be able to speak to animals! I was just walking in a meadow and they captured me!"

They took a moment to think about it. But then they nodded. *"What do we need to do?"*

"First of all, I need you to stay vegan for a short period of time. Once everyone gets out and has a chance to make a home, you can go ahead and eat meat. Got it?" They nodded. "Can you pass it on to other meat eaters? Oh—and by the way, my name is Safire." They turned around and began to gossip about it.

I turned to the monkeys that were above me. "Hey monkeys!" I said to them. They looked down at me. "I know it's weird that I can speak to you guys, but since you guys are sneaky, I need you to do something. If you do what I tell you, you will be able to get out of here, along with everyone else in this room."

They looked at each other, deciding. *"What's your name?"*

"Safire."

"What do you need us to do, Safire?"

"Okay, I'm going to try to find a way to get you guys out. I need you to sneak through the cages, get to the cameras and turn them off quickly. And to get the job done faster, try to get some help. You need to do this fast, because they might see you."

"How will the people watching the cameras not suspect something? After all, you can talk to animals."

"This room is pretty loud," I said. "As far as they know, I'm talking to myself."

The monkeys nodded. *"How are we supposed to get out of these cages?"*

"I'm looking." I searched my pocket for something small that could open the locks. I picked out a tiny piece of wood that must have come from the woods and stuck to my shoe. "Got it. Now, try this piece of wood on the locks and let out a couple of other monkeys. And *please* don't do something weird that makes everything get messed up." I handed them the wooden stick by stretching my skinny arm into the monkeys' cage. "Go!" I said. They unlocked their lock and crawled out.

I turned back around facing the cheetahs. "Did you spread the word?"

"Yep."

A smile came to my face. Maybe, for once in my life, things would go my way. "Okay, your job now is be the messenger. I need you to—"

CLICK CLICK CLICK CLICK! I looked at the security cameras and saw the monkeys bouncing on them, pushing random buttons. Because pieces of the cameras were falling down, I thought the things would turn off.

But, all of a sudden, my gut twisted around. I faced the cheetah and I started to talk fast. "Quickly, tell the birds to save those monkeys—and check for any other

243

security cameras!" The cheetahs went to work, clearly enjoying this for some reason.

CAW CAW CAW! The monkey with the wooden stick tossed it over to a big red bird. It caught the stick and opened its cage. Fortunately, there were several other birds in the same cage. *CAW CAW CAW!* They flew wildly out of the cage, helping the monkeys to unlock the other cages, including mine.

After I slammed my cage open, I stretched out quickly and looked around the room. *"Thank you!"* said a little baby coyote. I nodded and gave him a quick rub.

"Listen up, everyone!" I called over the crowd. "Everyone needs to destroy every single security camera so—"

The alarm rang through the room as men trickled into the room through the locked doors. I ran around the room, avoiding the humans and helping the wounded animals. The meat eaters launched at the humans, and the birds pooped on the humans' heads. Never have I thought that humans were the best race in the world. Animals just try to survive, but humans kill each other for sport and trap creatures for their own good. They don't care about anyone but themselves.

CHIC CHIC! BOOM! I turned around to see a bunch of men with guns. I had an idea that would save the animals, but possibly kill me. I sighed and ran in front of the guns, putting my hands up. I edged myself to the middle of the room, where I could block the guns easier.

"STOP!" I yelled. Every one froze, even the animals.

"What are you doing, Safire?"

"No! Don't do this!"

"What's going on?"

"If you let them go, you can have me," I said.

"You are kidding me, right? Why do we need you?" one of the men said.

"Why do you need all these animals when you can have *me*—someone who can communicate with animals, run super fast, think super fast, heal people and animals…" They looked at me like I was crazy. "Oh, and I'm an empath! So think again." I ran behind them, quickly pushed their guns out of their hands, and ran back to my original spot. "So, what do you say?" I said forcefully.

One, Mississippi.

Two, Mississippi.

Three, Mississippi.

Four, Mississippi.

Five, Mississippi.

Six, Mississippi.

Seven, Mississippi.

Eight, Mississippi.

Nobody moved. I lost track of the Mississippis, so I started again.

One, Mississippi.

Two, Mississippi.

Three, Mississippi —

Then, one of the men began to speak.

Igneous

CHAPTER 28

"Hello, Igneous!"

It was a voice in the vast darkness. A high-pitched girl's voice. "I've been—I mean, we've been waiting for you."

My heart beat like a drum with a fast tempo. "Um…"

"Oh sorry, you can't see? One second…"

I drummed my fingers on my lap as I waited. Then suddenly, I could see a dark shape.

"Who are you?" I said in a weak tone.

"I am Agapi. I am one of the Colossi," Agapi said.

"Oh?" *Was this real?*

"Let me show you the Colossi. They will figure out where you are staying."

My heart beat in excitement. I always wanted to see a Colossus!

"Um…is this really the Wrath of the Colossi?"

"You must never tell the creature that wields the staff about this: the staff is a portal between its world and the Colossus world."

"Oh…"

"Follow me." The shadow of Agapi walked away with her back facing me, so I followed her. Every now and then, she would glance back at me. "Here we are."

I didn't like this Agapi person. She seemed fake and weird. There was obviously something she was hiding from me. My gut told me she wasn't trustworthy at all…

There was a sudden burst of light that made my eyes feel like they would burst. We were standing before a HUGE pair of doors. The doors had all types of carvings that glowed. On the other side of the doorway was a BIIIIIIIG room with a throne in the middle, but the room was plain white.

"What is this place?" I asked. My eyes had recovered from the blinding light, so I whipped my head around to look at the hallway that we had been walking in earlier.

Instead, my jaw took a drop as I looked at Agapi. She had brown hair with a perfect wave that reminded me of the waves of the sea. She also had soft, blue eyes that sparkled like the sun. Her eyes perfectly matched her dress and its small sparkle belt. The shimmery belt matched her high-heeled sandals that were also covered in sparkles. To me, super pretty girls are creepy because they always have makeup caked on their faces. But sometimes it's fine. With Agapi, it was creepy. You could see—

"He's here!" Agapi called.

All of a sudden, a man with long black hair and

black, serious eyes walked through the second door next to the throne. "HELLO, AGA—" All he was wearing was a pair of skimpy little white shorts. I realized they were… underwear.

"*Dad,*" Agapi said. "I keep telling you, you cannot do that when visitors come over, especially if you want people to respect you after that War." She spit on the floor.

"Well, then…" The man disappeared.

"He shows off," Agapi told me.

"Who is he?"

"You don't know who my father is? You don't know the *ruler of the Colossi!?*"

"Oh! That Colossus!?" He really didn't seem like a good leader. I expected him to be a soldier or something. Yes, I may have wanted to see the Colossi, but they seemed so weird. Wouldn't they have a lot more people there? I guess I expected a grand palace with tons of servants and good food…

"Yeah. Who did you think it was?" Agapi said.

At that moment the man reappeared, with more clothes on.

"Ahem…I'm sorry. Hopefully this outfit will appease my daughter," the Colossus said.

"W-what is your name?" I stuttered.

"Seven," the Colossus said simply.

"Okay. Um…now what?"

"YOU, my son, are going to stay here for now. And we will try to get you back to where you came from! Now Agapi is going to show you to your room; it is right next to hers. Please go to Agapi's room at

10,304,381,329,489,971,187 o'clock." I frowned, confused. "That will give you enough time to get comfortable with your room. Then Agapi will be able to show you around. See you later!" And Seven walked away.

I wanted to ask why I was there, and why they seemed stuck in this place, too, but I couldn't get myself to ask.

"Okay. Don't mind my dad. Come on. I'll show you to my room." Agapi walked to the door with the big, fat, bronze doorknob. As soon as she touched it, we teleported to a long hallway with three doors. One was Agapi's room, and another was mine. *But what was in the other one?* "Okay, this is your room," she said. "You can design it any way you want by tapping the screen in your bedroom—wait. Do you want to play around and decorate the room together?"

"Sure!" Agapi and I walked to my empty bedroom. It had nothing but white walls, a white ceiling and a white floor. This felt weird.

"This is the screen." Agapi pointed at a tablet that had a wire connected to it. "It works by connecting the wire to your head. Wait for about ten seconds and a room for you will come into this space. Let me show you."

Agapi took the wire and touched the tip to her head. A purple room started appearing. The walls transformed into bright white, with blossom branches with real blossoms on them. The ceiling was the same. The ground was covered in silky, soft purple carpet. There was a white bed with purple sheets with a white bedside table and a purple lamp, plus a white wardrobe and makeup center. Purple must be her favorite color.

"Let's see what's in my window. It shows your dreams. Let's see mine—" She stopped in her tracks. The window showed Agapi and me in a garden, sitting on a bench...*kissing?* She smiled. "Heh...um...now it's your turn!"

She shoved me over to the screen and plunged the wire onto my head. *Did she seriously want to marry me or something?* I was SOOOOOOOO creeped out, I couldn't stop listing all the creepy things in my head.

Agapi's room turned into a huge gaming room, probably because I like Earth's video games. The walls turned grayish blue and the carpet turned into a regular blue carpet. Yellow bean bag chairs appeared with an awesome T.V. and tons of gaming systems. On the other side of the room was an office with a computer, a file cabinet, an awesome lamp, a black, spinning chair, and a book that said "diary" on the cover. There was the bed with a blue comforter, a wardrobe and of course, the window.

"Wow, that window is really taking its time to make the perfect dream," Agapi pointed out.

I shrugged. "Yeah—"

Agapi's eyes opened wide. I turned around to look where she was looking. The window showed Safire and me kissing. That wasn't a surprise for me, but Agapi screamed, and then apologized. Her jaw dropped down like she forgot something important. "Oh. Um...I'll be back. See you later! Bye!" Then she dashed out of my room and slammed the door behind her.

I sat down on my bed so confused. I zoned out, with thoughts swimming around in my head. I felt like this place was a jail. I wondered if this place was where Obsidian Slag kept all the people he didn't like or that disobeyed him. *Was this all staged?*

Glancing at the clock, I got up and saw that it was 400 minutes. I walked out of my room, confused and curious, and knocked on Agapi's door.

Safire

CHAPTER 29

"So, what do you say?" I repeated.

I really needed these animal thieves to capture me so the animals could get away. I would be able to slide out of their grasp—

"Fine," the main one said. He sighed. "But you have to do *anything* for us." He had a wicked grin in his eyes. I nodded, scared of what they were going to do.

One of the men opened a door that led outside. Once every single animal had gotten out, they shut the door. I stood there in the middle of the room, barely able to stand. My muscles tightened up. These people weren't good people. Now they could do anything to me. I waited for instructions. Then I had an idea, I was fifty percent likely to die.

But I did it anyway.

"Okay everyone, put your guns away," the main guy said. Everyone put them away. "We are going to train her to be like us. But she will be trained harder than all of you babies. So—"

I jumped on the guy who was talking. I pushed my

feet off him and had my hands around his neck. When my feet landed back down at his back, I pushed extra hard and he fell to the ground. I jumped up and watched the guys racing towards me.

I was so glad that Igneous—I cringed at the thought of the name—had taught me some moves. I raced towards them, sliding on the slippery ground, grabbing the closest guy's legs and swinging them at the others. *THUMP!* They all fell.

Some more soldiers came. I braced myself and threw a cage at one of the guys' heads. He fell back and started to bleed. I hated hurting people, but at this moment, I needed to. I still cringed every time I hit someone.

THUMP! I kicked someone next to me and hit him in the crotch. He collapsed into the path of a guy running towards me. I turned around and dodged a blow. I took my attacker's arm and twisted it around. He cried in pain and I pushed him away. He staggered to a door.

"MOVE, MOVE!" a man shouted. A bunch of men came out of the doors charging at me. I was pretty sure that they planned to kill me.

I took an injured man's legs and slid him quickly across the floor. All the men dodged. I cringed, feeling hopeless. They started to throw punches at me. I managed to dodge most of the blocks, but one hit my face, my arms and then my shoulders, making me bleed. Blood slowly dripped down my face as I threw more and more useless punches.

"Safire!!!" someone screamed. I stopped fighting

and looked over my shoulder. Nobody else seemed to hear the scream. Somebody punched me, catching me off guard.

I tumbled to the floor. The men seized me.

I cried for help…but nobody answered.

Why did I hear that voice?

I wanted to die at that moment.

Why did I have to be the one who got chased by doctors?

Why did I have to be the one who had to survive by myself?

Why did I have to be the one who was betrayed and lied to so many times?

Why did I have to be the one with the weirdest life ever?

Why is the world this way?

What was in store for me? Death? Suffering?

Why me?

And then I blacked out.

. . .

When I woke up, I was in a small white room. There were a bunch of different weapons lining the walls. I shuddered as I took everything in. I was chained around my chest to a thick post. I looked in front of me to see two chairs sitting there.

CREAK! A man opened the door and sat on one of the chairs. I tried to get a good look at him, but the post obscured my view. "I am going to ask you a few questions," he said. "If you don't tell us the truth, you will be punished."

I cringed. I finally got a short glance at him and saw that he looked normal. He was new to me. I spoke up. "If you know whether I'm telling the truth or not, that means you probably know the truth. So...why do you need *me* to tell you these things?"

He ignored me and kept talking. "Why did you come here?"

"You brought me here!"

"I said, WHY DID YOU COME HERE?!" he snapped.

"Because you guys brought me here. I never meant to bother you people."

This seemed to make him even madder. He walked around the post until he was behind me. I closed my eyes and waited.

THWAP! He hit me with something similar to a rope—a whip. My back bent under pressure and began to go numb. I could feel my backbone cracking. I kept myself from crying out in pain.

"Next question!" His voice seemed completely calm. "What were you doing in that meadow?"

I hesitated before speaking, looking for the right words. "I was camping with my family when a wolf chased us out of our tent. I don't know where my parents went." My voice trembled.

"There are no wolves in that area."

I could hear him get ready for the next whip. *THWAP!* I felt some muscle and bone crumble. My back began to bleed and I began to feel dizzy. But I fought to stay awake.

"Why did you fight back?" he asked.

"Because it's the right thing to do."

He hit me again. He had said that he would only hit me if I lied. I wasn't lying on that question. He must have liked to whip me.

I heard a door open. "We need to transfer her to room six-six-six!" the man said. A bunch of men rushed into the room and carried me out. They shoved a blindfold on me as I lay helplessly in their arms. I closed my eyes, knowing that I was probably going to die. My mouth was so dry and numb—I hadn't eaten or drank anything for three days.

When the men set me down, they put me face down on the ground and took my blindfold off. They slammed the door and I was left alone.

I felt like I wouldn't be able to use my back ever again. I looked up and saw a bowl of water. I hesitated, then chugged it all. I still needed water, but it would do. I held onto the wall and tried to get up. I slowly got to my knees, then a bending position and finally, a standing position. I just needed the wall to support myself.

I took small steps and walked around the room once, twice, three times, four times…too many times to count. I could use my back now. But once I got too tired, I stopped.

. . .

I don't know how long I was there. Every now and then I would get some soupy food and water. It was gross but I still ate it.

I thought back to movies where people were stuck inside rooms. *What do they do?* I thought to myself. The first thing I thought of was weaseling through iron bars and windows. I looked around. There was no windows or iron bars. I thought about the next thing: strength. I was so injured that I almost immediately skipped that. When I tried, I ended up making my knuckles throb and my wrists hurt.

I rested for another day before trying something else. *What else?* Tricking the people *outside* the cell. This was the one I knew was going to work. These guys seemed pretty stupid, after all.

I screamed at the top of my lungs and waited for somebody to come in. "Stop screaming, little baby," someone said. "You aren't going to get us to go in there. You can't trick us!"

I screamed again. "STOP!" someone yelled. I stopped.

I heard some shuffling outside and food was brought in. I savored the food and decided that I wasn't going to scream anymore. After I finished eating, I laid on the cold, hard floor. My mind wandered for a while, trying to think of what to do. *Was I going to be stuck there forever?*

I fell into a light doze, but I almost immediately woke up. I remembered one of the things people did to get out of those types of situations in movies: find false blocks that lead outside. I got up slowly and pushed all the blocks that made up the walls. I got to one that made a weird, creaky noise. I pushed it again.

CREAK! I pushed it for the third time. *CREAK!* I kept pushing the block until it fell out to the other side. I winced as I pulled my hands away, right when the other blocks were about to come down on my fingers.

I heard the door being unlocked. I kept pushing the blocks to make the opening big enough to crawl through. *BANG!* The door slammed open just as I jumped outside.

I placed my foot on the wall and shoved off to run down the hill as fast as I could. My heart beat like a drum as adrenaline pumped through my veins. I noticed a forest stood in front of me. It was like when I had to run away from home, getting chased into the woods by random people. I was so used to running from everything…

I shook my head, getting rid of the thought. I realized that one of the guys had a grip on my thin black jacket that I bought all the way back at the fake city. I escaped his grasp by taking off my jacket and running for dear life.

The trees around me turned into a green and brown blur as I leaped past. Not a minute later, I stumbled. "UFF!" I cringed as I heard shouts of the men chasing me. I found a stick to use for walking and soon was far away from their factory.

I knew I wouldn't be lucky every time I got stuck some place. I needed to be way more careful. I made a mental note to run if any man—or woman—jumps out of a bush.

I walked on into the woods, thankful I was in a place where I felt almost completely safe. After all, I was used to the woods.

Igneous

CHAPTER 30

I walked stiffly to Agapi's bedroom door and knocked.

"Ahem...who is it?" She opened her door.

I was shocked to see what I saw. Agapi's hair was all over the place, and her makeup was flowing down her face like blood. I looked around her room, and all I saw were posters (and more posters) of...*me?* She snapped her fingers quickly and everything went back to normal. Her face and her room.

"Hey, whatcha doing here?" Agapi said. Her cheeks were completely red.

"I...I just came over here to ask you if we were doing the tour."

"Oh. Sure." She walked out of the room, slammed the door and waved at me to follow her.

After a little while, we came to what looked like a dining room with a long table with ten seats and a beautiful tablecloth with candles to top it off. "So, this first room is the dining room," she explained. "Every evening you have to come down here for dinner. For breakfast and lunch, you can go to one of the kitchens and pick something up. Let's go to the kitchen."

She headed off again, but this time, we went towards our rooms and into the room right next to Agapi's room. This room was a little kitchenette. It had a see-through refrigerator with snacks and stuff. It had a little sink and counter with cooking knives and butter knives that were in a knife block. Above the counter were dark wooden cabinets that held all types of foods. But this didn't seem right—it was too much like the Earth I had visited.

"This is the room where you can prepare and grab lunch and breakfast. You might be spending a lot of time here," Agapi said. She told me what was in each cabinet. "Down this hall, you will see a trapdoor. If you go down it, you will end up in the yard. You can relax out there. Sometimes there will be gatherings."

As we walked out of the kitchen, she looked me in the eye. She looked kind of bored. "And sorry, there is no way out of this place. There are scanners everywhere, so if you try to get out, you're dead. See you later." Then she ran to her room and slammed her door.

What is wrong with that girl? I thought. After a few seconds, I walked to my room. This place seemed so odd. I jotted down all the weird things on a piece of paper.

1) This place has a yard, a kitchen and a dining room (they don't even have different names for them)
2) Their food is like Earth's
3) They don't have any guards (they

261

might have them, but I haven't seen or
heard about any)
4) There aren't any other Colossi (I don't
know for sure, I've only seen two)
5) There are no creatures or weird animals
(I don't know for sure)
6) There just aren't any things that weren't
on Earth when I visited it
7) They don't even have any high
technology (except for the room thingy)

I didn't know if they really were the Colossi, or if they were in my dreams. *Am I awake?* Everything got stranger every minute. This place was definitely not right. *All I know is that I have to get out of here.* So I decided to take my mind off of the topic and explore the yard.

When I got out into the yard, my eyes were instantly blinded. I didn't realize how dark it was inside until I had walked out. Suddenly, I felt this strange heat. Not heat, like comfortable heat, but heat as if I were in a volcano. *What?*

"Is that you, Igneous?" someone said in disbelief.

I recognized the voice instantly. "Xed?" I asked. He put sunglasses on my face. "XED?" He nodded. I jumped up and down and hugged him, but he pushed me away. I took the sunglasses off and blinked hard. The only thing that I could see was the shape and face of Xed. "But... where have you been all this time?"

"I was captured by Obsidian Slag soon after we

had that 'fight,' because he wanted to know more about you. Unfortunately, he didn't get the information he wanted from me, so I got stuck here…" All this confirmed my thought that this place was Obsidian Slag's prison. He slowly unleashed a breath. "This place is creepy."

"Yep."

"How did you get here?"

"Oh, now THAT is a long story."

"Make it short."

So I told Xed everything (the long version), from the moment Obsidian Slag took me to that ship to that very second. "Are you a servant now?" I asked Xed. He nodded. "So you don't eat with us?"

"Yeah…I get the leftovers. I really don't get why you're living normally, and I'm a servant."

"I don't either, but I'll make sure I leave you some," I said. I gave him a thumbs up.

"Thanks. You have never given up on me, have you?"

I shrugged. "Well, anyways, that was a long story to tell," I said.

"Do you think you will ever see Safire again?" he asked. "Do you think you'll start dating, if you do?" He cringed. I rolled my eyes and we headed out of the grassy yard.

I went to dinner after that. It was a pretty bland dinner—it was just Seven, Agapi and me. I saved food for Xed and put a note with the leftovers:

Dear X,

Meet me at the yard at 600 minutes everyday.

If I don't come, I'm probably in some crisis with Agapi.

LOL. >w<

From,
Ig

Other from that, the rest of that day was boring. Most of it was thinking and hoping—hoping that this journey would come to an end.

Safire

CHAPTER 31

It had been hours since I had escaped from the factory, and I was completely exhausted. I hadn't taken a single break. I just felt like there was a place I was meant to go to. But I didn't know what it was.

So I just followed my mind's ways, and that was that. It's like movies: stupid people will do stupid things, and while you are watching, you say, "No! Don't do that!" (I don't know... maybe right now *you* are thinking this about me.)

The trees got thicker and thicker.

I got hungrier and hungrier.

The number of animals got larger and larger.

And the cloud of smoke from the factory got smaller and smaller.

The moon was starting to climb up into the sky, and the sun was starting to climb down beneath the land.

I could start to see a city's lights. The city grew and grew until I was standing there, on a sidewalk. The sidewalks sparkled. One by one, the lights in the buildings turned off. The city was in complete darkness, except for the spots where the streetlights shined.

I saw a light that went around and around a long distance away. *What was it?* A number of things came to my head. A lamp. The imaginary deathly wheel with lights. An illusion. Magic stuff? No—it was a *lighthouse!*

I was near a beach! I felt like this was where I needed to go. All I had to figure out what beach this was. I walked through the streets like a zombie following a human. And soon, I got to a small dock. The dock had three boats tied to the dock. They reminded me of Goldilocks and the three bears: there was one big ship, one medium-sized ship and one small one. I was so close to the lighthouse—

"Shoo! Shoo! Get away from my ship! &%#&^&* little #$%^&*!" a man said from inside a nearby log house thing.

"Do you do rentals?" I asked.

"What?" the man said. He had on a blue vest with a striped black-and-gray shirt and some jeans. His dark brown eyes matched his hair, which was mostly gray with some brown strands of hair.

"Do you do rentals for your boats?" I repeated.

"Yes, I do. But not for you, little scum. Now shoo!!!"

"Do you have anything that is broken or anything I can do to rent the boat?" I asked politely.

"Yes, I do but you would never—"

"You have yourself a handyman, then?"

"Scum! Then let's let your little hands do something. Fix my boat! All three!" he ordered.

So I ran to the smallest boat. All I needed to do was oil some gears, change some old wires to newer wires, and...*voilà!*

"Polish it and paint it!" the man ordered. "And my name is Leland."

Leland was a bit mean but turned out to have a sad story. Apparently his wife died in a car crash, and his sixteen-year-old kid died of cancer. It almost made me cry. But I didn't have a headache or anything, because I could finally control my Empath ability. Thankfully, Leslie taught me that.

After I had polished the first boat, Leland had me try it out. The boat happened to be a two-person speed boat. When Leland saw that it worked, he immediately put me to work on the next boat. So I fixed that one, and tested it, and it worked. Now, all I had to do was fix the biggest boat, I would be able to get to the lighthouse.

"Now, all you have to do is fix the next &^*% boat and you are all good," Leland said. I could tell he liked my company. He was rude about it, though. All he does is tell me what to do. I'm thirteen years old! He isn't even my parent.

Ever since I first ran away—a year ago now—everything has been so crazy. First I had to live in the woods, then in a random city, then I did those tests in the woods. After that, I got put in jail, then lived in a hotel for a month. And it goes on! I crash into a pole and get imprisoned in a hidden factory. Then I escape and get here, working with a drunk boat man because I'm trying to get to a lighthouse...

"GET TO WORK!!!" Leland surprised me. So I ran to the big boat and opened up the metal protector for the engine. The moment it was cracked open, smoke flooded the area and into my lungs.

"UGH!" I coughed hard and quickly shut the protector. "How long has it been since you have used this boat?" I yelled at Leland.

"Ten years. Why?" Leland said from inside his little shack.

"Something must have burned. I don't know how, but something did." Then I had an idea. "Do you have clips and plastic wrap?"

"Yeah, why?"

"Can I use it?"

"Sure." I heard him opening and closing some cabinets. I waited patiently until four clips and a roll of plastic wrap came rolling toward me from the shack.

I clipped each corner of the plastic wrap. Then I was ready. I quickly took the door off the protector and put the clips on the corners of the box so the plastic wrap covered the smoke. But I made sure there was a tiny hole (the size of a sharp pencil tip) so the smoke would go away, but not all at once.

So I waited. Every ten minutes, I poked another hole for the smoke to come out. By the time all the smoke was gone, there were seven holes. I slowly peeled off the plastic wrap as Leland watched.

"Smart. Huh?" he asked me.

"Yeah. I...took classes," I lied.

"'Kay," he said. "Polish it. And done."

Sigh. I never seem to get a rest. "Okay." I polished it, got a paintbrush and painted a name:

SMOKE

I could have named it Smoky engine, Smoky, or Smoky butt. But *Smoke* means something to me. I just don't know what it is. (Also, I didn't want it to sound too much like a cigarette.)

"Are you done yet?" Leland said.

"Yes, I am."

I saw tears come to his eyes. But he forced them to go away. "Well…" His voice cracked. I knew what to do. I ran to him and hugged him. At first his arms were out, not yet embracing me, but then he slowly put his arms around me. His shirt smelled really weird—like boat oil. I let go, wrinkling up my nose.

"Can I rent the small speed boat?" I asked.

"Yes! Yes of course." Leland went inside and came out of the shed with a paper bag full of something. "Take this bag and don't open it until we are parted," Leland said poetically.

"Why not open it now?" He gave me a look that told me I should obey him. "Okay, then. Bye?"

"Bye. Please return my boat, even if I am not out here." he said stiffly. As I walked away, I could feel his eyes burning into the back of my head. Who knew what he was thinking.

I was sorta in a hurry to get out of there, both to get to the lighthouse and to open the bag. So with just a wave and a goodbye, I set out for the mysterious lighthouse.

. . .

At first the waves were smooth. A little bump here and there, nothing big. I was using a paddle because I didn't know how to use the actual engine.

But after a few minutes, I was in the middle of what seemed like a hurricane. I only say that because I wasn't used to fifteen-foot waves towering over my super small boat. Half the time, the boat was going straight through waves. It was not one bit as fun as you probably think it would be.

As I was being sucked under the waves, I looked at the full moon in the air. Right now, you are probably thinking, "Why in the world are you doing this?" The question I'd have for you is: Why would I be telling you this story if I die?

Here is the real reason: I saw the shape of Liginia— a shadow—in front of the moon. It looked like the figure was heading to the lighthouse. That made me even more motivated to get there. And especially get through this storm.

A few minutes later, the storm stopped abruptly. I was about to crash into a huge wave, when the water turned as smooth as stone. When I reached over to touch the water, it felt normal.

As I got closer and closer to the lighthouse, I opened the paper bag that Leland gave me. The first thing I saw was a huge turkey sandwich with mustard and tomatoes.

After I gobbled half of it down, I found a note with a picture.

THIS IS MY DAUGHTER. BYE.
- LELAND

Clipped to the message was a picture of a girl with perfectly wavy brown hair. She has smooth peach skin and deep navy blue eyes.

Emotion hit me like a wave. *Family.* A mother, a father, a brother, a sister. Things I have never had. Well—I sort of did. That life is behind me now. Buried on a faraway land, like a treasure. And I'm a pirate, on a boat that keeps me stabilized. Searching the waves and looking for any land. To rest. To find the treasure. But now, my boat has capsized. I have fallen away and floated away. Lost and never to be found...

Since I had a lot of time to think, I looked back at my bad life decisions.

I think about how I disobeyed Liginia, when she's pretty much the only one that I can trust in this world. How I should have never trusted Igneous.

I remember how my mother used to sing me lullabies:

Here on the meadow,
You will be cozy and safe.
This is where the warm wind
Tickles your face.

Hear the crickets who will sing you to sleep.
Watch the animals run past and eat.

Here on the meadow,
You will be cozy and safe.
See the butterflies land on your fingers.
Smell the great blossoms
As they bloom in the spring.
Listen to the great splash of the wild rivers.

Here on the meadow, you will be cozy and safe.
Forget about your worries
And everything will be okay.
La la la, didi da, la la la la, didi da.
La la la, didi da, la la la la, didi da.

Now fall asleep and you will meet me.
On the other side of the dear meadow.
This is where we met, in the dear old meadow.
La la la, didi da, la la la la, didi da.
La la la, didi da, la la la la, didi da.

I know it's cheesy, but it reminds me that I can go into my own world when things are troubling. It's just…I haven't really been free. I'm always running from something. And it chases away my memories.

But then something huge happened.

Something I didn't know that was coming…

Igneous

CHAPTER 32

Every day I felt more and more uncomfortable. Everything had become more and more awkward. And even if I got out of this place, the same feeling would follow me—though the feeling would take me hours to explain.

One day, I felt so exhausted for some reason. Seven had come into my room to ask me some questions.

"So, what do you think of this place?" Seven asked.

"I-I really love it," I lied. "But I still miss my home," I added.

"I need to tell you something. The owner of the Staff of Colossi said that you can get out of here if you do one thing for Agapi. She is going to come here any moment now to tell you what you must do!"

My jaw dropped. *Why was life so weird?* "She can make me do *anything?*" I whispered.

"Yep."

I closed my eyes, trying to think. "Anything?"

"Yes. Definitely, yes," he confirmed.

I wanted to puke. "So like… anything? Even something like, kill myself?"

"I'm sorry, but yes. You don't deserve it—you are a good man."

I almost felt like rolling my eyes. It didn't matter if I was a good person. It was all happening whether I liked it or not. I leaned in. "Are you sure I can't get out of it?" I asked.

"I'm sure. But what could Agapi possibly—"

Agapi burst into the room. I flipped around to look at her. She was wearing a pink robe, and her hair was nicely brushed in place. Her bare feet thumped across the room to me.

"Let me make this quick," I said.

"My wish is for…it's a surprise!" Agapi said. "Igneous, can you meet me in my room in an hour?"

"Um, sure?" I said. I looked at Seven as the door closed.

"That's a bad sign. Usually if it is a bad idea, she puts it on hold for an hour." He walked out of my room. *Thanks for really* not *comforting me, Seven,* I thought.

Over the next hour, I just laid there in bed looking at the ceiling. But, of course, the end of the hour came fast.

"Hey, Agapi? You in there?" I opened the door.

She ran to the door, looking really dressed up. The first thing I noticed was the dress. It was a long, flowing dress that was white at the top and faded to yellow at the bottom. The dress ended at the floor. Then I noticed the makeup. Her lips had smoothly applied, shiny white lipstick. She had a ton of blush on her cheeks.

Bleh. I don't like makeup. Girls are already beautiful without makeup. It just covers who they really are. *Girls…Safire…*

"Hello. And how do I look?" Agapi said. She gave me an I-am-so-pretty-and-you-have-to-think-so look.

"You look amazing," I lied again. "So, where shall we go?"

She forced me to hook arms with her. "To the garden." Then she walked away from the yard door.

We walked down random hallways that I had never seen before. We came to a beautiful garden that I had never seen. It was full of flowers of all kinds. Beautiful, glimmering ivy creeped up the marble walls. In the middle of everything was an amazing, shining gazebo. If you squinted, it seemed to shine light onto the walls of the garden. It almost felt like a dream. Warm and sweet scents filled the air as the calls of songbirds echoed through the wonderland.

"Follow me, gentleman." She led me through the flowers as I put on a lopsided grin. This was completely the opposite of what I was actually feeling. I felt like she was about to kill me herself. Or… *The window she had in her room,* I thought to myself. *Oh no…*

"Please sit down here." She patted the seat next to her in the gazebo.

I had a bad feeling about this. But I was glad that at least I wore a plaid shirt that was nicely ironed and looked nice. So maybe she wouldn't suspect anything—if her wish was even remotely close to what I was thinking would happen.

"So," she said. "I can make you do anything. Literally, anything." She forced me to take her hand. "So you could leave, if I wish it. What I...um..." She leaned forward and kissed my mouth.

I pushed her back into her seat. "Ahem?" I gave her a look.

She blinked. Her face was completely wiped of any emotion. "So..."

"Just get to the point!" I barked. I meant it.

"Well. What I want you to do is stay here. We shall get married. And then you may leave a couple of years after that." She smiled.

Then it all just came out of me. "WHAT? What the heck, lady?" I yelled. "You first flirt with me, then you ask me to *marry* you? That's deep! And...SCARY!"

"Well then. FREEZE!"

As soon as I tried to move, my body froze. All I could do was whisper. "You...you can't do this." I struggled again.

"Well, sweetie, I think I just did." She smirked and kissed me again, but for much longer. The sensation kept sending icy tingles down the back of my neck. Her lips were soft. But they were too soft. It made me want to squirm. "Hey, Xed boy!" she called. "Come get the prey!"

Two seconds later, Xed came into the garden and solemnly bowed.

"P-please don't do this..." I gasped.

"I'm sorry, Igneous... I'm sorry..." By the look on his face, I could tell there were thousands of apologies that were unspoken. He set me on the ground and punched my frozen face over and over and over again.

I went unconscious.

Black. That's the word.

· · ·

After I don't know how long, I woke up. I was in a dark room with one chair. I was lying against a wall. I quickly jumped up but a pain shot through my body as soon as I tried. A voice spoke. "How are you doing, sweetie?"

Agapi. "Hey, what's your problem!" I yelled.

"I don't know. Sweetie." Agapi came over from the shadows and planted a kiss on my cheek. "Please don't yell at me. Aren't we getting married? Oh, and I forgot to tell you that I scheduled the wedding. It's in a couple weeks! Isn't that exciting? Well, we have to go dress shopping, honey!" She said this as if I were actually her husband. *How weird could this woman get?* "And I made it so that if you try to tell someone what happened earlier, they won't believe you!"

"You…" I cracked. I was getting more and more hopeless and desperate. How in the world would I get home now?

"Honey, I don't care. Let's go clothes shopping!" She snapped her fingers and we transported to a fancy shop. On the racks were tons of dresses. Small dresses, puffy dresses, super long dresses, brown dresses, white dresses, black dresses, pink dresses… Anyway, this place had not a single person, just the devil-like Agapi and me.

I tried to get up from the seat I was sitting on, but I couldn't get up.

"Now. Look at this." She snapped her fingers and a purple dress with a bow on it appeared on her body. She snapped again and a rainbow one appeared. She kept switching through dresses, muttering comments to herself. Pink with stripes. Brown with spots. A Snow White costume. Teal with a hoodie. White with a hole in the back. Fungus-colored. Yellow. Silver. Gold. Gray. Orange. Sunset-colored. Hot pink. Lavender. Metal? Black. Tech-designed. Green. Blue. Super bright green. She switched them faster and faster until I couldn't take it anymore.

She stopped at a crimson dress. The dress was the color of a devil. She even had a trident along with it. *She is the devil.* For a moment, she stood there looking at me. Smiling. Smiling like she had some plan to do something bad. It was super creepy.

She came toward me. I tried to run, but she put me in locked position. *Great.* My heart thumped as her high heels clacked against the floor. Then she snapped her fingers.

My eyes closed, and I fell into what felt like a dream. (I couldn't tell if it was a dream or not, but I do know it wasn't such a nice dream.)

I was in a jail-like room. "Hello? Is anyone there?" I said.

"Igneous! You have to get out of there!" a voice said. *"Agapi is trying to control you!"*

The voice...it was Safire!

278

"What are you doing here?" I said.

She ran out of the shadows and hugged me. The warmth from her body felt so real. My face felt hot. We let go of each other. "What —"

To my horror a spear shot through the air, targeting Safire's back. "UGGH". A gruesome noise came out of Safire as the spear went right through her back. It went all the way through, so the head was poking out of her stomach. Weird sounds came out of me, too, as Safire fell to the floor. A pool of blood collected around her as she tried to breathe.

For some reason this didn't feel real. I watched as Safire's body disappeared and turned into a hawk. The hawk landed on my stiff shoulder and turned into a songbird. The songbird began to sing in my ear.

"Here on the meadow,
You will be cozy and safe.
This is where the warm wind
Go your face.
The crickets will sing *to* asleep.
Watch the *lighthouse* run and eat.

"Here on the number,
You will be cozy and safe.
See the *one* land on your finger…"

I didn't hear the rest. It sounded nice, but there were weird words in the middle of it. Wait. Go. To, Lighthouse. One? That sounded weird. It sounded…like a message. I need to go to lighthouse one! *I heard it's near an island on Earth…*

"ACKK!!" I woke up. The dream. It was weird.

Did…Safire die in reality, and is this dream telling me something? My heart rate surged. A chill ran through my spine. I know I'm not supposed to have feelings for her because of Obsidian Slag and Agapi, but…

"Hi sweetie. Are you awake now?" said the all too familiar voice. *That devil.* Agapi. She stood in front of me, tossing her hair and putting her hands on her hips. Her shoes made a *clickety-clackety* sound as she walked towards me. The sound echoed through the large room, with wooden poles every ten feet.

"Would you please be quiet?" I said in a nice voice. Completely opposite of what I was feeling right then.

"I was watching your dreams, fiancé. Your girlfriend is dead. She's completely gone." She came over to me and stroked my face. Of course I couldn't move again because of that freeze trick, or spell, or whatever you call it. Anger boiled up inside me as I strained myself.

Agapi ignored me and kept talking. "Now it's you and me. No one will be able to take us apart."

"I will run from you. That's what I will do, little brat!" I shouted at her.

"How can you?" She kissed me. I don't know why, but kissing at all reminded me of Safire. The sensation made me break the spell, and I tried to punch Agapi. She caught my hand two inches away from her stomach.

"I'm sorry, baby, but you can't get through me. Try again." She pushed me against the wall, walked over to a vanity, grabbed something and put it in her pocket.

I feared it could be a knife, so I looked around the

room. I had an idea. "You wanna go for a dance?" I said.

"Sure!" Agapi and her accent transformed into Safire.

Why did she look and feel and even smell *like Safire?* I had to battle this. I put one hand on her hip and the other in her hand. We slowly waltzed around the room. I could tell Agapi thought this was a real "I love you" dance. But it was the only thing I could think of—

She twirled around behind me, jumped onto my back and up onto my shoulders. Her legs were wrapped around my neck, and she slid to my front. She quickly unclasped her legs from my neck, glided them down my body and fastened them around my waist.

She looked at me, slowly raised her hand to her head—and did something that only a crazy person would do. She held a gray, electric razor and placed it on her head.

BZZZZT... She gently pressed the power button and large pieces of hair fell to the ground, covering my feet. When she was done, she gently put her head down and grinned. I began to try to slip out of her grasp, but she was too strong. I began to regret not trying to learn fist fighting because I could have tried to punch her or something.

"Like my hair?" she asked.

"Nope." I tried to tug Agapi's legs off my neck, but the more I tried, the tighter she held on.

"Sweetie..." She swung herself around my neck until she was on my back.

"Get...off..." I started coughing and wheezing. She

was putting pressure on my neck, so I leaned over. She wasn't thinking I'd do that, so she fell off my back and slid down into the hair pile.

Now, I understood she wanted to fight.

So I got ready…to fight.

Remembering my plan, I quietly and quickly took a piece of string on her dress and pulled. A long piece of yarn came out but there was still more of it. I pulled with all my strength as Agapi kept rolling over and over, uncontrollably. The dress she was wearing unraveled. Soon I had a string as long as the room…and then one that was the length of a house…and then it became the length of a two-story house..and then a three-story house…and even up to a five-story house!

"Oof! Ow!" she yelled. Yank! *Crack…CRASH!!!* The string broke and Agapi was swung into the wall. I was glad she had on a tank top and shorts under her dress. Otherwise… (Bleh, it's gross just thinking about it.) I stuck my tongue out in disgust.

When I looked at Agapi, I knew I was in trouble. Her face reddened and her nostrils flared. Her veins popped through her forehead. She slammed her arm into my leg and a pain shot through my leg up into my arm. I flailed and fell. Agapi pinned me to the ground. It was a mystery how she could do this stuff.

She grinned. "Now you can see…I'm not as weak as you think." Color rose up to my cheeks. That *was* what I had thought.

She took a knife out of her pocket and scraped the sides of my face so that blood dripped down into my hair.

I almost yelped but I held it in. She gave me a devil-like smile and snapped her fingers. A devil's trident appeared in her outstretched hand, as a red sequin dress suddenly draped her body.

"Thank you, sir, for helping me show my real self. As you can remember, you can marry me or not. If you marry me, you will be with me and we shall rule the lands together! Forget my fake father—come with me to your new home." She glared. "If you *don't* marry me, you will be immortal and in pain for the rest of eternity. Now, please. Let's dance. More like, *practice* dancing. Oh…and we captured your *former* girlfriend. You know who that is?"

She's not dead? "No…" I whispered. No-o-o!

"It's Safire…"

Safire

CHAPTER 33

WHOOSHH!!! A huge wave rushed over top of me. My boat sent me flying out into the water with a big *SPLASH!!!*

BOOM! The sound of explosions pierced my ears as I fell deeper and deeper into the unknown ocean. My lungs burned as I tried to keep my breath. My whole body shouted for me to rest, to stop kicking to try to reach the surface. I struggled to rise like the lucky bubbles floating to the top of the water. I stopped flailing and looked up. I watched the world disappear from my eyes. I tried and tried to stay awake, to say goodbye to everything.

Goodbye forests. And the fake City. And Aenon. And Liginia—I mean Mom… And life. And the boat I was flung off of. Goodbye… Igneous.

Then the world blackened.

. . .

"Where shall we put her? She must be here for the marriage."

"I don't know. Why are you asking me? And besides where is the bride?" said another voice.

"I'm here!" said a girl's voice. "The groom is tied up. He's in room 193749, put her there. I shall make them hate each other so much, that he won't be in love with her anymore. Then he shall be *mine.*"

I heard lots of shifting. The first person walked away. I think.

"Okay, madam. Shall we wake her up?" said the second voice.

"Yes." The girl's voice was cold and commanding.

My eyes shot open. I was in a hospital room with white stone walls and blinding lights. *No...* To either side were sharp hospital tools and—a girl. A bald girl about my age, with a blood-red dress and a blood-red trident.

"I'm glad you are awake," said the girl with a crisp voice. Her piercing brown eyes drilled holes in my soul. She looked and studied every inch of me. My hair. My nose. My eyes. My lips. My feet. My chest. My body. At least I wasn't naked: I was wearing an undershirt and a pair of black leggings.

"Who are you?" I croaked.

"Oh. My name is Agapi." She plucked a strand of my hair. I tried to lift my hands, but they were frozen, as if by magic.

I had to get out of this. "What groom are you talking about?" I asked. My heart raced as Agapi's jaw dropped dramatically.

"You don't know who your ex-boyfriend is?"

"No." I meant it. I never had a boyfriend.

"Igneous," she snapped and walked out of the room, like one of those mean, popular girls. Her hips swayed side-to-side with each step.

Rage filled me. Suddenly, my bed lurched forward, out of the room and into the hallway. The moment the bed stopped speeding, I fell off in a *THUMP* and rolled uncontrollably. The bed screeched off into the hallways. What was going on? *How was this happening?*

I clutched my shoulder and rolled until I could stand up. I looked around at the room. There were wooden posts on opposite sides of the room and…a pool of blood.

"Who is there?" A voice echoed through the room. It sounded familiar.

"Who are you?" I echoed. I stood in a protective position, with my feet firmly glued to the ground and my hands ready for action. My heart thumped like a drum. I stood with my back to the wall. My eyes searched the room—

"Safire?"

"Igneous?" I spat. He appeared from behind the farthest post. I clutched the door handle, trying to balance myself. Anger rose up again. But when he said my name, a warm tingle went down my spine. I ignored it.

"Safire! I—" he started.

But anger took over me. "GET AWAY FROM ME, BEAST! After what you have done, YOU DESERVE HURT! Get away from me with your 'oh, I'm a little prince, and I can do whatever I want and it won't hurt anybody' act! GET AWAY FROM ME!" I screamed. I didn't care about anything or anyone right now. All I wanted was for Igneous to feel the emotional pain he had inflicted on me.

"WHY CAN'T YOU JUST FORGET ABOUT WHAT HAPPENED! Can't you see that I'm not who you think I am? I'm not a cheat! I *have* lied to you BUT I WAS TRYING TO FIGURE OUT HOW TO TELL YOU CERTAIN THINGS!"

"WHY WON'T YOU JUST ACCEPT THAT I HATE YOU!" The moment the word 'hate' came out of my mouth, I froze. I ran over to the only door that possibly let out of this cold and annoying room. I could hear footsteps outside.

"Agapi?" I said. "Agapi? Is that you? Can I please tell you something?"

"Yes?" she said. I could hear her shifting so she could hear me clearly.

"Open the door. I want to properly say that I'm surrendering."

She hesitated and slowly opened the door. I quickly ran behind the door to hide.

"Oh brother, this is a stupid trick. I know you are behind the door," she said. But when she looked, I was already out the door, running—

"MFFF!" I moaned. With one gesture and a flick of her wrist, Agapi had completely frozen the hallway floor. My feet were freezing, planted in the ice. I couldn't move them, no matter how hard I tried.

"If you haven't noticed, there is a thick layer of ice on the ground. I use this to trap anyone who gets out of my grasp. Don't you feel so useless right now?" she said. Her voice was as cold as the floor made my feet.

"No wonder you have ice powers. Your heart is basically made out of the same material," I said to her.

"What did—" She was cut off by a line of flames melting the ice below me.

I followed the fire with my eyes to find where it was coming from. Igneous stood in the hallway, with flames beaming from his fingers. He looked determined and tough.

Agapi screamed and tried to freeze me again. But I ran around her Freeze spells using my super speed. This time I could control how fast I was moving.

THUMP! Igneous came out of nowhere and tackled her to the ground. I gathered my bearings as Agapi started to overpower Igneous. My hands began to shake. THUMP! Igneous knocked her to the floor again, putting his hands around her neck and his foot on her back. CRACK! I could hear Agapi's back cracking under the pressure.

"Get away from me," she growled. With that, she elbowed him really hard, and he collapsed to the floor. Before I knew it, she had her feet on his arms, and she punched him in the chest and face. I stood there, petrified, not knowing what to do. His eyes closed, and he looked lifeless.

She stood up to face me. Blood dripped down the side of her face as she rubbed the swollen bruise on her cheek.

She gave me a wicked grin. "FREEZE!" I dodged

her spell. "FREEZE!" She kept shooting spells, and I had to slide all over the place to avoid them. I was moving so fast that everything around me turned into slow motion, including Agapi and her spells. "FFFRREEEEEZZZZE!" Agapi yelled.

Each time, she would slowly flick her hand and send a tiny ice ball at me. But I was able to dodge each and every one of them. I was moving so fast she could never even get close. She sent one at my stomach—I jumped up. She sent one at my leg—I somersaulted away. I felt like I could do that all day—

"ACK!" I screamed. I tripped on a little ice block that must not have melted all the way. I lost my concentration. I closed my eyes, my heart beating loudly, knowing that Agapi was probably going to take this chance to freeze me. I waited, knowing I couldn't do anything...

"FREEZE!" I opened my eyes. She may have said 'Freeze,' but *it didn't work.* The world around me went back to normal, and it was no longer in slow motion. I looked at Agapi and saw her staring in annoyance at a person in front of me. I looked where she was looking— and my heart stopped.

There stood Igneous, standing firm, his arms and legs spread out, looking like he was trying his best to get frozen. Adrenaline pumped through me. *What is he doing?* Was he trying to save me? *If this is true, maybe I am wrong about him,* I thought to myself.

Warmth flowed through me as I tried to regain my concentration. I jumped up to my feet and ran, at lightning speed, out of the hallway. *Where did I last see a fire?* I asked myself. I ran to the closest room. I scanned the white, empty space for a sign of some type of fire. I saw a fireplace on the far side of the room and dashed to it. I carefully picked up a long stick of wood and dipped it into kerosene I found inside an old lantern. I lit the tip of the stick and it began to feed the fire as I rushed around looking for a knife.

THUMP! I crashed into a wall, I rebounded into the next room and found a knife there. I ran back to the hallway where Agapi and Igneous had been, to find that Agapi had finally succeeded. Igneous was frozen.

Sizzle… I pressed the torch against Igneous, trying to melt him. Agapi started shooting ice knives at me. I dodged all of them, except for one. It barely hit my back, but it cut lots of skin off and I collapsed. When I got back up, I saw Igneous pick up the knife on the floor and throw it at Agapi.

"AIIIIYYEEEE" She screamed when it cut through her stomach. Blood pooled at her feet. She ran away, and a tiny trail of blood followed her.

I sat there with my mouth wide open.

"I guess…we did it?" Igneous whispered.

"Yeah…" I responded. We both stared at each other. I felt on top of the world.

"Um…also—"

THUMP! A cute bird flew into the hallway and fell between us. It looked like a whiskered treeswift. It had weird, whisker-like things around its large, deep, black eyes. It had a small orange tuft of feathers behind its eyes, and its head and wings were blue, but the body was a darker bronze color.

"Do you know how that got in here?" Igneous asked?

I shook my head in answer.

"*Hello, ya!*" The bird turned towards me.

"Hi, what's your name?"

"*Melody…how come you can talk in my language?*"

I shrugged.

Igneous stared at me. "How can you talk to that bird, Safire?" I ignored him and bent down to talk to the bird some more.

"*Who is that? Your BOYFRIEND?!*" she asked.

I rolled my eyes. "Where did you come from?" I asked.

"*Can I trust you?*"

I nodded. "I don't think someone you can't trust would be able to talk to you…"

She sat quiet for a few seconds, deep in thought. "*Ok…well…I was flying around in search for food…and I found this weird door and went inside. I flew down some halls…but I couldn't find my way back. Then I found you guys!*"

"Um…"

"Safire, we have to go!" Igneous whispered. "I can hear someone's footsteps, let's go! It could be Agapi!"

I looked up at him, then at the bird. "Do you want to come with us?" Melody nodded and jumped on my shoulder. I followed Igneous, quietly. (The whole time, I obsessively thought about him.)

"Jump when you get to the edge!" he whispered. He must have known to go this way the whole time—but why didn't he escape, then? Without hesitation, I opened the door he told me to open and jumped.

"WHEEEEEEEEEEEEEE!" Melody shouted. We hit the ground in seconds, and no pain shot through my legs, I had a new energy. Around us was a huge meadow with very tall grass that went up to our chests. On the edges of the meadow were tall trees. The grass was so tall that, when we crouched down, we were hidden. The soil was soft.

I turned around to look for the door we jumped out of. In the air was a lone white door that was not connected to any walls. *What???*

"Safire, you look tired," Igneous said, concerned. I may have had a new energy, but I was still tired. I nodded. "You should go to sleep, the sun is going to set soon. Me and..."

"Melody," I said.

"Yes, *Melody* and I will be here to protect you."

I laid down on the ground. I felt so overwhelmed, it felt good to take a break. Plus, it was a dreamless sleep. Yay!

. . .

"Safire. Wake up!" Igneous shook me awake.

The sun blinded me, so I covered my eyes. I groaned as I got up. It was the afternoon. The grass was damp and the soil was gooey. I was covered in a nice leaf blanket with Melody in my arms.

"*WAKE UP, SLEEPYHEAD! YEAH!*" Melody shouted. I grinned. It was good to hear her eager voice.

"Safire, it's gone!" Igneous pointed to where the door once hovered in the sky.

"Must have been magic," I mumbled. Igneous grinned.

"*SOOOOOOO??? What are we to do, ya?!*" Melody sang.

"We survive," I said. An unusual adrenaline pumped. Stronger than the tests. Stronger than when I fought Agapi. "Although Agapi is probably still out there."

"*I know what we should do! We should journey that way! Come on, ya!*" Melody nodded towards the faraway mountains that I hadn't even realized were there.

"You're right!" I said. It may sound cheesy, but I must say, my smile reached to my cheeks.

I told Igneous what Melody had told me. "I'll pack up," Igneous said. "You guys get fruits and berries for the journey."

"*So…so you like him? I mean, you just let him guard us while we were sleeping,*" Melody said, when we went out of Igneous' sight.

"I do not!" I argued.

"*Sounds like somebody who is in love,*" she sang.

"*When she seeeeeeees him,*
Her eyes look longinglllly.
Watch her eyes chase him

Wherever he gooooooes.
Seeeeee her eyes!
Seeeee them long for him…
SSEEEEEE her love for the booooooyyyy!"

Then she posed. I rolled my eyes as she giggled. My face was heated, too. *It was true… in a way.* I wasn't mad at him like before, that's for sure. We had fought Agapi together. We were a good team.

We collected berries in silence. *No distractions, just survive,* I repeated in my head. I needed to concentrate. When we got back to the meadow after our journey to find food, we started out on our *real* journey to find a new *home.*

．．．

We climbed high up into the mountains. A steady wind was blowing, so I could never enjoy the beaming sunlight.

"BRRRRRR…" I shivered. My goosebumps seemed to have goosebumps on them. Igneous—well, he was fine. He can make fire with his bare hands, after all. Melody sat in my arms as she shivered, too. Her feathers quivered. My face grew blue and my hands quaked.

"Uh…do you wanna stop?" Igneous asked. He scratched the back of his head. I could tell he needed something.

"*Yeah!*" Melody said.

"Follow what she says," I said.

"What?" Igneous said, clearly confused. His

eyebrow raised.

"Follow what she says."

"Um…what did she say?" Igneous asked. I had forgotten that only I can decipher what Melody says.

"She said, let's stop," I said.

"Oh. Um, Safire, can I talk to you?" Igneous said, nervously.

"Sure." *What was he gonna talk to me about?* "Melody, can you sit there? I'll be right back in a sec."

Melody grinned. She flew out of my arms onto a log. *"I'll be right here! Ya!"* Melody gave me a wink and looked up at the sky. (She must have been bird watching or star gazing.)

"Okay. Let's go over there." Igneous pointed to a little clearing as I followed him.

"So hey, I'm sorry about the whole…you know… just everything?" he cringed.

"I know. It's fine."

"I know I will never be able to make it up to you…" He just couldn't seem to finish his statement. No one spoke for a moment. It felt like an eternity.

I put my hand on my arm, staring at the floor. "So…"

"We can destroy him," he said all of a sudden.

"WHAT?!" My brain seemed to jump. "What do you mean?"

"We can destroy Obsidian Slag."

"Who is that?"

"The bad guy behind pretty much all of this."

"Oh…" I nodded slowly. This all felt odd.

"Sooo…" he said.

"Yeah. I think I know somebody who could help us," I said. *Mom.* "One sec. I think I can communicate with her if I try. I could finally control my speed with Agapi, so I can probably get to her, if I put my mind to it." I closed my eyes and concentrated. I tried to block all of the other sounds around me. It's like my mother always taught me when we did yoga and meditation."

"Mom…" I called in my mind. Nothing.

"Mom…" I called again.

"I see you have gotten a hold of communicating with me in your mind. All the people that live on our true planet can do —"

"I'm truly sorry about yelling at you when we were in the city."

"And I'm sorry for lying to you your whole life."

Nobody spoke for a moment.

"I forgive you," I said. *"And Mom?"*

"Yeah?"

"Do you think you can get Igneous, Melody and me to our true planet? We need to get out of here. It isn't safe."

"Yes! Of course!" I could hear the excitement in her voice. *"I can't wait to see you. It's called Planet Azul."*

"Thanks, Mom…"

"Huh?"

"Thank you for everything you have done for me, even when things got hard and I yelled at you. I know you were always trying to teach me, even when we were both on Earth…"

I heard a muffled cry. *"Okay. Gather your friends,*

and I'll send a transport." she said.

With that, her voice was gone.

"Igneous, come on!" I yelled. We ran over to Melody as a stream of purple and white light shot down on the ground with a *BOOM*. Mud splashed everywhere.

"WHAT?!" Melody shouted.

"Melody, just go into the purple light!" I shouted over the booming noise.

Igneous jumped in the purple light and disappeared. Then, Melody jumped in with a *"YA!"*

I looked around me. This could be one of the last times I see Earth. (Too bad the loud sound of the transporter ruined the moment.) I took a handful of soil and it blew away in my hand. Feelings poured through my heart. I was going to leave the planet Marissa would be on forever. It would be a while until I would see anything that even remotely reminded me of her. It felt like I was truly leaving her.

One foot after the other, I took small steps to the purple light. A hand popped out of the purple light stream. I took a deep breath and grabbed the hand as it pulled me in. All of a sudden, a warm cookie smell came into my senses.

"IT'S REALLY GOOD TO SEE YOU, SAFIRE!"

Igneous

CHAPTER 34

"So, that was how it was," I say to Liginia as I finish the story. We are in a room with large red velvet chairs and cozy white walls. Safire and I sit in two chairs in front of Liginia. We have come a long way.

"Huh. Livinius…Livinius is *still* alive?" Liginia asks, confused.

"Yes, Livinius. He said he was your brother," I say. "I just didn't know who you were at the time."

"Livinius. I didn't know he was still alive," Liginia repeats, choked up.

I glance at Safire and I happen to hear her whisper. "Aenon." *Who is that?*

"Is Livinius that guy Igneous met in the cave that had the potions?" Safire asks. Liginia nods.

"I know he's your brother, but is he gonna be trouble?" I ask. I don't like that I have another enemy.

"Livinius had a tough time, when we were growing up. Only time will tell where his loyalty lies."

"So what about Obsidian Slag?" Safire butts in.

"Yes. yes…our signal radar has been picking up

his ships."

I lean forward over the control panel as Safire's jaw drops. "So he is here?" I whisper, pointing to the largest ship on the radar. *The ship closest to us.* On the radar, it looks like it was almost on top of us.

My voice is shaky and my finger has a hard time tracking the ship. I lean back in deep thought. Thoughts of Obsidian Slag swim through my head. Before, I used to think he was just a shadow trying to lead my people, but now, I am so frightened of him. I know what he is capable of.

"Yes, he is here. I'm gonna get you, Safire and Melody a safe place to stay," Liginia says, trying to comfort us, uncertainty in her voice.

Safire stands up and gives her mother a fierce look. "No! I'm going to fight with my people!"

"No." Liginia says.

"WHY?!"

"Because."

"BECAUSE WHAT?"

"BECAUSE YOU AREN'T TRAINED!"

"Then train me."

"It is not that simple."

"ALL YOU HAVE TO DO IS *TRAIN* ME!!!" Safire shouts. Her veins look like they are popping out of her head. She glares at Liginia, arms crossed.

Liginia sighs. "Fine."

Safire looks surprised. "Can we start now?" she asks, jumping up and down like a little kid waiting to get a popular toy.

I zone out, not paying attention to what they are saying. Liginia and Safire are always happy together, even if they don't know it. As I watch them talk, I hope that I'll see Xed someday. Besides Safire, Xed used to be the only one that could make me happy, even when I was having a dark day. Will we ever be able to get that friendship back? Can I ever trust him again?

"—but you two can meet some of the other kids your age, in your generation," Liginia informs us. Before I know it, we teleport to a room with a bunch of kids. It's so crowded that I can't see the walls or anything. Wall-to-wall kids, some talking loudly, others standing patiently and quietly, not knowing what to say. "I'll leave you to it!" Liginia says—and she disappears.

Safire and I look at each other, confused. "Uh... should we go—"

All of a sudden, loud party music blasts through the room. The walls begin to open, and we're suddenly in a room that's a hundred times bigger. The ceiling disappears to reveal the night sky. The stars and moons are our only source of natural light. On one side of the room a big stage appears, and a bunch of random people start playing music on it. In the middle of the room is a big dance floor that has tons of neon lights. The room is lined with Earthy food trucks, with tables and chairs in front of them. In one corner, there are bars with bartenders shaking up drinks.

"Why do they have bars here?!" I shout to Safire. We squeeze through the crowd to get to the tables.

"Maybe some people in our generation are over

twenty-one!" she shouts back.

"Um…now we have to potentially work with alcoholics?!" I shake my head, knowing that we need all our warriors to be smart and awake.

"Why did my mom have to torture us with this… party?! I wish we could have skipped it."

"Yeah—"

Safire frowns. "I'm starting to wonder if those people are real!"

"People actually do that, Safire!" I shout over the loud music.

"And now some classical music for all the lovers out there!" the DJ says. The music changes from heavy metal to classical. A bunch of couples twirl around on the dance floor. The music starts to make me sleepy.

"Are you tired of this music?" I pipe up, after a moment.

"Yeah?" Safire says.

"Do you want to change it?"

"Huh?"

"I said, do you want to *change* it?"

"What do you mean?"

I smirk and hold up the fifty notes that Liginia handed me to pay for stuff. They are dark bronze with some weird symbol on them. They feel rough to the touch.

"I'm in," she says. "But how did you get those fake notes?"

"They're not fake. Your mom gave them to me."

Safire grabs one to see what they look like. "Okay,

let's do it!" she says, jumping up and down.

We walk over to the DJ stand. It seems a little different than the ones Safire had told me about before. The DJ guy looks up at us. I can't make out any facial details because there aren't many lights in this corner.

"Can we change the song?" I ask.

"Nobody ever does that," he responds.

"I didn't ask you if people do it, could we please change the—"

Safire pushes me aside. "I'm sorry that he is being so rude. We just wanted to change the song because it's making us feel tired," she says politely.

The guy considers it. "Fifty notes," he says. I hand the money over. "What genre of music do you request?"

"Rock, please," Safire says. The song shifts into rock and she nods, satisfied.

We walk onto the dance floor and begin to jump up and down to the music with everyone else. I can't remember the last time I had this much fun. Things had been so hard this last year. This is the first time in so long that I can remember feeling relaxed.

We meet a couple of people. One of them is Zam, and she has the power of controlling and making Voids. She explains that Voids are holes that you can teleport through. I'm guessing they're kind of like the one Liginia used. Zam seems nice and sweet. Safire seems to like her a lot, because they go off to talk about "girl stuff."

While they are talking, I let myself walk up to a guy who is sitting by himself. "Um...hey!" I say to him.

"Oh! Hi. Sorry, I was off in my own world. I didn't

even notice you."

I sit down. "Lonely?"

"Sorta." He turned to look at me. "What's your name?"

"Igneous."

"What's your power?"

"Lava, Fire, and I can throw knives."

"Oooh! My name is Kal, and my power is Annoyingness!"

This sounded about right—he just went from quiet to obnoxious in one second.

"I'm just kidding, bro! I'm not really sure what my ability is, but I guess I'll find out some time, right?" I don't know what it is about this guy, but I knew that I kind of liked him.

We talk for a little bit, until Safire comes back. "Hey guys... Zam went off to go dance with her friends."

"It was nice meeting you, bro. I'll leave you two alone," Kal says, while pushing his chair towards Safire. He disappears into the crowd.

It's just Safire and me again. We sit down and munch on some tiny sandwiches that have some random stuff on it and talk about random things. But most of the time, we sit there in awkward silence.

"Do you want a soda?" I ask her.

"Sure. Here—" We both reach for our empty glasses, but instead, our hands bump into each other. We look up at each other. We exchange glances and look down at our hands. I think we are both confused. I reach up and brush Safire's hair out of her face. She is a true beauty, inside and out. She isn't a snobby rich girl or a mean girl. She is truly special. She is perfect to me.

She studies my eyes, looking for something. I want her to lean forward, but I wait. If we kiss, everything will be different. Maybe wounds will be healed. Trust will be rebuilt. But it all overwhelms me. *I'm only fourteen! Is now the time for all of this?* I struggle to say something. "Yis nook retty," *Big fail. BIG FAIL.*

She frowns. I'm counting the seconds in my head, my heart beating so loud I can't hear the music anymore. I count to ten.

Her face softens, and my heart beats even louder. Our eyes lock. She leans forward. I take that as a cue to lean forward, too. Her soft forehead touches mine. I can feel her heavy breathing on my cheek. I run my fingers through her soft hair. But my hand gets stuck in a tangle. I cringe and take my hand out of her hair.

She tilts her head to the side and puts her arms around my neck. She turns her head up, making her soft lips touch mine. I take it all in. I feel free from all my worries as we hang on to each other. I want it to stay like this. Her eyes flutter shut, and so do mine. I feel the hunger for more, but I control myself and try to focus.

Liginia whispers, "I hope—oh!"

We separate quickly and see Liginia staring at us.

Safire

CHAPTER 35

"Now let me show you to your rooms," my mom says. She skips along the halls as Igneous and I follow her.

Everything feels so awkward after our kiss. We barely look at each other and focus on every word she says to distract ourselves. "Now, the moment you go into your room, shout your first name and last name. Then your room will appear."

"This sounds an awful lot like Agapi's place," Igneous mutters.

"I know," I reply, feeling the only hesitation I have felt since seeing my mother again. My hesitation shifts, quickly. There is so much excitement rushing through me. I skip into my room and yell, "Safire Waters!" Slowly, inch by inch, photographs of my journey cover the walls. They appear like fast-growing ivy. I wonder how anyone even took them. I thought I was alone throughout all of these experience. I didn't see anyone sneaking up—or any cameras.

The first picture is of me, climbing over the fence of my former home, out into the wild. I really didn't know what I was in for then.

The next picture is of me by the waterfall, during the flood, on my bed raft. Funny. I snort and my eyes shift over to the next picture.

It makes me quiver. It is a picture of Marissa and me sharing an ICEE at the local convenience store. Right now, I wish I could talk to her, tell her about my new life as an alien…

I wish I could say…

Hey, Marissa. A lot has happened since you died. I had to run away from my home, because doctors were basically going to take me away forever and do these tests and stuff. So I survived in the woods for a while, then I found this city which happened to be an illusion that was made by my mom, who was also Liginia (apparently I'm an alien!). So then, I went into these challenges where I met this guy named Igneous (he was the same exact guy I met through these Lavagraphs). He got us sent to jail, where we met this guy named Joe. We got out of jail and lived in a hotel. I found out that Igneous was actually spying on me, so I ran into a meadow and a man found me. This guy apparently worked for a factory that captured animals. He captured me, and I had to fight my way out of there. I got out and I found a REAL city that had a guy who had boats. I wanted to get to a lighthouse for some reason, so I fixed his boats and took one myself. I went toward the lighthouse, but when I was halfway there, my boat capsized. I mysteriously got to this other planet with this girl named Agapi, who was evil. Apparently Igneous was there, too, because he did something bad…or something? And we ended up defeating Agapi. Then we got to my true home planet, the place I'm at now, and…

I wish I could tell you about Igneous. I may have been wrong about him. At first, he may seem weird, but once you get to know him... He makes me happy.

I hope you will forgive me for saying this, but, yes, I miss you so much, and I wish that you didn't die...

And, also, remember when I used to complain about not being normal? I was dumb. This last year has taught me so much. I feel like I've grown up by ten years. I'm kind of loving that I'm different now. It sets me apart from everyone else. Besides, no matter how normal anyone tries to be, we are all different in our own ways. Does the idea of being normal even really exist? Everyone has something that sets them apart from everyone else...

I push my imaginary conversation with Marissa to the back of my mind, trying not to cry.

I glance at the other pictures and look around the room. My bed is the same bed as I had when I was at my former home. The carpet is the same, too.

There is also one picture that is black and looks like a screen. I'm not sure what it is, so I tap it. I quickly confirm that it is a screen, because when I tap it, a keypad appears. At the top of the screen, it says, "Type the name of someone you know, then you can watch whatever they are doing."

I raise an eyebrow. I type "Liginia." My mom appears on the screen. All she is doing is walking along some hallways. I hit the back button at the top of the screen and type "Igneous." It shows Igneous in his room. It looks like the room he described when he was with Agapi. All he is doing was sitting there, talking to himself.

307

"Arg! Why can I not stop thinking about it!" he says. Then he stays silent.

I turn off the spy thing and flop down on my new bed. I sigh. Then, without a clue that I would, I fall asleep.

. . .

It's been a while since I've had such a peaceful sleep. Imagine not having a truly good nap for a year.

I open my eyes to see Melody standing over me. She is just staring at me. When I get up, she starts clucking. *"YOU HAVE TO GO TO THE CONTROL ROOM!"* she shouts in my ear. *"FOLLOW ME!"*

"What did you say?" I groan, still feeling groggy from my nap.

"You. Have. To. Go. TO THE CONTROL ROOM! Follow me!"

She tugs on my shoe, and I stumble across the floor like a zombie. I grow more awake as I take more steps. We power walk along the halls, occasionally seeing a person the same age as us (or just some random alien that I assume lives on this planet). We stop at a door at the end of the hallway.

"Here we are! I'll be by the door if ya need me!" she yells. She salutes, jumps up and points at the knob for me to open the door.

I swing the door open to see my mom and a bunch of other aliens in a large room with computers and other technology that I don't recognize. They are far more advanced than anything I have ever seen.

There are huge screens on the front wall. The screens show a planet that has green and blue water around tiny, bright orange islands. It is beautiful—it must be the land we are on now.

But then my eyes jerk over to a radar. It's beeping, and the beeps are getting louder and louder. Obsidian Slag's ships look like they're right on top of us. I swallow so hard I almost choke.

"Safire!" My mom's standing near the door, watching me intently. "Come over here. We need your fingerprint for recognition here. You're new, so…the central intelligence needs you in our system."

She hurries me over to another machine and presses my finger onto it. It makes a tiny *beep.* "Now, Safire, you need to stay safe, because Obsidian Slag is here. You can't go wandering around. You understand me?" She looks and sounds different, but, yep, that is the mom I grew up with.

"Yes." I nod and stare at the radar.

"Swear on your life."

"I solemnly swear I will not wander around—"

"Without anyone accompanying you," she finishes. "And, you will not see Igneous for a while because you need different types of training." *What?!* My heart races. "And don't worry, we will take care of you. If you find something you think I should look at, tell me. Always have Melody with you. She knows first aid and how to power simple weapons. She learned while you were asleep."

I tap my foot impatiently. "How long was I

asleep?"

"A week. But it is okay. Now keep yourself safe."
She starts typing wildly on her pad. She pauses, turns
around and looks me straight in the eye. "Safire, I know
you have been lied to a lot—"

"Yeah…"

"So I want to tell you some things. First, Agapi did
bewitch that one guy who threatened your friends not to
talk to you, back when you were in school and had a
semi-normal life on Earth. Apparently, she can use her ice
powers and control people. If we are going to fight her,
we are going to have to study her."

"That Agapi!" I scream.

"What did you think of the city I made, by the
way?" my mom says. "Pretty beautiful, huh?"

"Stop trying to change the subject," I say. "Was all
that food I ate fake?" (Her plan to change the subject is
working—I'm hungry.)

"No, it was real. Pretty tasty, right?" she smirks.

"How many disguises do you have that I've seen?"

She switches from a ball of light, to the old lady, to
my mom and finally to Fred, the guy who hosted all of the
tests.

"WHAAAT?! You were a boy?" I ask.

"It was the weirdest transformation yet." Her face
grows pale. My stomach twists around, I don't like that
look. I've seen it on her face before, and it always means
that she's about to tell me something that I won't like.
"Safire, I don't want to tell you this but…Agapi-killed-
Marissa," she slurs.

At first I don't understand what she is saying, but then my face grows pale. I should have known... *THUMP!* My legs buckle, making me fall to the floor so fast I can't catch myself. I bump my head on something and it hurts. It reminds me of all of the headaches I used to have before my powers would kick in. Now that I can control them, I haven't had a headache in a while.

She tries to help me up but gets distracted. "Um... ma'am? There is a problem with the connection to the Azul Planet System," someone says. My mom walks over to their floating screen. I blink hard and slowly get up.

"Well, reboot it!" she says to the woman who gave the warning.

"We already did."

"Who is breaking the connection?!"

"The ships, I think."

"Huh. Tell everyone to stop and look at the screen. Let's see what they do."

"But ma'am—"

"Please," she says.

"Fine." The woman shouts to everyone to look at the screen.

Another voice comes from the speakers. "T-test... te...in..." A large shadow appears on the screen. "Hello." *Obsidian Slag. It has to be Obsidian Slag.* He's exactly like Igneous described him. A shiver is sent down my spine.

I walk down the stairs to the second row of floating screens. I start to feel panicky. *Breathe in, brea—*

But my breathing stops when I see Aenon, Leslie and Agapi standing next to Slag. My muscles tighten and

I hold my breath. My mind screams, "Take a breath!" But I don't.

Slag's voice continues over the speaker. "I know you hate me and don't want to talk to me. But I'm willing to make peace. I will give you something, if you give me something. I'm willing to do a trade with you."

Everyone gasps. People whisper.

"If you give me what I want, I will leave your planets alone, and you will never see me again," Slag says. "But you must give me this before the week ends, or something terrible will happen."

"What will it be?" somebody whispers. I nearly faint. I'm so paralyzed that I can't move or take a breath. My eyes start to flutter shut.

"SHHHHHH!" somebody else shouts.

"What I want is…**IGNEOUS STONE and SAFIRE WATERS.**"

And then, blackness.

About the Author

Aria Sindledecker loves to read dystopian and sci-fi books, write and swim. She is 11 years old and lives with her mom, dad and dog named Wicket. Aria is inspired by women who have grit. Her favorite subjects are math and science. She wants to be a doctor when she grows up so she can make a difference in people's lives.

Made in the USA
Coppell, TX
08 January 2020

14243046R00185